Copyright

Catatonia

C.S. Crane

Copyright © 2023 C.S.Crane
All rights reserved.
ISBN

CONTENTS

Chapter One	Rain man	3
Chapter Two	Black is the color of cowardice	22
Chapter Three	Sincere admirers	38
Chapter Four	Who Cares?	57
Chapter Five	Nema Nema	72
Chapter Six	The greatest of all crimes	83
Chapter Seven	The first disciples	110
Chapter Eight	Dodging a bullet	124
Chapter Nine	So very French	136
Chapter Ten	Bats	148
Chapter Eleven	Living dead men	154
Chapter Twelve	That God does not exist	188
Chapter Thirteen	Visits from the police	207
Chapter Fourteen	Revelations	211
Chapter Fifteen	A warrant is served	217
Chapter Sixteen	In the hour before dawn	223
Chapter Seventeen	The new man	231
Chapter Eighteen	A legal strategy	235
Chapter Nineteen	A surprise arrival	241
Chapter Twenty	Behind closed doors	248
Chapter Twenty-One	In the middle of nowhere	257
Chapter Twenty-Two	Visitors day	262
Chapter Twenty-Three	The Coming Out party	268
Chapter Twenty-Four	A death in the parking lot	282

CHAPTER 1 | Rain Man

At the intersection of two busy city streets, a man stood in the pouring rain on the sidewalk unmoving. His head was bent forward, his eyes focused on a spot below in the puddled sidewalk. His clothes were soaked and blackened. He wore no raincoat or jacket, just a cotton t-shirt and jeans. Long strands of black hair clung to his face. Pedestrians splashed and scurried around him. Blinded by umbrella edges, the man's legs would suddenly appear beneath their blurred line of sight. Then they would jump aside to avoid him or occasionally, seeing him too late, barge into the figure blocking their path. The standing man was collecting bumps and curses by the minute but seemed completely unaware of any of it. He was also unaware that a young woman was videoing him with her phone from several yards away.

"What's this? A protest of some kind?" she thought, water dripping off her baseball cap. "Well, at least he's not going to set himself on fire. Not today anyway. Performance art? That could explain anything and everything these days."

Another pedestrian, a Catholic priest, had been watching the stationary man with growing interest from the protection of an awning covering the entrance to a bodega. The young woman noticed his approach and shifted to bring the priest into the frame. The crisp white square of the Roman collar at his throat glowed in the dimness of rain and spray and mist. Weaving his way to the man through the streaming crowd, he arrived beside him and lifted his umbrella higher to shelter them both.

Minutes passed as they stood together, silent and wet. Then the priest, juggling his umbrella, removed his black raincoat and placed it gently over the other's shoulders. Passersby slowed to wonder at them but buffeted by the determined flow of the crowd were forced to move on and they quickly forgot the odd couple.

"Move for Chrissake!" a voice growled at the young woman. She hopped off the sidewalk and into the street. Even a man standing motionless in the rain could be an Instagram hit, #whatisawtoday. The priest's act of kindness prompted a more compelling hashtag, #kindnessofstrangers.

Noticing her, the priest's face lit up. He waved at her dramatically to come closer. Still videoing, she joined him, but slowly and frowning.

"Oh, thank you for joining us. I can't seem to rouse him."

Now, close up, the priest reminded her of an actor, of that Irish actor, Peter O'Toole.

"Who is he?" the girl asked, turning off her phone and sliding it into her back pocket.

"I have no idea," the priest answered. "Do you?"

"No. But I think he's faking it," she said with a skeptical eye on the priest.

"Oh no, I really don't think so. I did think so but I've been watching his eyes. I'm pretty sure he hasn't blinked."

4

"I think you're faking it, too, by the way," she said. Her earlier suspicion that she might be witnessing performance art when the man was standing alone seemed even more plausible now. This 'priest' was altogether too animated, too creepily eager to please. If indeed he was an actor attempting to persuade her to believe he was a priest, he was a bad actor. She expected the two of them would break out laughing any moment.

But the priest went on, committed to the part. "Oh GOD yes!" He answered her accusation with a large smile that could have been seen from the back of the house. Rather than defending himself, it was if she had handed him a most appreciated compliment.

"I've been faking it all my life. So clever of you. You see right through me."

"So you're not a real priest?" she said, with a smirk of satisfaction.

"Well, yes I am," he insisted. "I have the documents to prove it. Somewhere. But yes, yes, I've been one for forty years. But I've never in all that time felt like one. Whatever one is supposed to feel who is one."

"You mean, a priest."

"Yes, one of those. Just never felt like I fit in in real life." He went on in a confidential whisper. "So I've felt like a fake priest every day for forty years."

Perhaps he was a real priest. Perhaps he was a bad actor pretending to be one. She didn't care.

"This is all too weird--sorry--but don't you think we should, like, do something?" she said nodding toward the man.

"Oh PLEASE," the priest said, lifting his head as if dodging a projectile, "don't say 'like'!"

"'Like?'" the girl said, too surprised to be offended.

"Yes, well, no. Not the word. The usage! It should be banned by Papal decree!..You seem an intelligent person and I was just getting to 'like' you. Yes, but I used it the proper way. When you used it, you might as well have said 'Do you think we should, I'm stupid, do something?'"

For a moment, the young woman thought she was going to turn and walk away leaving him to do whatever it was he might decide to do.

"Oh, I'm sorry. I've overwhelmed you—"

"Certainly not," the girl shot back at him.

"Forgive me anyway, won't you? When I'm nervous I come on a little too strong. Then to answer your honest question, I have no idea what to do. Which is why I'm nervous. Why don't you try?"

"What can I do? We don't even know what's wrong with him."

"Catatonia?" the priest suggested with a lift of his eyebrows and a questioning smile.

"You mean, he's, I'm stupid, stuck like that?"

The priest roared with delight at this but caught himself quickly in deference to his new friend's condition.

"Oh my God, you are a treasure! But, yes. I think so."

"Isn't it rare?"

"Oh no," the priest protested smiling even more broadly now. "I have a classroom full of catatonics."

Evidently this was intended to be a great joke. The girl frowned back at him, shaking her head. She moved closer to the silent rain-soaked man and bent slightly to peer up into his downturned eyes.

"He's not dangerous, is he?" she asked. "I mean, he's not going to wake up and knife me or anything, right?"

"I don't think so. I hope not," the priest said, the first note of seriousness creeping into his voice.

"Thanks. That's very reassuring."

But suddenly, the priest reached out and pushed her back a step. There was concern in his eyes. "Hold on a minute. Listen. I feel I've been very irresponsible. Neither of us are equipped for this. I should call 911."

"So he could be dangerous?" the girl asked, unnerved by the priest's sudden reaction and now feeling there might, in fact, be real danger here.

"Well, we just don't know, do we?" the priest said. "What if he harms you? I wouldn't be able to forgive myself. We've been having a jolly little talk here under, as you say, the weirdest circumstance in which two people meet for the first time. I--I don't even know your name! I'm Jim Flynn, by the way. And I desperately want to avoid our next meeting to be in the parousia."

"Wait a minute, you're Father Jim Flynn. From St. Augustine's?"

"Yes!" the priest nearly shouted but caught himself again. With the slow-dawning realization that he had so stupidly allowed this pleasant, unsuspecting young woman to put herself at risk, her abrupt and surprising reaction to his name came as a gift of grace (as he liked to think all things came) and in his typically dramatic fashion, left him enraptured. "How do you know me? Isn't this the most incredible of coincidences? It's wonderful, isn't it? Sometimes I think coincidence is more like a god than God. Perhaps coincidence *is* God. It resembles a hand of fate at times so convincingly, even the modern Epicurean must wonder, don't you think?"

"Yeah, well, whatever," the girl said. It was clear she hadn't understood a word he had said. "But how I know you is, my brother talks about you. He's a junior at St. Augustine's. Richard--Richard Benfont."

"Yes, of course, Richard...Oh dear," the priest said, placing the name. "Oh dear, oh dear."

"What?" the girl asked anxiously.

"A classroom full of catatonics, I said. I'm so sorry! Once again, for perhaps the millionth time in my life, I have to abjectly apologize for my big mouth. I was just making a joke, a bad joke. Richard is not one of my catatonics. Your mind may rest on that."

She noticed that he was suddenly looking at her in a new way, as if trying to place her.

"Father, look, I'm just going to touch him softly and if that doesn't work I'll wait with you until an ambulance comes. I don't know where he'd hide a knife if he had one...I'm Bella, by the way."

Now the girl reached out slowly, pushed aside the raincoat and touched the man's bare wet arm, rubbing it gently up and down.

"Hello in there. Anybody home?" she offered softly with a weak nervous smile.

At first, there was no reaction, but as she continued rubbing his arm it moved. Slowly, slowly, his arm drifted up to wipe the hair from his face. The girl stepped back. She saw that his lips were thin and small, too small for the width of his jaws. His cheeks were flat, almost indented, making his face seem like a mask. His nose was long and straight--a good nose. But it was his eyes that disturbed her. Too close together, perhaps, in that flat expanse of dead-grey tissue but so black it seemed impossible any light could penetrate them.

Having brought her into focus, the man's face took on a mean and threatening expression. He turned to the priest who was leaning in toward him, his face close and anxious. The man stepped away in alarm.

"Ah!" said the priest, "you've returned to life. Welcome back. Can we help you in any way? Wouldn't you like to go somewhere and get warm? Dry off? You must be so uncomfortable. I know we are and you've been standing here much longer. Come, come with me. You, too, Bella." And he gently took the man's arm. But the man pushed his arm away roughly. With his drenched hair like black slashes across his face, he became a truly threatening vision. The priest moved away from him under the pressure of it but Bella stepped even closer and took the man's arm, which he allowed or perhaps did not feel or notice. The rain had stopped.

"I'll take him wherever he has to go, Father," she said, removing the priest's raincoat and handing it back to him. To the priest, she sounded calm and capable and he was much relieved by this. Yet, ironically, Bella Benfont was now herself acting a part--that of a confident, level-headed, not-easily-frightened young woman. The truth was that, for as long as she could remember, she had lived in fear of her own cowardice and for just as long had fought it with very mixed results. In the last few minutes, she had felt the old enemy rising again. She could not bear the thought that it might win this round, not in front of this priest. So she had stepped forward, acting quickly and without thinking. Shaking but determined, she turned and led the man away. The priest watched them go.

"GOD BLESS YOU BELLA!" he called after them. "AND YOU TOO YOUNG MAN!"

After a few steps, her charge shrugged off her guiding hand and sped up unsteadily, leaving her behind. But very soon he was staggering badly yet he kept going even picking up his pace and not once looking back at her.

"Hey," she called after him. "Are you OK now?"

Up ahead, the man's hands had begun to tremble and his body was shuddering violently. A moment later he collapsed on to his hands and knees, breathing fast and shaking all over. Bella ran to him and dropped down beside him, throwing her arm over his back. The flow of pedestrians had fallen off and they were nearly alone on the street.

"You saw," the man mumbled into the pavement.

"Yes," Bella answered softly.

"It happens...when it wants to happen."

"You're freezing! I mean, God, you're completely soaked through--c'mon, let me help you up--can you stand?--I'm going to call an Uber."

She heaved the shivering figure onto his feet and fumbled her phone out of her pocket. She ordered the car and looked around to see that the man had staggered several steps away and seemed to be heading blindly into the road.

"Hey-hey-hey! Wait up. I've got an Uber coming. Just stand here." She sprinted up to him and grabbed his arms. Now she held him close as they both stood by the curb.

"I-I-don't b-b-believe in g-g-gratitude," the man suddenly said but his voice came with very little force and Bella did not hear him.

"Don't talk. I didn't realize. . . I mean, this thing you've got, it's really awful, isn't it?"

"This is what happens. After. Don't need a car. I live just d-d-down there." He pointed across the street with a shaking finger.

"OK, c'mon, I'll walk you home." She took his arm, holding it firmly, and with her other arm around his back they crossed the street looking like a pair of lovers.

A few blocks down a street with several boarded up houses on both sides and almost all of the rest run-down and shabby, they stopped in front of a dirty white single-story ranch that had two entries, the front door for the main, larger part of the house in which all the windows were boarded up, and another door which seemed to be a secondary entrance to an addition or attached apartment set back from the front of the house. There was a window beside this door which was not boarded up. The man listed onto the dirt path leading to this door and together they mounted a broken step to a small porch.

    The man opened the front door (it was unlocked) and they entered a scene of dishevelment and decay that took Bella's breath away. It was a single large room with a single door in the back wall into a bathroom. This door was open, or rather the doorway was open, as the door itself leaned against the wall beside it. It had been ripped from its frame. Bella could see pieces of the wooden doorframe still screwed into the hinges. Nails had been pounded into the door from which hung several pairs of jeans. In the main area, sweaters and sweatshirts and T-shirts, socks and shoes, were scattered across the floor and piled onto every surface. The long low couch along the right wall evidently also served as the man's bed. A sheet and blanket were crumpled up in a pile near one end with a throw pillow peaking out from between them. A low coffee table in front of it sat at an odd angle to the couch, as if the man had kicked it out of the way upon waking. The center of the room was taken up with a large square table and three matching chairs. There was a laptop computer on the table crowded into one end by a chaos of dirty plates, used coffee cups and drinking glasses and assorted silver ware. A hotplate at the table's other end, surrounded by cans and jars and three stacked cooking pots with handles, was connected to an extension cord that ran across the floor to the single outlet in the wall opposite the couch. There was no rug on the floor and no ornamentation or artwork on the walls. There were no bookshelves or closets. The walls themselves as well as the ceiling were stained with years of grime, possibly from a former heavy smoker, and the yellowed and filthy wallpaper was peeling off in several places. In the ceiling over the table hung what must have been the original fixture. An old and fraying electrical cord extended from a hole in the cracked ceiling and twisted down toward a small ancient glass globe covered in dust and grime. Inside, dead insects threw spotty shadows on the table top.

It was several moments before Bella recovered from her first reaction of disgust and even alarm to notice that the furniture beneath all the detritus was in fact new and very expensive. It might have been lifted straight out of a Crate and Barrel showroom. The rocking chair positioned in the corner in front of the one window which looked out onto the street was sleek and minimalist, with a tubular frame wrapped in light blonde leather. The couch was long, low, grey, and uncomfortable-looking in classic Swedish design. Both the table with its matching chair set and the coffee table were made of blonde wood with tubular steel legs.

As the initial shock wore off, Bella's first clear thought was that she had made a terrible mistake. Her constant battle with the charge of cowardice which she was so quick to level against herself and in which she had won her most recent round back on the street, had gotten her into this situation. "What have I done?" she thought. "What am I doing here? Look at how he lives! What kind of a crazy bastard have I got myself hooked up with! Oh God, I just want to go home!" Without realizing it she had begun to back toward the front door. She bumped up against it and pressed herself into it.

"Go ahead, run away," the man murmured in a dead voice. He had stumbled into the room and now stood weak-kneed, propping himself upright with his hands pressed and splayed against the table top, his head hanging loose.

"Well, what do you expect?" she responded with a defensive glare.

"I expect you to run away," he murmured. Then he turned slowly, leaning his back against the table edge for support, slid along it to the nearest of the three chairs. He fell sprawling onto it, legs fanned out, hands between his thighs, his head thrown back as if it was too heavy to hold up. Bella knew that he was watching her, though because of the angle, it appeared that his eyes were closed. A slight twitch of his lips greeted her.

"You. Look. Ridiculous," he said, each word requiring its own breath to escape.

Bella felt that was exactly how she must look and, ashamed, stepped purposefully away from the door and into the room. She searched for a dry towel and found one tossed in a corner.

"If you want to see ridiculous, look around," she said, throwing the towel over his shoulders. She could not see those black eyes and was glad of it.

For a long time neither spoke nor moved, but finally with an effort the man began to adjust himself into a more normal sitting position. His breathing had become less labored and color was returning to his flat mask of a face. He began to study her more closely. His eyes moved over her as if he was seeing her for the first time.

She had dark brown hair cut short with a natural curl that softened her square jaw and accented her brown eyes. She was not pretty in any conventional sense. Most people would not notice her in passing. But there was something about her that acted on certain people very strongly, those that happened to be face to face with her like store clerks or pizza delivery drivers. If anyone afforded her more than a mere glance, they would sense a kind of aura of femininity about her. It was a subtle effect. She was not outgoing and did not expect to be noticed or particularly wish to be. But in the way she held herself, in the unconscious movements of her body, and especially in the loveliness of her hands, which were long and thin with beautifully molded fingers, she displayed a kind of genius for evoking sympathy and good-feeling in others. Yet--and adding to the effect--of all this she was completely unaware. In fact, her own image of herself was as a very ordinary, inconsequential person, unattractive but at least not repulsive, unintelligent but not a complete dope, flat-chested, narrow-hipped, with a nice enough smile and decent teeth.

"What," the man challenged as he watched her eyes assess the space.

"Nothing. I mean...how can you live like this?"

"Rich parents," he said with a sneer.

This produced an involuntary snort of nervous laughter. "Wow, it's a wonder what money can buy these days," Bella said with a sideways glance anticipating some kind of reaction but he ignored the comment.

"I told them I'd disown them if they didn't support me without question. And of course they did. But I will disown them anyway." This he pronounced with evident pride.

They were silent for a moment, each now more at ease with the other.

"Why did you think I was going to run away?" Bella asked at last, hoping her voice sounded matter-of-fact, indifferent.

"I'm surprised you're still here."

"What's so surprising about it?"

He tilted his head and peered at her from half-closed eyes, contemptuously but also somewhat amused. Earlier that morning, before his fit had stopped him in his tracks, he had been on his way to a meeting with his uncle whom he had not seen in years. He had been anticipating this reunion with a nearly frantic intensity. Of course, now he had missed the meeting but was only waiting for the after effects of the attack to end before starting out again. His amusement arose from her question, to which the answer was that her presence had truly surprised him. In his weakness, he had been forced to abide her help and now as he regained control of himself, his contempt for her was only surpassed by his contempt for that weakness. But, then again, he considered, perhaps there was...Yes. Why not? Let's have a little test.

"Since you're not going to run away, sit down."

Bella moved to the far end of the couch, the only space free of tossed off clothing, inspecting it critically, perhaps for bugs or evidence of mice. She wiped at the fabric while not actually touching it then lowered herself onto its edge.

The man had watched her movements with interest, but Bella was growing accustomed to his penetrating manner of looking at her.

"Isn't it about time you told me your name?" she said.

"You first," he said.
"Bella."
"Bella what?"
"Benfont. Your turn."
"Nicholas.
"Nicholas what."
"Shelley."

"Would you please change into dry clothes. It's uncomfortable trying to talk to someone who's uncomfortable."

Nothing in his demeanor changed and she at first wondered whether he had even heard her, but then decided his silence was due to a kind of ongoing assessment, as if he were trying to make a decision about her candidacy for some project or purpose.

Finally, he stood and, steadier now, walked through the clutter to the bathroom. He emerged dressed in a black hoodie with the hood up, black pants and black Chuck Taylors. Sitting on the edge of the couch with her elbows on her knees and hands clasped, Bella involuntarily jerked upwards.

"Oh! Now I get it," she said half-smiling with sudden insight. "You're Antifa! Where's your balaclava?"

He came to an abrupt halt in front of her, as if he'd walked into an invisible wall. Standing only a few paces away, between her and the table, his mouth hardened and almost disappeared as his lips tightened and shrunk. He turned the nearest of the kitchen chairs toward her and sat.

"First of all, I am not antifa. Let the children rage. They are inconsequential. In the extreme!" He paused, regarding her with his attitude of precise and focused attention.

"Here's a situation and I'd like to know what you think of it," he finally said. It was clear to Bella that some kind of decision had been made, and in her favor.

"OK," she said, taking a deep breath of relief and leaning forward.

"You are sitting at a red light," he began, "waiting for it to change. The oncoming cars have an advance green light so they get a head start of a couple of seconds before your light turns green. You are bored and turn your attention to the drivers in these cars as they slowly accelerate toward you. Maybe only three or four cars pass by you before your light turns green, but in those few seconds it dawns on you that you are a whole universe unto yourself, not a part of any other, and they are too. And you realize that all along you've taken it for granted that your universe is the only one that matters, because of course it is the only one that matters. And yet there they go, those other drivers in their cars, unconsciously secure that *their* universes are each the only universes that matter, each one representing an absolute denial of your own certain existential knowledge that there can be only one pure universe--your own. Of course yours is the only universe that matters! How dare they exist! And with that, the light changes and you drive off to pick up the milk, feeling a little sick in your tummy."

He stopped and Bella watched him, waiting for some direction, but none came. "I don't know what you want me to say," she said. "What am I missing?"

Nicholas didn't answer but rose in disgust from his chair and turned his back to her, then planted his hands on the table top again, leaned forward and dropped his head, the same posture he had taken earlier.

Bella was all too aware of the inadequacy of her response but was so completely baffled by his 'situation', what it meant and what he expected her to say about it, that she couldn't even feel guilty for having disappointed him. She felt lost and suddenly very tired.

"I--I--" Bella began, but he interrupted her.

"No, no, don't speak."

"I should go. I don't feel--"

"Run away," he demanded into the table top.

With effort, Bella lifted herself off the couch and shuffled to the door. She reached for the doorknob but stopped and turned back into the room and joined him at the table. She scanned the rubbish, found a torn-open envelope and a ballpoint pen. She wrote on the envelope, slid it between his hands and left.

"Bella 737-8550"

After several minutes, Nicholas raised his head (his eyes had been closed the whole time) and saw the note on the table top in front of him. Absently he crumpled it up and rolled it away, just another item of rubbish. Alone now, his eyes swept over the disorder in the room and he found that it calmed the disorder inside him. In fact, he used the room and its chaotic contents as a kind of touchstone to remind and reassure himself in those moments of doubt which he was struggling to make less and less frequent. To remind himself that he had risen above the human rubbish all around him. And to reassure himself that an occasional slip backward--as with the little test--was only to be expected. He smiled. He was rather impressed with himself, remembering how the early doubts, so intense, so debilitating, had left him longing for the comfort and warmth of the rubbish heap of ordinary life. And why was that? Because of self-pity! And cowardice! Now, months later, he could call up the memory like an anti-Muse, not to be inspired by but to be repulsed by. And thus had he won significant victories over himself.

He glanced up at the wall clock. He would be very late for his uncle but he didn't care. He was fully recovered now and there was a small precious flutter of excitement in his stomach.

"Breathe. Just breathe." He closed his eyes and took several deep breaths. When he opened them again, they fell upon the crumpled note on which Bella had written her cell number. With a quick, sharp motion, as if trying to hide the action from his conscious mind, he retrieved it and hurriedly stuffed it in his pocket. Then he left slamming the door behind him.

CHAPTER 2 | Black is the color of cowardice

    Bella walked back to her car and drove toward home as if on autopilot, troubled but also intrigued by her inability to a get a grip on this odd man, to categorize him. He didn't seem to fit in with the culture around her, a culture which she frankly disdained. The insidious and, to her, preposterous belief in the rightness of every opinion, no matter how lightly held--a belief strengthened precisely because it could be held with such ease, for no other reason than that it was held so easily by everybody. But this Nicholas person was..different.
    "That's quite a compliment, coming from you!" she thought. "Probably that sickness. Could explain a lot. There's definitely some kind of weirdness there. He doesn't fit at all...Am I judging him now? Who am I to analyze somebody else who I don't even know and only just met?...God, what is it about him that makes me feel guilty about thinking about him? I can think about anybody I want to think about. That doesn't mean I'm passing judgement. Stop being so sensitive. It's not a judgement, it's a fact. Face it honestly--he's a weirdo...wasn't it strange, that situation? I mean, how do you come up with something like that? Can't be that illness. It's like his brain is different...that could be because of his illness. But ordinary people aren't like him...ordinary people? Who's ordinary today?

This fucking culture! Nobody believes anything and everybody believes everything!"

Back at home, Bella entered by the front door, still lost in thought, and moved absently toward the kitchen which was behind the stairs in front of her. Out of long habit, she glanced into the dining room on her left which was usually empty at this time of day. It was mildly surprising to see it occupied. At the dining room table sat her mother and her younger brother Richard with the newspaper spread out in front of them. Her Aunt Eleanor, her mother's older sister, stood on the other side of the table, looking down at them.

"What's going on?" Bella asked, sensing a definite tension in the room. Aunt Eleanor answered without looking at her, her gaze fixed on her nephew, Richard, who was leaning forward on the table with both arms crossed and a wry, insolent smile on his face.

"There's some news that isn't funny," Aunt Eleanor said boring into the boy with her eyes. "But it's no big surprise." Now she turned to look at Bella. "Another priest scandal."

Aunt Eleanor looked years younger than her age as very large people often do. With her fine white skin stretched tightly over her round fat face, her thick dark hair trimmed close, her big brown eyes that shown with the confidence of the true skeptic, she was an intellectual and physical dominatrix. There was a story she never tired of telling about the time her late husband, Arturo—a first generation old-school Italian—had slapped her face. It was shortly after their marriage. Eleanor had had the temerity to serve Arturo a sauce of her own invention instead of using the recipe given her by his mother. She had slapped him back, knocking him off his chair. As he looked up at her from the floor she had withdrawn a piece of paper from her housecoat pocket—her mother-in-law's sauce recipe—torn it into small pieces and sprinkled them over Arturo's plate of pasta "like grated Parmesan".

"Ignore the brat son of yours, Angela," she said to her sister, who gazed at Bella now with pathetic entreaty as if at a savior. Behind her large round glasses, Angela Benfont's soft brown eyes were moist.

"Hello, honey," she said in a dull tone. Her hands clasped around her rosary beads rested on the table and her shoulders slumped forward. Bella had rarely seen her mother in such a sad state.

She too was a large woman but shorter than her sister and she carried herself with less assurance, perhaps from growing up in Eleanor's dominating shadow. Her mind, however, was all her own. She had the Antonelli's brown eyes but hers gave off a gentle questioning glow which could flare up into wonderment at ideas that pierced her heart, and she was prone to heart-piercings. Her children could always tell when she had been pierced because her hands would jump to her heart, fingers intertwined as if to catch the shot itself and hold it firmly embedded there. She seemed to have been born with an innate thirst for those rare moments when, out of the endless meaningless stream of life's trivialities that passed through her leaving no detectable trace, a single thought or idea might collide with her heart and explode in her eyes. Yet, to her older sister, this was a failing which had set them at one another from their earliest days. Even as they adored her, it was difficult for her children not to see that Aunt Eleanor must have been sorely tried through the years by their mother's willingness, even an eagerness, to see the other side of every question. To a woman of Eleanor's judgmental character, it could only have been by an effort of monumental self-control to accept her younger sister as a person worthy of her respect. Yet, were someone to act disrespectfully toward her sister, to mock her or laugh at her or even look at her as if they thought she was odd or stupid (and, God knows, Angela was good at producing such reactions in people), Eleanor would suddenly rise to her defense. It was, perhaps, caused by a sense of guilt boiling up against her own transgressions, and perhaps too, a real though unacknowledged affection and even tenderness for her sister and her annoying weaknesses.

Here it was again, the exhaustion that made Bella feel as if she could fall off into deep sleep at any moment while facing them all, especially her mother. It was the same effect people often report feeling at times of intense trial, very often at funerals.

"Mom, you don't know these guys," her brother was explaining in an urgent voice, "but I have to live with them every day." As he spoke, his eyes which were wide with excitement continually flicked back and forth from his mother to his hovering Aunt Eleanor as if to find some encouragement there, but she only glared at him with distaste.

"They're all phonies. They're all fake news. Believe me. And this guy's the worst. Everybody loves him. He's Mr. Smileyface around school. All the kids go to him for 'talks'. His classes are great, he's a cool guy. But that's the perfect M.O. And it explains a lot, actually. I mean, the other priests don't like him and we always thought it was because he was so popular, because he had this cool attitude toward stuff, almost like he was one of the guys, like he wasn't one of those old boring priests. That probably had a lot to do with it, but what if they knew something or suspected something and that's why they didn't dig him?"

Richard Benfont might have been Angela's adopted son, so little did he resemble his mother. It was his father who could be seen in all his features. He was seventeen but looked younger, one of those people whose youthful appearance stays with them for many years into adulthood. He was not tall but well-muscled, wiry, and quite strong. He was his school's top wrestler in the 145-pound weight class. Lately, he had taken to wearing his thick brown hair long, letting it curl freely and crawl over his forehead and around his ears. It was a style that drove his Aunt Eleanor crazy and she constantly bothered him about it (though his mother quite loved his hair and thought he looked like an intellectual). His face was narrow and long with a sharp long nose and small eyes close together. His lips were thin and finely, even delicately, shaped. Unusually, however, they had a persistent upward twist on one side that gave his face a kind of impish impudence that had gotten him into more trouble with authority than he deserved. Teachers and Principals had only to look at him to believe he was a trouble-maker and needed to be watched, even though he rarely got into any actual trouble. He was not particularly good-looking, though one could see that he might be considered handsome as he grew and his face filled out.

"C'mon, Mom. What do you think, these guys enter the priesthood because they're good people?" Richard continued, his voice rising in excitement. "They're not good people. They're just guys who are afraid of women. Or they're gay. I'm telling you, you don't know them."

While he had been talking, his mother's face had slowly, unconsciously, contorted in pain. "Oh, Richard. Don't honey," she pleaded.

But Richard seemed not to hear her. It was doubtful that he saw the pain in her face though his eyes were bright and eager as he stared directly at her. These were thoughts he had held for some time, keeping them close and developing them inwardly but never expressing them in his mother's hearing. But now with this revelation in the papers, the proof of the rightness of those ideas had been thrust under his Mother's nose from an outside objective source. The hurt it caused her did not touch him. Rather a thrill of exhilaration coursed through him. To express his ideas openly, under the imprimatur of the news article, freed him from restraint and blinded him to all but his own feelings of triumph.

"Think about it. Why do they dress in black? You know why? Because that's what they think life is like, all the black things in life, death and suffering and pain, what life would be like if they had to live like the rest of us! So they go into the priesthood, where they don't have to worry about keeping a job, or where their next meal is coming from, or living side by side with an actual woman all the time. I mean, c'mon Mom, they're cowards. Black is the color of cowardice. You don't know them like I do."

Suddenly, Aunt Eleanor slapped down her hand on the table and everyone jumped. Her face was red and her eyes were slits which burned into her nephew.

"That's enough!" she commanded. "You insensitive little bastard. How can you say she doesn't know these guys? Have you forgotten your mother cooks and cleans and shops and probably even puts on their slippers for them over there at the Rectory? I wouldn't be surprised in the least if she did. And as much as it galls me to think of her slaving and scraping for those two priests, she never complains, hardly ever. She thinks it's some kind of holy vocation. OK, I'm not saying she isn't half-crazy but she's my sister and your damn mother. I've never been a lover of priests or the Catholic Church and haven't got any fonder of them over the years. And if you ask me they can shut down the whole operation and good riddance. It's done more harm than good, if you ask me. But I've never willfully tried to hurt your mother like that. And now here's me, who in fact agrees with every word you say! Yes, they are arrogant and cowardly too, like all men underneath that masculine baggage we load them up with and then kick them out into the world to trample everything like rampaging elephants..don't you laugh at me, you insolent little pachyderm, don't you laugh at me."

Richard had been watching his aunt closely, enjoying himself immensely. He was very fond of the big woman and never more so than when--and it was not rare--some comment by one of them would send her off into these highly comical paroxysms of anger. Inevitably they would find the episode too funny and break down into laughter in front of her. At which she would jam her fists into her thick sides and glare at them until she too could no longer resist and her big body shook with laughter instead of anger. It was this that endeared her to all of them, that a woman who's natural attitude of unassailable dominance could so easily accommodate within herself such a seemingly contradictory virtue as the generosity of spirit to laugh at herself.

"Oh! You make me so mad!" she said because, once again, they had made her see herself through their eyes.

"Eleanor, Eleanor, please, don't be angry with him," Angela said. Her voice was weak and there was great sadness in her eyes, though she too had had to smile.

"I'm not angry," Eleanor said breathing hard. She needed to be off her feet (which were always killing her) and catch her breath. She pulled out a chair and sat heavily. "If he were my son, I'd slap him across his insolent face."

"I know, I know, and I'm glad he's my son and not yours," Angela said gently. She smiled at her sister and wiped her eyes with a tissue. Turning back to Richard, she leaned close to him. She took Richard's hand and stroked it gently.

"My beautiful son," she said in a quiet voice. "You're taking too much joy in all this, sweetheart. But, honey, you're so intelligent and so clever and you see many things and understand them better than I do. And I'm so proud of you. But in this case you're wrong." She patted his hand as if to apologize for criticizing him. "Thank you, Eleanor. I do know priests, if I know anything. I see them when they're alone and out of the spotlight, when they're just two ordinary men who live together in loneliness. Terrible loneliness, Richard, so terrible." Her eyes began to water again as she spoke and her hands pressed tightly into his as if she could imprint the empathy she felt for the priests into his heart. "I do love the Church and I do love the priesthood and I know there are bad men that are priests. I'm not blind. But I know, I know in my heart, that there are really good men in it. And I know I sound ridiculous to you, Eleanor, when I talk about it so I try not to, just like you try not to talk about it to me. Isn't that funny?"

"Well, Angela, we're sisters," Eleanore said, calmer now and somewhat deflated having caught her breath and relieved the pain in her feet.

"But I often think I'm wrong to not talk about it, Eleanor," her sister continued. "I've often felt that way around you." Turning back to her son, she went on. "Sweetheart, I love you and I will always love you, and when you hurt me I love you even more because I know you don't mean it and I know someday you will come back to the Church--no, no, don't say anything. I am your mother and I know you better than anyone. You are my son. Sometimes I think my love for you is too great, but then I think, can love for my son ever be too great? Was Mary's love for her son too great? Yes, it hurts me when you speak about the priests that way but I'm wrong to feel hurt. Yes, Eleanor, it's wrong, I'm quite sure. Richard, you make me believe that much of what you say is true. I never thought of it that way, the way you put it. And it really only goes to show what a beautiful and mysterious and wonderful thing the Church is, that we can find everything in life inside it, everything good and everything bad."

Eleanor's temperature had been rising the more Angela talked. Her anger-fueled sympathy of earlier had leaked away to be replaced by the old and by now very worn, frayed and familiar irritation with her sister that she was wholly unable to control.

"Stop it now, Angela," she said with authority as if talking to a child. "I can't listen to any more of this. I like you better when you keep all this business to yourself. I mean it now. Too much information. T.M.I like the kids say. Who wants to hear it? I don't. I really don't. I find it indecent. Yes, indecent! I really think that at your age you should know better. Nobody appreciates it when you expose yourself like that. Don't look at me all wide-eyed and innocent! Why make everybody uncomfortable?"

"She's not making me uncomfortable," Richard chimed in.

"Shut up, you," Eleanor said without looking at him and continued to bore into her sister. She raised her heavy arms and let them fall thudding onto the table. She leaned into the space between herself and her sister, her face reddening. "And why now, huh?" she challenged Angela. "What's gotten into you. You'd think this was the first priest ever charged with molesting kids! Is that it? Is it something about him especially?" she said, pointing at the newspaper. She sat back and wiped her forehead which was showing lines of perspiration under her hair though it was not warm in the room. "Oh, never mind. I'm tired. You wear me out. Really you do. I'm going home," and with an effort began to heave herself out of the chair. Once up on her feet, she glared down at Angela. "And another thing. You seem to forget you have two children. While you've been slavering over this brat who doesn't deserve you as a mother there's poor Bella standing there." She raised her hand in a gesture that meant she would say no more about it, accompanied by a chin raised in imperious dismissal, and turned to go.

"Wait, Eleanor," Angela said. She too had risen from her chair. She seemed anxious that her sister should not walk out in such a mood. There was also a distinct impression felt by them all that she was suffering some kind of inner distress, caused by something more than her sister's dressing-down. She was visibly uncomfortable. She looked like a little girl caught out in a lie by grown-ups.

"What is the matter with you, Angela?" Eleanor said. As often happened when their relationship reached a certain tension, as it had now, her eyes were stretched wide with authority as if to browbeat the truth out of her sister. But now 'the look' was darkly tinged with worry. Irritated, she turned to Bella.

"Bella, why don't you sit down, for God's sake. You're part of this family. Unfortunately."

At first, Bella had stood in the doorway hardly registering what was being said. But Richard's description of the abusive priest as 'Mr. Smileyface' had caught her attention. Her fog had lifted and she drifted into the room.

She was certain that he must mean that priest, Father Flynn. After all, the priest had told her he taught at Richard's school and knew her brother. And she could well understand, after meeting him that morning, how he might be described as 'Mr. Smileyface' (though it was such a childish phrase, like baby-talk, that she cringed in embarrassment for her bother). He himself had admitted to being a 'fake priest' and seemed quite pleased with himself to tell her so. Still, it was strange that a weird priest she had met only an hour ago entirely by chance should be the subject of tense conversation right here in her own dining room. Hadn't he said something about 'coincidences', that it's more like God than God, or something like that?

She had entered the room with the intention of impressing them with her news. It was, she felt, an immature impulse, this jealousy for attention, which in any other circumstances she would have chastised herself for not having outgrown. But she gave herself up to it nonetheless as she waited for the right moment to speak.

The right moment never arrived. Angela turned to Bella, whom in fact she had forgotten about. "Yes, Bella. Come sit, honey." She offered Bella the chair beside her and they both sat.

Her mother frowned and pushed the newspaper away from her as if it no longer held any interest for her. Addressing Eleanor, she said, "I know there are good priests and I know Father Flynn is one of them. Before you ask me how I know, it's because I've been meeting with him for several weeks." She shifted her gaze to Bella then to Richard. "About your father."

"I don't believe it," Eleanor exploded. "Another counsellor? How many priests have you burned through already and now you're meeting with a pedophile?"

"He's not a pedophile," Angela said with conviction.

"And how would you know?"

"I just know. It's not true. I know it's not true. I heard him give a sermon one Sunday when he was helping out at the parish. And I talked to him after Mass and I liked him very much. And I asked if I could speak to him about..well, anyway he agreed and he's been really wonderful."

"Good God, Angela, how long are you going to drag this out? Please, we're all sick of this drama. Just divorce the sonofabitch and get it over with."

At this, Richard jumped in to support his Aunt. "It's true, Mom. Get it over with already. Seriously. He's like a ghost around here anyway. We'd all be better off without him."

Bella spoke up now at last. "I just met this priest, him," she pointed at the newspaper, "this morning."

"Father Flynn?" Her mother jumped at the mention of his name. "You met him? How? What did you think of him?" she said, emphasizing the 'you' as if she felt that Bella would certainly corroborate her impressions and that her opinion would be decisive.

With her daughter's first words, her mother's face fell. Bella shook her head. "Wow. Why am I not surprised? Of course, you know him," Bella said.

"What do you mean, Bella?" Her mother, who was one of those people who are incapable of disguising their feelings, gazed at her daughter with the fearful eyes of a woman who knew betrayal too intimately and could smell its approach.

"Oh, I don't know. I don't know," Bella said, still shaking her head. "It's just..it's just I'm so tired of all this constant drama between you and Dad. I don't even want to come home anymore. I feel like there's this, I don't know, this dust everywhere, this emotional dust all over everything, and it's making us all sick and all we do is talk, talk, talk. I'm so sick of talking."

"But honey, I'm trying--"

"No, Mom, you're not. You're just you. This is just who you are. The problem is, Dad's not like you, he's just an ordinary guy, just one of the elephants. He can't help it. I'm telling you, marrying you ruined his life."

"Oh, Bella!"

"Admit it for once. You're the problem, not Dad. Have you been listening to yourself? All that stuff about the Church and lonely priests and this guy who, frankly, is a first-rate weirdo and a fake priest, too--he admitted it to me, that he's a fake priest. Oh, he was only trying to be charming and he wanted me to like him because now I realize he knew I was your daughter, but he made my skin crawl. And what do I find when I come home? There's more dust! Dust piled up to the ceiling! This is the guy my mother idolizes! This fake priest! My mother, who's been trying to divorce a guy who isn't a fake anything, just a poor dumb slob who had no idea he'd married a woman who'd rather sleep with a rosary than her own husband."

Richard, unaware that he was breathing with his mouth open, watched her with admiration and fascination. Aunt Eleanor sat with her arms crossed on the table, leaning forward, unblinking, her mouth tight. Angela, who like the others could not take her eyes off Bella, at first had seemed to shrink under the onslaught. But gradually her whole demeanor altered so that it became far easier to see her resemblance to Eleanor at her fiercest. Bella knew her mother's anger when aroused was not explosive like Eleanor's but was nevertheless the more corrosive. It lurked and sulked inside her, was slow to dissipate and left scars.

"What's going on here?" Eleanor finally said. She was livid. "What kind of little hellions are you two? I've never heard such treachery come out of the mouth of a child."

"Oh, please, just be quiet Aunt Eleanor," Bella said wearily.

"No, I will not be quiet. Your mother--"

But Bella had stood and pushed back her chair. "Yes. She's my mother. Poor me."

CHAPTER 3 | Sincere admirers

In the past few weeks, he had found himself thinking more and more about his uncle, Benjamin Shelley. Seven years ago, Ben Shelley had become something of a malign celebrity in the financial world. He was accused of "engaging in multiple schemes to ensnare investors through a web of lies and deceit" according to news reports and had been sentenced to seven years in prison for securities fraud. Having served his sentence, Ben Shelley had set up as a lawyer specializing in clients with a prison record (and those who might be acquiring one soon without his help and inside knowledge). They had spoken several times by phone recently and very quickly and naturally resumed the connection that had existed between them.

He set out with an overwhelming sense of expectation to see the man who had been an inspiration and a kind of guru throughout his life, to the consternation and strong disapproval of his parents from whom his uncle had been estranged for many years. This fact alone had made of his uncle the sentimental hero of his youth. But that youthful hero-worship had grown immeasurably in his imagination for it was Ben Shelley alone who would be able to appreciate a certain document he had written, a kind of manifesto, entitled "Who Cares?". He had sent it to Ben three days ago and the meeting today was both a reunion and, for Nicholas, a validation.

Now, hurrying to Ben Shelley's office for their first face-to-face meeting in years, Nicholas was beside himself with anticipation to hear the praise he was sure Ben Shelley would heap upon the manifesto and him. There was no doubt in his mind that his uncle would be awestruck. He still marveled at the grandiosity of 'Who Cares?' From such a small seed to such an explosion of genius! Because of it, his whole previous history had instantly been validated in his mind. He saw it, this genius of his, struggling to burst forth, until one day it had simply *bloomed* while he sat at a red light idly gazing at the drivers passing him in the other lane on an advance green. And suddenly it was as if every nerve in his body had been dazzled. His mind reeled. His eyes closed. The police had had to break the driver side window. He came to himself in the ambulance.

Since then, he had spent every waking moment in contemplation of, in awe of, what had struck him that day only to be disturbed by his occasional fits. They erupted randomly, as this morning when on his way to his uncle's office for the meeting to which he was now heading. Yet, even these fits he had come to believe were the fate of genius.

His uncle's office was in a dingy strip mall close by the Argyle neighborhood, a distressed agglomeration of blocks far down the list (if it was on the list at all) of locations ripe for gentrification. Nicholas scanned the eight storefronts that made up the Argyle Mall, a dry cleaners, a pizza joint, an H&R Block, a comic book store, a barber shop, and three empty locations with greasy clouded windows.

As this was the first time he and his uncle were to meet in person since his release from jail over a year ago, Nicholas, standing across the street from the Mall, saw no sign or indication of a lawyer's office. However, there was a just discernible light penetrating through one of the three greasy windows over which an old and faded metal sign announced 'J's Argyle Market'. Nicholas crossed over toward it. Coming closer, he saw a small wooden plaque beside the glass door. There was no name on the plaque, only a badly hand painted image of a bright yellow bird with black stripes circling its body.

"Oh, very clever!" He thought. "The jail bird lawyer! Clever bastard."

The door buzzed releasing the lock and he barged into a large open space. He was taken up sharply by what he saw. The big room had been left in a shambles by the former occupant and it appeared the new occupant had spared every expense to keep it that way. Cardboard boxes were kicked up against both side walls. Yards and yards of broken down shelving were piled nearly to the ceiling just inside the front door. The space was weakly lit by ranks of overhead fluorescent fixtures that hummed monotonously and blinked at random intervals. Two large, dust-covered meat freezers projected into the space, one from each side wall. Between them, four feet of open floor space served as the formal entrance to the actual office which was crowded into the furthest back corner. A desk made out of sawhorses topped by an old wooden door held an ugly old black computer, a desk lamp, some reference books and folders of various thicknesses. There were two hard-back chairs in front of the desk and a large office chair behind it and behind this a beat-up grey file cabinet. The entire affair could easily have fit within a small bedroom, yet here in an area so large, it gave the impression of a hiding place, and perhaps that was intentional.

To his intense disappointment, there were clients in the office. Two men sat in the chairs crammed up against the front of the desk in conference with Ben Shelley who sat in the large desk chair. This was to have been a happy reunion of like minds, culminating in the validation he so ardently desired from the one person who mattered. The shock to his pride launched him in a speed walk toward the office.

"Look who's here! Hello Boobala. Boys, this is him," Ben Shelley said jumping up from his chair and rushing to embrace his nephew. But Nicholas pushed him away.

"This was supposed to be our time! *Our* time!" His voice was harsh and piercing and rose to a high pitch.

"Yes, yes, of course," his uncle said, draping an arm over his nephew's shoulders and guiding him to a chair that one of the two men had dragged up to the desk. "But I thought you forgot. Better late than never. Hello, hello. It's good to see you again, Nicky. Come. Sit. Sit."

Ben Shelley was in his early forties, had short black hair going grey, blue-grey eyes and a long thin neck accentuated by a loose-fitting open neck work shirt. He had about him a kind of disarming vagueness, a charming inoffensiveness, which produced--at first glance--the impression of a weak mind. He was fully aware of this and had found it a valuable asset when dealing with certain people. For example, it had served him well during his years in prison where he came to be trusted for his inoffensive personality and proven expertise in financial law, and most importantly, in how to use it for personal gain.

"Haven't we been sitting here all a-twitter in anticipation?" Ben said, retaking his seat and leaning forward over the desk to speak more directly to Nicholas whose anger had subsided but who remained deeply disappointed. His uncle seemed not to notice. His face was suffused with good will.

"I..I was unable to..something came up and I was--" Nicholas mumbled incoherently.

"Oh hey. No problem at all. No problem at all at all. We're all here for you," he explained, waving at the two men as if introducing actors to an audience. "Shiney aka William Shine and Art aka Art Gross."

The men nodded as their names were mentioned. The one called Shiney was also in his forties. He was lean and angular with sharp thin narrow shoulders that poked at the seams of his V-neck sweater. It was an old and tattered sweater. His whole wardrobe--an over-fancy term in this case--was generally disheveled and moth-eaten. He wore wire-rimmed glasses and a cravat around his neck. But for all that, in his eyes there was a real intelligence at work, not the foggy, bemused intelligence of an academic but the sharp, calculating intelligence of a gambler. Sitting too close beside him (all three men were shoved together in front of Ben Shelley's desk) Nicholas could feel his gaze which had been fastened on him unnervingly from the moment he sat down.

The other man, Art Gross, had been sitting uncomfortably sideways with his elbow balanced on the back of his chair and his head resting on his hand with his legs crossed. He had thick brown hair cut short and a full beard. His ruddy face was wrinkled and blotched with red dots that might once have been freckles. Unlike Shiney, Art Gross showed no interest in Nicholas. His dull blue eyes were fixed on a point above Ben Shelley's head. They peered out from beneath the baseball cap he wore and there was a look of intense dislike on his face. He was not a big man but he was more sturdily built and thicker set than his companion. It was clear that he considered this meeting a complete waste of his time. He exuded contempt.

"What do you mean, they're here for me?" Nicholas asked, a note of anger rising again in his voice.

"We'll get to that but for now, I have to say...that document of yours. It's really rocked the boat. Hasn't it, fellas? We're feeling kind of honored even to be in the same room with such a mind. You know, I always knew you were a smart one. I could see it even back then when we were still a family. Oh yes, you've certainly proved me right on that score, oh yes. I knew you'd do something, I didn't know what, a good something, a bad something, but something. You had it in you, that part. The brains you got from your father. He was the smart one, I was the clever one. Though if I'm honest, he was cleverer than me as it turns out. It wasn't me that came up with the code, was it? But back then, who had any idea that it'd make him rich? But *somebody* had an idea, didn't she? You were too young at the time. But water under the bridge. Anyway, to make a short story long, I see the genius of it now after reading it. I should say, after devouring it."

"If I may jump in here," Shiney said, glancing at Ben Shelley who nodded briefly. "Your piece, you know, it stung me. I can still feel it. It's become a kind of itch in my brain. I know we're here for--well, never mind, but, really, I just wanted to meet you, Nicholas. Can I ask you, please don't take this the wrong way, but can I ask you, did you develop this on your own? I mean, was there an influencer perhaps, you know, Nietzsche maybe, or, or, Foucault? It's just that those fellas, well, I've always thought they never crossed the finish line. Their nihilism never got to where you've got to. 'Who cares?' indeed! In two words you said more than Marcuse, more than Althusser, more than Baidou, more than Lenin even! I mean, you've made a leap here, Nicholas. A great leap, in my opinion."

Nicholas sat back in his chair and even slid it a few inches away from the man sitting so close he could smell his breath. He was not aware that he was doing this. It was rather an unconscious reaction to this disturbingly fulsome assessment by this disheveled stranger.

He had never heard of these other 'fellas' but the detestably simple-minded suggestion, triggered by the mention of Lenin, that he had jumped on their spongy old ideas using them like a trampoline to propel his 'great leap' angered him even further.

Art Gross, who had been shifting in his seat with agitation, now spoke up.

"Sounded to me like the ravings of a spoiled brat," he blurted out. His face had gone red. His partner's remarks had annoyed him beyond endurance.

"Art, no call for that," Shiney said, quickly turning to Ben Shelley. "Am I right?"

Art ignored him. "I've been sitting here all day. I thought we were going to be discussing the other thing. I will say this. You were right, Ben. I was wrong. Now I see him, you were right."

Nicholas stood up now, slowly, decisively, as if the very motion of standing was to be seen as commentary. Yet he didn't say a word but glowered down his nose at the two men. His eyes burned and his hands trembled at his sides. In fact, it was impossible at that moment to think of the first word to say. He was painfully conscious of how ridiculous he would very soon appear if he didn't think of some way to respond, but the seething contempt he felt for their pretentious comments overrode the personal betrayal he felt toward his uncle and completely disordered him. His mind was a hive of swarming, buzzing thoughts. It seemed an eternity before the single idea that had been his touchstone rose through the clamor.

His throat was tight with resentment. His words were squeezed out in a squeak of rage.

"How dare you speak those two words like some supercilious adjunct trying to impress the class," he said speaking to Shiney. "And you," now focusing his rage on Art Gross, "Who are you to judge me? You have no idea. No idea!"

Ben Shelley, seeing that a crisis was at hand and afraid for reasons of his own that Nicholas would end the meeting, came up out of his chair with an exaggerated show of rescuing his nephew.

"Now, now, Nicky, don't take offense," he pleaded, grasping his arm with one hand and with the other caressing the back of his neck. "C'mon now, buddy, you're among friends here, isn't that right, Shiney? Isn't that right, Art?"

"Yes, of course that's right," Shiney agreed. "Friends and if I may so, sincere admirers."

Suddenly Art pushed his chair back and stood up. "Why are you encouraging this kid?" he demanded. "Don't look at me like that. You know what I'm talking about. He's teetering on a cliff edge and what do you do? Cheer him on! Can't you see the kid is unstable? I mean look at him. That--" he flicked his chin at Nicholas, "wrote this--" he picked up his copy of the essay from the desk, "and nearly--".

"Now, Art, let's just take it easy," Ben Shelley quickly admonished him.

"When are you going to tell him? Let's get this over with."

Nicholas, even as he was the subject of their argument, began to feel himself detached from the drama, floating above the scene. Having found his voice had provided a certain measure of relief. Now, the thought that had been squirming anxiously in the back of his mind all along forced itself forward opening a flood that raced around inside his head. "Why are they here? Who are they anyway? What are they all up to? What am I missing? This is very strange. Nothing here makes sense. It only makes sense if--" And suddenly he saw how it might make sense. "This is all because of *them*! It's unbelievable but that must be the reason."

He settled himself, oddly calmed by this insight, and now looked at them all with what seemed to him new eyes. The tight frown of anger and embarrassment that had been making his jaws ache melted away to be replaced by a scouring smirk. He looked and felt once again like the superior human being he knew himself to be. For the first time since entering the building, he knew for a certainty that he now controlled the situation. The change in him caught the attention of the three men nearly simultaneously, so startling was the transformation.

"I see it now," Nicholas said, looking down upon them. "Or should I say, I see through it. Family, friends, praise from people like you, it's all rotten lying and betraying. For a minute there you made me forget that I don't need any of that. And my disappointment--in you, Ben, especially--teaches me that I haven't yet reached the pinnacle. But I will. I will."

"Oh, Nicky, what's this talk? We're only concerned for your well-being. Believe me."

"I smell my parents in this. How else to explain these two? A coincidence that you invite them here for our first time together in how many years? No. It stinks to high heaven of those washed-up geeks and their millions. I'm with him: let's get this over with. If you can say three words together and one of them isn't a lie, maybe I'll believe a word you say."

Ben Shelley nodded slowly. "Won't you sit down then, please, Nicholas. No? You want to stand there lording it over us? Looking down on us as if we're some sort of evil cabal? Fine then. Fact is, you've brought this on yourself. Yes, you're right, your parents have, I guess you'd say, enlisted our services. You see, I didn't know this until very recently, but your behavior in recent months has alarmed them. More like scared them to death. What with your erratic comings and goings and the demands you've made on them, and then, uh, that certain incident and of course this..disease. I mean, honestly Nicky, I wouldn't have believed it of you. I didn't believe it at first. But then, you sent me your, what should I call it? You call it a manifesto. Art thinks it's more than that. I have my own interpretation. I call it a reflection of your state of mind. As I said, it really rocked the boat. For the first time in decades, I found myself in a very uncomfortable position. I never wanted to speak to your parents again and would have done anything to avoid it. But then...so I forwarded it to your father. Yes, I did that. You can believe I betrayed you but, you know, nobody writes such a thing unless they expect someone to read it. I was worried sick about you and what you had become, that the boy I loved had grown up to be able to write that. Frankly, I was afraid of what you might do--no, no, you asked for this. There's history, after all, OK? Don't interrupt. The other day, your father called me and we talked. He brought me up to date on all that's been going on with you. He was very worried and very scared. To be honest, he's not changed much. Still the scaredy-cat, still a coward, worse than before, it seemed to me. But I gather your mother stiffened him up to propose an idea to me. She always did have the balls in the family. And I have to tell you, it took quite a set of balls to ask me--me, of all people--to help them. But I agreed. And here we are."

"And these two? What's their part in this..whatever this is?"

"Witnesses."

"To what?" Nicholas asked, alarmed.

"To your state of mind, Nick. To your state of mind. This document--your document--makes it clear to us, Nick. I have to tell you it breaks my heart to do this, but you've brought it on yourself. And the way you glory in it! I mean, my god, this is not normal, Nick."

"So, it's my state of mind you're all worried about?" Nicholas said, as a shiver ran through him. "I'll tell you about my state of mind. First of all, you have no idea about my state of mind. No idea at all. You will never understand me. That's my state of mind for you! I never intend that you should understand me. You are all insignificant, of no importance whatever, you and my silly blasted parents. Go ahead. Tell me your plan to try and stop me."

"OK, that's enough," Art gross finally said. "That's enough for me. My god."

"No, wait," Shiney said. He had been listening with great interest. His eyes had never left Nicholas's face while a queer smile, perhaps of appreciation but with a tinge of condescension, played on his lips. "This is fascinating. This might, you know, this just might be a new thing. Listen to what he's saying. I mean, see it from his point of view. The three of us, who are we? Symbols of everything no longer worth saving. The disintegration of society. The corruption of authority. The scraping. The grasping. The hustling. The stink of the world of dead ideas. We all know it's a disgusting way to live but what do we do about it? Well, this is what it looks like when somebody stands up and says, 'Not me! I refuse to run with the lemmings. Kill all the lemmings!' Why shouldn't he hate the very sight of us? We're the defeated enemy and all he wants from us is to sign the articles of surrender. This is exciting!"

"Jesus Christ!" Art growled. "You're as sick as he is."

"Are you sick, Nicholas?" Shiney asked. He was still watching him intently, bearing in on him with an irritating suggestion of having achieved a kind of common ground with the younger man. "Or are you the only healthy one here?"

"Ha! Is that what you think?" Nicholas snorted. At last, his cherished sense of disdain returned with a vengeance, having found its grounding again, this time not merely in his imagination but in the person of Shiney. "I'm not surprised. You think I'm you, a petty revolutionary. You don't understand me at all. You can't understand me. I'm an Evolutionary! The first to go where it points. The first to see where it points! And the first who's tired of waiting for it to get there. I'm leaving you and all of it behind."

"Well," Ben Shelley said sadly, "I think we know what we have to do." He opened a folder and took out a legal document that he slid across the desk to Shiney and Art. Each one signed the document and returned it to him.

"Nicholas," Ben said in his practiced professional voice, "Shiney here is a psychiatrist and Art is a nurse practitioner. They are witnesses to this order that I have drawn up on behalf of your parents. This is the gist of it. It stipulates that in the opinion of the medical witnesses who are qualified to judge these matters, you are not competent to live as an unsupervised adult due to the danger you present to yourself and the community. Therefore, in accordance with the wishes of your parents, and in order to protect them from damages that might arise from actions taken in your present state of mind, they hereby renounce all parental rights and privileges regarding you. They further direct that Benjamin Shelley be appointed your legal guardian with *in loco parentis* responsibility for the monitoring of your personal activities. And that's about it. The rest is legalese, but you see now how profoundly worried you have made everyone. I'm sorry, Nick. I really am."

"And my allowance? You'll be cutting that off, too, I suppose."

"No, no, Nick. Certainly not. That will continue."

To their surprise, Nicholas began to laugh noiselessly while shaking his head in disbelief. "Do you honestly believe I care about any of this?" he said, surveying them pitilessly. "This whole fiasco? And what are you getting out of all this, huh? No, never mind. I don't care. But I hope you had the brains to soak them for every penny they've got."

Art Gross said, "This guy is a piece of work."

"Then I can tell them we've reached an understanding?" Ben Shelley said.

Nicholas stood up. "Tell them whatever you want. You think I don't see what's really going on here. You're using me against them for some purpose. I don't know what it is but you can't seriously expect me to believe this is for my own good. Good luck with it. You think you're clever. A slithering snake, making plans, hatching intrigues. But I tell you you're just three dumb rocks. But you see, the rocks will get turned over and what's underneath will surprise you. It will finally be free, a new thing will spring up from the mud and you won't recognize it."

"Oh, listen to the Biblical prophet!" Art Gross exclaimed. Now he stood up, seething with anger, his arms outstretched, his eyes burning at Ben Shelley. "Have you ever heard anything more ridiculous? Can this be over now? I can't stand listening to him for another second."

Shiney pushed his chair back and stood beside his partner. "I must say, Ben, this has been an exhilarating experience. I wouldn't have missed it for the world." The two men turned and walked toward the door without so much as a glance at Nicholas.

Finally alone with his uncle, he found he had nothing to say. In fact, the man before him was not his uncle of fond memory but some vile doppelgänger, a thing of no more interest than a rock.

Feeling the awkwardness between them, Ben Shelley shifted uneasily in his chair, craning his neck to look past his nephew toward the front door as if expecting someone any minute. He repeated this action several times as they sat in silence, hoping that Nicholas would get the hint, get up and leave. But the younger man seemed content to stand in front of him, motionless and silent.

"That was quite a speech you gave," Ben said, unable to withstand Nicholas's diffident gaze. "Listen, I admit, OK, I admit this whole thing has a deeper purpose. You know the history, right?"

"They never spoke about you..after we were no longer a family."

"Yeah, I'm not surprised. There was no way the truth would make them look good. But you've got to understand, I've spent the larger part of my life since then consumed with the idea of getting a part of that pile they're sitting on, that your mother has locked up against me. I admit it. It's a low, mean way to live. Nothing so elevated as your idea, whatever it is. But I really don't care, honestly, what you're cooking up. I don't understand what's happened to you nor do I want to. I have my own obsession to deal with. But in that way, we are alike. It's just that mine is much more practical than yours. All I want is money. Not all of it, not all their money. I don't deserve that, but I deserve *something*! I was there when it all happened."

Nicholas again raised his eyebrow.

"Look. Back in '90s, your father and I were still great friends. Kit was already getting colleges crawling all over him, throwing all kinds of incentives and scholarships at him and I was proud of him. He was a genius at writing code. Then the whole Y2K thing erupted and the whole world was freaking out about how the change in the date to a new century would fry every computer in the world. Your father, though, devised one of the most ingenious pieces of code to protect those computers and suddenly he was in business. I had just passed the bar so we teamed up. God knows he needed a lawyer. There was a lot of negotiating that had to be done. Businesses were skeptical of a startup and, well, anyway, he couldn't negotiate his way out of a paper bag so I became his head of sales. Man, I landed him some big deals! We were on a roll, we needed people. So who do you think was his first hire? A dumpy coding wiz with stringy blonde hair. I could tell right away, this chick had eyes on him from day one. Within months, she had cleaned herself up, lost weight and grew her hair out. Bam! He married her two years later. The now very delectable Edith Mary Schwartz...Aha! You didn't know that was her real name? She'd left that name at home and never picked it up again. She'd done her own personal Y2K transformation and from 2000 on, she became Marigold. Just Marigold. They became inseparable and I was cut out with a knife in my back. But now, Nick, after all these years, I'm going to get my share. Thanks to you. And all I have to do is pretend to give a shit about you and protect those two from any blowback you could cause. And that's it. The whole story. Not very pretty, but truth never is."

At first, Nicholas had listened to this story with open contempt but slowly, as his uncle went on, a change occurred in him. A genuine smile grew on his lips. He leaned down straight-armed to rest his knuckles on the desk and peered into his uncle's eyes. The smile corroded quickly into a disdainful smirk.

"This is absolutely perfect," he said, surprising his uncle who had been expecting the worst. "I have been pondering what to do about those two. And you, Ben, have made it clear to me, even providing the opening. I think they deserve a visit, don't you? Yes, a visit. A final visit. They have disowned me and I have disowned them, long ago. They just don't know it yet. Only fair, then, right, that I should reciprocate with my own disavowal of them. Yes, yes. And thank you." He turned and walked out of the office.

Outside, he crossed the parking lot to his car and slumped against the driver's door. He dropped his head in his hands. "Look at me," he thought. "Why do I still feel this rotten disappointment. It's crawling around in my head still! Goddamit! How could he? He of all people! I was so sure!..The old Ben would have appreciated it, would have praised it. But who is he now?..This is what I needed," he reasoned, catching at a way out of his misery. "This has been a test of my abilities. I have to expect this. Will the road ahead be potholed with betrayals? So be it. If that's the price, then that's the price..but goddammit!" and he slammed his fists into his pockets. His hand felt the crumpled piece of paper. He brought it out. For a long moment he stared down it, hardly breathing. Slowly he spread out the scrap on the hood of the car and smoothed it. For an even longer moment he wrestled with a thought that had come to him. At last he said aloud, "I can get back at him this way." He took out his phone and typed Bella's number in the message app then attached the PDF of the manifesto. His finger hovered over the message. Even though he was the self-sufficient Apex of Evolution he was still quite capable of self-deception. In the back of his mind lurked the knowledge that without praise and adulation from the rubbish heap he could not advance. "Will she be another pothole...or, maybe...I'll fix him." He hit 'send'.

CHAPTER 4 | Who Cares

Bella had gone to her bedroom and thrown herself on her bed. She felt drained and despondent. How cruel she had been to her mother! Why had she said such an awful thing? Her body wanted to sleep but she felt she must stay awake. Stay awake and care. About something. About anything. To stay awake *spiritually* so that she could go downstairs and hug her mother and apologize. She was too tired, too sad, too ashamed. She closed her eyes.

Within moments, however, her phone buzzed with a text message. Bella saw the number it came from but did not recognize it. There was an attachment with the title "Who Cares?". She tapped it and read:

Who Cares?
By
Anonymous

Why should I tell you my name? So you can make a judgement about me? Deduce an insight into my motives? Get a leg up on me?

No thank you.

You believe you deserve to know who I am. Why? Because it's your privilege as a reader. You expect to settle in with all your prejudices intact, just as you settle into your comfortable chair. Isn't that the bargain all readers make with writers?

That's not a bargain I'm willing to make.

A shibboleth. One of many you have no right to assume. Let's get this clear right at the start: there is no privilege, there are only shibboleths.

Now that we understand one another, I will tell you something about myself. Why? Because this is my page and it's my right.

I have not taken up this task because of the withering disdain I have for you, a disdain so intense that I am often physically sick with it. When I pass you on the streets I relish the idea of slapping you across the face, but I can't be bothered. There are too many of you and eventually my hand would break.

No, I take it up because it's time. I have waited long enough. I cannot contain the joy any longer as I contemplate your reaction. Disdain has its rewards. And this project is my reward. And your ruin.

While you were out playing golf, watching Netflix, skimming your timeline, following your Twitter feed, driving the kids to school and soccer practice, having sex, attending Sunday services, and on and on and boringly on, I was imagining a new world. A world where I would be free of you and all pre-existing human conditions. A world of my own design, shaped by my own desires, unconstrained by your rules or any rules.

Where had it come from, this idea of a new world? I trace it to a time when I was one of you. A time when I could still feel pain and terrible anguish. A time when my grandmother lay dying in her hospital bed. Then, she was a woman who affected me--don't call it love. Yet I wondered at this as I grieved for myself without her. She existed and would soon not exist. Why should I care?

In her hands she clutched her rosary and mumbled. My hand lay on her arm and pulled at it gently to dislodge the beady thing but she resisted weakly and I pulled harder. Her hands parted and I lifted the thing away from her. Her eyes opened and she whispered, "God forgive you." Then she died.

For I don't know how long, I sat by her bedside. I watched her features slowly wither and recede away. I had no tears for her but driplets of disdain were pooling up inside me. Finally I stood. What followed was a moment I shall relive forever. From her dead body there rose up a kind of fog that coalesced into a speck of bright dust which in its turn luminesced into a hot spark that electrified every cell in my body. It shot out of me and into the world, and with a bright laugh and a tear of joy in my eye, I uttered the anthem that I now can say to all of you and to all of life as my grandmother knew it:

Who cares?

Yes. So simple but yet profound, because beneath it and supporting it, giving it life and meaning, there rages a molten lava core of the greatest beauty. You see, I had invented Evolution!

Oh please, not that simpering shibboleth of Darwinian brainwashing. My new Evolution is non-biological, it is purely attitudinal.

I call it Evolution Of The Individual.

See if you can follow this with an open mind--because I intend to close it!

In the beginning there was no such thing as an individual. First you were a part of the natural world, an undifferentiated part of all that was and would ever be. (Which explains why no ancient wall painting anywhere ever depicted a human face!) Slowly, you began to have intuitions of your dark and dangerous differences from the natural world. And the world became dark and dangerous in your reflection--though of course the world had not changed at all!

To protect yourself you came to recognize your safety lay in the those closest to you, first the family, then the tribe, eventually the class. But as your intuition of your difference matured, some among you felt the stirring of a new feeling. Or rather the stirring of a new question:

"Why?"

And a new human attitude was born, but even in greater distress than in the pains of childbirth. "Why" is the key that unlocks the unthinkable. "Why?" is the precursor of "Who Cares?"

With the "Why?", a new evolutionary rubicon had been crossed. "Why?" gave birth to the unthinkable. Or rather, "Why?" undermined every shibboleth and with that one word all transgressions were set free. Predictably, the cost of transgression was--required--expulsion, from the family, the tribe, the class, to live alone. To live as an individual. As we would say now in a moralistic attitude, individuality was born out of transgression--thus was 'sin' introduced into the world. And to know yourself as an individual was to know yourself as a 'sinner'. Humanity had discovered Individuality, a new and terrifying attitude that could only be found and only expressed in 'sin'.

Evolution proceeded. And you understood that not only through transgression had you become a new being, nature itself had been transformed. Dark and dangerous no longer, you discovered its primordial and eternal 'nature', now as different from you as you from a rock. A nature wholly itself, free and correct in every way, unable to "sin" by virtue of its unconscious perfection. A pure individual in all its magnificence. How could this be 'sin'? Had nature also transgressed?

And suddenly, in this new mirror you saw the reflection, not of yourself, but of the self you could become. You saw reflected there the reality of the natural world and wondered how you had strayed from it, and your own internal natural world seemed small and meager and you were disgusted with yourself for seeing in the perfection of nature a sinning world in all its innocence. And you rebelled. You said "No! This cannot be! What I see there is something else, something new."

And thus the idea of freedom came into the world as a temporal and undifferentiated good that all could share, as it was shared by the rest of nature. As it was DEFINED by nature! Moreover a good that owed it's existence not to a family, or a tribe or a class--or a god--but to nature itself, and thus also YOUR nature!

The first of all freedoms came into the world, which today is defined precisely this way: as natural, unearned, thus undeserved, thus unrestricted, thus universally available. So as humans could only 'sin' as individuals, now they can only be free as individuals.

And since 'sin' has evolved into freedom, and there is no longer any 'sin', there can no longer be any transgression. And since there can be no transgression, there cannot even be individuals. There is only AN individual. Me.

Now you understand the depth of and reason for my disdain. For the further decimation of your faux priviledge, I offer this little anecdote. Don't recognize yourself in it? Liar!

You are sitting at a red light, waiting for it to change. The oncoming cars have the green light, and you are bored and start to look at the drivers as they pass. And you start to feel that they are just like you, in your car, aware of yourself as a complete and separate universe. Haven't you had this feeling? That you were a whole universe, not a part of any other, and they were too. Didn't it make you a little sick to your stomach? Here you are, lazily and unreflectively taking it for granted that your universe is the only one that matters, because of course it is the only one that matters. And yet there they go, those other drivers in their cars, like thieves in the night, unconsciously secure that THEIR universes are each the only universes that matter. Each an unquestioning existential denial of your own certain existential knowledge that there can be only one pure universe--your own. OF COURSE yours is the only universe that matters! OF COURSE each of their's is the only universe that matters! And then the light changes and you drive off to *pick up the milk, feeling a little sick in your tummy.*

But did you ever ask yourself the foundational question:

Who did they think they were?

No no. Don't go there! You might drive yourself into a bridge abutment. Coward.

But you could feel it, and your whole life is a struggle against that feeling. In fact-- why I disdain you so thoroughly--it's a struggle against the Evolution Of The Individual!

By their very existence those other drivers were claiming for themselves the very right you felt was yours alone--the right to be unique. Singular. I cannot adequately express the outrage that wells up in me at this injustice, the appalling presumption of it. And this, as I at the same time concede the inevitability of their rights! Logic demands I do so.

As the light changed and you drove off, you abdicated the choice that was facing you: either accept the injustice imposed on you by logic, or deny logic altogether, now and forever.

I admit that I too had felt that sickness in the gut. Which was proof that I was only a short way on the road to the evolution that I am unfolding. Yet even then I was far ahead of you. So far ahead that I could even then proclaim--logically--that you should not and in fact do not exist. Why should I be cornered by rational evidence? Is it for me to bow to what is not exclusively mine? Who says so? Only I can say so for myself.

> *I am Evolution and I am One. I alone exist. I alone matter. Logic is what I say it is. iLogic trumps Logic.*
>
> *"But what about history?" you squeak.*
>
> *Ah, yes. What of history? That sink of delusion. That sly justifier of every shibboleth. What are we to say about history? Only this.*
>
> *There can be no history in Year 0 of The Evolution Of The Individual. Here. I have a gift for you. A piddling little thing. I leave you the "H". Do with it what you will. I'll take the rest for myself. There is and can only ever be istory. All that has gone before is of no consequence to me because there is nothing that has gone before. istory is all that matters, and it will be as I decide. istory is I.*
>
> *"Oh, the arrogance of this person!" you splutter. But look around you! What good is your history? What has it produced? You will cleverly answer, "You!" and think "Gotcha!" and I will laugh. Enjoy yourselves. The party won't last. Don't you see me coming? (Of course you don't.) But I am here and you are not.*

"Nicholas," she whispered. She had recognized the 'situation' he had proposed to her that morning. The document had a strange affect on her. A sense of exhilaration was rising inside her as she read, but at first she did not understand why. The feeling did not seem to fit with the ideas she found there which actually frightened her. But perhaps the fear and the exhilaration were of a piece. She had never heard such ideas expressed before and would certainly never have thought of them on her own. In fact, they were as far removed from anything she had ever thought that she wondered if she had grasped them at all. And it was this sense of having been initiated into a new way of thinking, a new way of seeing the world, that both frightened and excited her. Here was a completely new frame into which she felt drawn--and not only that, more importantly a possible way out of the frame in which she felt herself trapped. Was this a world for her? Could it become a refuge from *this* world? And immediately she thought, "No, this is nothing more than some kind of adolescent fantasy, like a little girl dreaming of life in a castle with pink horses, a Barbie dream. And who'd want to live in it, I mean really? And this Nicholas guy, who I don't even know, is all of a sudden my Price Charming? What is wrong with me? It's complete and utter nonsense. Good God, what a mess I am! Listen to me! Have I even got any brain cells left that actually work? I don't know who I am or what I'm good for, but so what? Who says I should be the only one who does?"

Just then, her brother Richard entered her room. At first, he crept in but seeing that she was awake he hurried to sit next to her on the bed.

"You were zonked out," he said, trying to control the excitement in his voice. "I looked in before."

"What do you want?" Bella asked in a tired, bored voice. She sensed his excitement and peered at him, forcing herself to concentrate on his face. "What's the matter with you?"

"So, I've got to tell somebody." There was apprehension in his eyes but also a kind of giddy hopefulness. His natural smirk was now a lopsided leer. "I never would have thought you'd be the one I'd confide in. For anything. But after that scene in the dining room, I mean, wow. I was kind of blown away. You. You were something else. Where hast thou been all my life, oh, courageous one? Art thou my sister, the pain of my ass? But, hark, I love thee again."

"Oh shut up, you idiot."

"We're doing Henry the Fifth. I'm infected with Bard mouth. Hahaha" he laughed. "I kill myself."

"Go away."

"Yes, yes. In a minute. In a minute," he said, catching his breath. As he spoke, his hand shot out toward her knee but stopped within an inch of touching her. He blushed and shifted on the bed. "Oh God, I'm feeling a little rickety. Look at me! I'm trembling!"

At that moment, looking at him, Bella saw her little brother as he was as a small child, always excited and bubbling over with happiness. She half-expected him to jump up and raise his hands and pump his legs, twirl around and fall down laughing, just as he did when he was five. A sweet sentimental sadness swept over her. She took his hand.

"Settle down, you dope."

"Yeah. Phew." Richard took a deep breath then leaned forward, still vibrating with excitement but now speaking in a conspiratorial whisper. "You won't believe what I've done, Bel. But after this morning--I mean, I just can't get over it. You meet him, Flynn, *this morning*! How crazy is that? Of all mornings. Of all meetings! It's some kind of a crazy fate thing, right?"

"Would you please--"

"It was me, Bel! I did it. It was me!"

"What did you do?"

"I got his picture in the paper!"

"What!"

"I know. So cool. Me and Kevin and Bradley came up with it. You know, as a way to fix the bastard. He so thinks he's better than everybody else."

"You mean you accused him of abuse?"

"Yes!"

"But wait--he didn't..."

"Fuck no. I would have killed him if he tried that shit on me. God. Fuck no. But listen. We hacked this registry of abuse cases and inserted one on him. Pictures and everything. Then we linked it to the reporter's email, that woman who's done some stories on this stuff. And she went for it! The paper fact-checked it and saw it was in the registry, and--voila!--the scoop of the year!"

"It's that easy?"

"The dark web, baby! It worked."

"But, Richard..what about Mom?"

"Yeah. That was a bit of a surprise. But hey, she's so wrong about him. I mean, I actually feel like I've performed a public service after listening to her down there. I love her but she's so clueless about so much.

Aunt Eleanor gets it. And even you agree with me!"

Suddenly, he jumped up and threw out both hands in a pantomime of grabbing her shoulders.

"But listen. Listen to this. This is the best part. Guess who's name I used."

"No idea."

"Jared Probst." His eyes went wide with the cleverness of it and joined with his wide open mouth to give him the aspect of a manic gameshow host urging on a contestant.

"Who's Jared Probst?" Almost, Bella hoped he wouldn't answer so that her eyes could linger on the ridiculously sweet site of his hair bouncing around his ears and the child-like flush in his cheeks. But beneath this sweetness, her heart had registered a small tremor that she had been ignoring, a fault line in that lovable crust, which she hoped was only her tiredness.

"A kid that went to Auggie."

"And?"

"He died in a car accident a couple years ago. That was Kevin's brainstorm."

This revelation was having an odd and unexpected effect on Bella. Slowly, watching and listening to her brother, she began to feel a twinge of something like hope which made her blink and wonder. She understood very clearly what he had done and in her mind saw it as an awful thing, a terrible prank. But there was such a ferocious adolescent energy in him because of it. This reckless, thoughtless act, seemingly free of the fear of consequences, seemingly free of any fear. Yet she knew that there should be fear--she was sure no one could commit such an act fearlessly unless they were somehow damaged psychologically. Which certainly did not apply to her brother. So there must be fear, there should be fear, there can be fear, there will always be fear. Fear is life. Her brother played with it. She cringed from it.

Suddenly, she didn't feel tired anymore.
"Wanna read something?" she asked Richard.
"What? No."
"I think you should read this. I want to know what you think."
"You want to know what I think? Who are you?"

Bella handed him her phone.

Looking at the screen, Richard said, "'Who Cares?' I like it already."
"Just read it."

Richard began to read.
"What's a shibboleth?" he asked a second later.
"And you go to Auggie? I don't know. It's like a way of thinking that nobody believes in anymore. Just read it for God's sakes."

Bella fell back on her pillow and draped her arms over her eyes. She waited, breathing slowly and easily.

Finally, Richard looked up from the screen. His face was a blank. Bella saw this and immediately cursed herself for making him read it. She sat up.

"What?" she said. "It was just a thing, don't worry about it. Never mind," she said and quickly reached out for her phone.

Richard let her take it.

"Who is 'Anonymous'?" he asked, his face now showed a kind of concern, with hunched brows and tight lips. To Bella it was almost as if he were concerned about her and the kind of people she hung with. Like a big brother.

"Like I said. Never mind. Just some guy I met. Forget about it."

"Forget about it?" Richard said, startled. "Are you kidding? I want to meet him! Who is he?"

"You do?"

"How could you have read that and still be sitting there calm and collected? Do you even understand what he's written?" Now, agitated once more, Richard stood up from the bed and began pacing the room in front of her.

"Oh my God!" he kept repeating as he paced.

"Richard, cut it out. So what do you think?"

"I don't know. I don't know. I feel like..I mean, I feel like I've never thought about anything before in my life. I mean..Jesus, Bella. Who is this guy? Do you know him? I have to meet him."

"Come here a minute." She brought up the video she'd taken that morning of Nicholas and Father Flynn. "I actually met him through the priest. Complete randomness. He was there when--well, just look."

And she played the video. Richard, leaning into her shoulder, watched without blinking. While he watched the video, she watched him. She had never seen him so concentrated, so drawn out of himself. She was alarmed at his intensity but at the same time wondered at it

70

as a creeping sense of repulsion seeped into her heart. Not at the video itself, but at the little brother, the happy, ridiculous, lovable boy who could have, somehow, become this..this--she could not put a word to it. She did not want to try. "What have I done?" was her only thought. The video ended and Richard stood up. Bella quickly shoved the phone under her pillow to hide what she had already let loose.

"That's the guy?" Richard asked unbelieving.

"Yes."

"What was he doing, just standing there?"

"The priest thought he was having some kind of catatonic fit."

Richard looked at her but Bella felt he was not seeing her. His eyes were vacant.

"Cool," was all he said. His voice was flat but it was clear that his mind was racing. "So it's a real thing, cata--what, catatonicism?"

"Catatonia."

"I thought it was a..a shibboleth." Now his eyes swung up to hers and he addressed her in a new voice, filled with decision and determination. "I want to meet him. I want to meet this guy. What's his name?"

"Nicholas."

"Nicholas what?"

"Shelley."

Richard turned away towards the door only stopping to say over his shoulder, "Send me that PDF and the video. I want to meet him." And then he walked out.

CHAPTER 5 | Nema Nema

Standing at the high reception counter of St. Augustine High School priests' residence, she confronted the receptionist with her gentle demand to see Fr. Flynn.

The woman peered up at her and explained, "I'm sorry Mrs. Benfont, but Fr. Flynn is unavailable."

"But you see, he is my spiritual advisor and I would very much like to speak to him," Angela said. She had slipped into her best attire--a green chiffon formal affair with a belt, white heels, pearl necklace, and white gloves--before leaving the house and had left as soon as Eleanor was gone.

"I understand that," the reception said, "but I am truly sorry but Fr. Flynn is--well, he isn't allowed..."

"Would you please just ring his room and tell him Angela Benfont is here? He'll want to see me. I know he will."

"Mrs. Benfont," the receptionist sighed, "I really can't do that, I'm so sorry, but the Rector has said no communication and he's the boss."

Angela pursed her lips, her most intense expression of frustration within the bounds of civility. "I'm sorry, too," she said and walked out into the broad hallway. But instead of turning left, toward the exit, she turned right.

"Mrs. Benfont! Mrs. Benfont!" The receptionist had leapt from her chair and now stood in the hallway behind her. "You can't go--oh dear," she moaned. "Crazy woman."

Angela hoped the receptionist would now inform Fr. Flynn of her arrival and evidently she had done just that because at the end of the corridor the double doors swung open and Fr. Flynn hurried toward her.

"Oh Father!" Angela whispered, tears welling up in her eyes.

The priest came toward her with his arms open and a warm smile on his face. He held her by the shoulders, peering into her eyes.

"Come, come, now," he said, wanting to reassure her. "No need for that, Angela." He took her by the arm and led her down the hall, back through the double doors and into a small empty office just inside the residence. There were two chairs set up on either side of a small table. On it was a vase with a small spray of plastic flowers, long since faded from sunlight and covered in dust. A statue of the Blessed Virgin appearing to Bernadette at the Lourdes grotto, small and unobtrusive and also greyed with dust, stood demurely at the far edge of the table. Father Flynn ushered Angela to the nearest chair and slid the other close up to her.

"Oh, Father," Angela began, taking her ever-ready tissue from inside her sleeve and dabbing her eyes. "I felt I just had to come and tell you that all of us who love you know it isn't true." She smiled at him, weakly and imploringly, hoping to embed her belief in his eyes.

"Thank you, Angela," he said, "thank you, thank you, thank you."

"I'm so afraid for you, Father, honestly, I don't know what to think or do. How could someone, some awful person, accuse you of such..such a thing? Oh, I know I must be making it worse for you, putting my suffering on top of yours and I didn't want to come for that very reason. This terrible thing that has happened to you, who could ever believe that someone could do such an awful thing. But I can't help myself because all of us who love you feel like it has happened to us, too. And...oh, Father, I don't know how to put this." The priest leaned forward and placed his hand over her clenched hands. "Oh, I'm going to say something too stupid, I just know it."

"Angela, it's all right. I'm listening."

"I could only say this to you," she said as she shifted in her chair to face him. "I know it's not stupid at all. It's what we're supposed to believe. But it just feels stupid when I say it."

"Well, let's feel stupid together. Let 'er rip," the priest said and patted her hands, then sat back in his chair.

Behind her large round glasses, Angela's eyes gleamed as they always did on those rare and precious occasions when it was possible to speak about what lay hidden, yet pulsing with the light of eternity, in the depths of her heart. Truly, in this small room with its meager furnishings and bad lighting, she felt as she always did upon entering a confessional, to her mind the closest one could get to God in this life, barring only the Eucharist. If it were allowed, she would kneel in the confessional in complete silence for hours, gazing fervently at the screen separating her from the priest as if Christ Himself sat there--as of course she believed He did. Now with no screen to separate her from a priest, her heart beat with exhilaration, for in this trusted and holy space she could confess openly and freely not her sins but her faith.

But strangely, now that the rare and precious moment had arrived, Angela hesitated. Her face clouded, her clenched hands rose into her throat, her eyes watered.

"Oh God, now that I'm here, in front of you, Father, I see that I'm not telling you the truth. I said I felt stupid but that's not right. It's not that I feel stupid, it's that I feel like such a hypocrite when I talk about these things." The priest's kindly encouragement had worked and the words now poured out of her in a torrent. "In my heart I know they are true and beautiful and they make me--I mean, they fill me with joy. But there's always this voice or a--a kind of presence--a tormentor that won't let it be a pure joy, that almost--"

She stopped suddenly and closed her eyes and turned her head away from him. When she opened them a second later, she was looking directly at the little statue of Bernadette kneeling before the vision of the Virgin. The sunlight shone on its worn and tired looking plastic. And this had an effect upon her that startled the priest. Angela began now to cry, openly and uncontrollably, her face buried in her hands.

"Angela," the priest whispered and leaned into her, placing his hand on her throbbing shoulder, "my dear, dear friend." He himself felt tears glisten in his eyes.

"I'm sorry, Father," Angela sobbed, now ashamed to look him in the eye. "I'm so, so sorry. I shouldn't have come here. I wanted to see you, I was desperate to see you. I wanted to tell you that Jesus loves you very, very much and that this--this terrible slander--is the proof that He loves you. And in my pride and complete hypocrisy I thought I could comfort you and make it all go away from you. You see? I'm here to comfort me, not you! And that's why I feel this tormentor laughing at me, calling me a hypocrite, because I am a hypocrite. But oh, Father, I do believe it! I do! I do! I believe that everything comes from Love, even this terrible thing that's happened to you, even this tormentor inside me, everything, everything, comes from Love. It must be so. I can't be wrong about that or else suffering and pain and wars and death and murderers and earthquakes are eternally true and eternally meaningless and Jesus died for nothing! It must be so as Lady Julian said, 'All will be well and all manner of thing will be well' and that's why I came, because it must be true, even if I feel like the biggest hypocrite to think that I can allow such thoughts to come out of this mouth. But aren't they true, Father, even if someone like me says they are? Isn't a true thing true even if--even if--oh Father! All I want to do is kneel before the Virgin for the rest of my life. I want to be Bernadette!" and she covered her eyes and sobbed. "Why," she whispered between deep sobbing breaths, "does everything, so beautiful have to make me feel so sad?"

"Oh Angela! Angela!" the priest said, leaning closer now and throwing a comforting arm over her heaving shoulders. "Of course, it's true! Of course! Especially coming from someone like you. *Please* believe me, Angela. I do so appreciate your love and friendship. But you know, Angela, this is my trial, my time of testing, and oddly enough--even for an oddball like me--I am not angry or afraid or depressed. I want you to believe that. I want you to take comfort in that. But if there was one thing I needed today, one single thing, it was to be reminded that everything comes from Love. Yes, Angela, even a priest can forget that. Believe me! So many of us do, so many of us live as if it wasn't true. But you, Angela, only you would put yourself in my shoes. Only you would love me enough to suffer for me."

Gently, the priest removed his arm from her shoulders and slowly, watching her with intense concentration, slid his chair back a short distance. While Angela blew her nose and wiped her eyes and went through the small motions of rearranging and composing herself, his eyes narrowed and he was frowning. Something was troubling him, as if behind his reassurances in this tender moment there was, moving to the surface, a decision he was loathe to take and had not expected to have to take, perhaps not at all, and certainly not then. And in fact, he had been badly surprised at her arrival just then, just at that moment.

"Angela?"

"Yes, Father?" she said slowly raising her eyes to his.

"Is there something else...?"

"Something else?"

"That you want to talk about?"

"I don't know what you mean, Father. But no, I don't think so. It's so selfish of me to unburden myself by adding to your burden, I'm almost ashamed. You're a saint, Father. You are."

"Perhaps--I just wonder, you know--how is everything at home. With your children?"

"Oh my children! My dear children!" she said as her hands flew to heart, "You know, as you mention them just now, my heart jumped and it's so strange. I suddenly feel ashamed of myself for--for what I said, about wanting to be Bernadette. I'm a mother, Father!" she giggled and the priest smiled at her. "That's my vocation. And there, don't you see, that's your genius as a spiritual director, Father. A word. Just a word from you, that one word 'children' and you bring me back to myself and change my heart with just one word!"

As she said this, her eyes widened and her mouth opened in a look of astonishment. "Oh my goodness!" she said raising her hands to her mouth. "You met my daughter Bella this morning! I'd forgotten. Yes, yes, she told us. I hope she wasn't...well, she's very opinionated, you know, at her age they all are, but--"

"I found her quite clever really," the priest said. "I think I could like her immensely."

"Oh, I'm so glad because you know I worry about her, that she may be losing her faith but of course they all lose their faith at this age, don't they, and a mother just has to be patient and trust that her child will come back to the Church after a time, after life catches up with them. She's running so hard to keep ahead of it and I try very hard to understand that and not be too worried. But--it's in God's hands, isn't it, how they'll turn out? And once again," she said beaming at him, "you seem to have read my heart again because, believe it or not, I had wondered whether I should talk to you about Bella, about her losing her faith. Isn't that wonderful? How things arrange themselves? How the hand of God is in everything? That's Grace, isn't it, Father?"

"And your son?" the priest asked after a short hesitation. It was the moment of decision he had been dreading. "Richard."

"Oh, Richard," Angela said. The question had surprised her. But she was immediately grateful for it and her head tilted to the side and her eyes gleamed with the chance to talk about Richard. "I don't worry about Richard, my little genius. He's too smart for his own good. You know him."

"Oh, yes. Like all the smart ones, he thinks all his teachers are dumb!"

Angela giggled with delight. "He thinks I'm dumb, too. Everybody's dumb but him! But he has a good heart. You know, Father, I'll never forget what the principal of his school told me when he was in fifth grade. That there were only four or five kids in the entire school who were born leaders and Richard was one of them...I've kept that talk in my heart all these years, the way Mary kept things in her heart about her Son." She lowered her eyes and straightened her dress. "Oh Father, I feel so much better. Thank you for seeing me." She rose and the priest rose, too.

"I'm glad, Angela. Pray for me?"

"Oh yes, Father, unceasingly!"

"And I'll pray for you. And for Bella...And for Richard."

After she left, Fr. Flynn sat down again, leaned against the little table, propped his elbow on it and rested his head in his hand. He closed his eyes and remained motionless for a time. Then he sat back and slowly drew from the inner pocket of his jacket a folded paper.

No more than half an hour before Angela had arrived, Fr. Bernardi had knocked on Fr. Flynn's door.

"Got a minute?" Fr. Bernardi said, entering the room with a sheepish glance at his friend.

"You dare enter the leper colony?"

Fr. Bernardi came in and shut the door, too intent on his mission to acknowledge the sarcasm. He held out a sheet of paper. "I think I need some advice."

"Sit."

Fr. Bernardi was younger than Fr. Flynn, and had only been teaching for two years. Currently, he taught AP English in the Junior year. He was Richard Benfont's AP English teacher. Nervously, he explained that he had had an idea for a creative writing assignment that he hoped the boys would find interesting and unexpected: to write a prayer. "After all, this is a Catholic school, isn't it?"

On reading through the papers the evening before, Fr. Bernardi had had to get up from his chair several times to keep himself from falling asleep. The papers were all mediocre with only one or two stray sparks of talent. Creatively, the new idea had been a bust. Nearing midnight, becoming more and more despondent but determined to finish reading all the papers before allowing sleep to put him out of his misery, he came to the last paper. Richard Benfont's paper.

"I know I tend to get fanciful," he explained to Fr. Flynn. "But I...well, I need your opinion. Am I being too fanciful? Should I--we--be worried about this kid?" and he handed Fr. Flynn Richard's paper.

Fr. Flynn sat and began to read:

How They Pray in Hell

Our jailer who art in heaven

Forgotten be thy name, thy kingdom rot,

Thy will be spurned, on earth as it is in Hell.

Living eternally with our hearts' desires,

We hate your angels as we love our own.

Deny us not our fond temptations,

But deliver us from all your saving graces.

Nema, Nema, Nema.*

(*'Amen' spelled backwards)

By Richard Benfont, 3B AP English

CHAPTER 6 | The greatest of all crimes

He had left his uncle's office with his mind seething. He could not hold one thought steady before it went screaming off to collide with another. So fast was his mind whirring and churning that his head ached badly and his eyes throbbed. And underneath it all was the ever-present threat of another attack, made worse by the fact that he had never been able to identify a single trigger that brought it on. It came when it came, for a reason or no reason, 'the fate of genius'.

The tumult continued as he drove, causing him to forget entirely where he had intended to go so that now, seeing a huge green sign hanging over the thruway for an exit he did not recognize, he took his foot off the gas, coasted onto the ramp and pulled to a stop against the guardrail.

"Wait. Where am I going--shit! No, no, no. No, no, no. These things are to be expected. Why are you angry? Disorder. Your mind is disordered. This is your strength! This is your way! Follow. Follow...Yes, pick it up, that coffee cup. Sure, why not? Pick it up. How long has it been there? Who were those two bastards anyway? Jail house buddies, no doubt. Sure, perfect sense, the jail bird lawyer. That's clever, that is. He's a clever crook. Turn the car off. Should I turn the car off?....but to let them read it! Them! Who are they to sit in judgement? That skinny neck sticking out of that shirt, why can't I get that picture out of my mind? Oh, how ugly people are! With their necks and their beards and their...their...Oh yeah, I was going to pick up that cup....but, oh! Why couldn't he see it? I was sure he would see it....my genius, The Evolution of the Individual!...and so all this will be new and terrible. OK but *trust*! That's all you need. Trust in disorder! Disorder begins at home! Hah! Yes, that's true. That's the way forward. That's the path. So be disordered! Be lost! Be confused! Be tormented with indecision! Let confusion rule! You're the new normal."

He put the car in gear and drove to the end of the ramp, turned left and then left again onto the entrance ramp and back onto the thruway in the direction he had come.

"Did she get it? Did she read it? And why do I care? See, this is pure immaturity, nothing else. Yes, you are. You're immature. And so you are a danger to yourself. Stay with this, stay with this. Why do you care? Because...because you want acknowledgment? Do you need acknowledgment? See? This is pre-evolutionary thinking! "Who cares" is the touchstone, always come back to that, don't let anything come between you and "Who Cares"...--that goddam cup!" And with this he finally reached down for the cup but it rolled out of reach. He stretched further taking his eyes off the road. His left hand, still on the wheel, was pulled to the right and suddenly there was a vicious jolt as the car scraped into the metal abutment and bounced violently. Nicholas's head shot back up. His eyes wide with terror, his hands crushing the wheel, he muscled the vehicle back under control. For many minutes his breath came in gasps and his whole body shivered as his nerves prickled. At last, in a sour temper and exhausted from the aftermath of such an intense rush of adrenalin, he let his arms relax and his shoulders slump. His foot barely touched the gas pedal. Out of the corner of his eye, he saw the coffee cup roll across the passenger-side footwell. Squeezing the wheel once again, he took in a breath of air until his lungs overflowed. Then he screamed at the top of his voice until his throat ached. After which, he felt much better.

"Go ahead, roll you little bastard!" he said with a sneer to the offending cup. "Roll! Roll, I said!" and he yanked the wheel and the cup obeyed. "Ha! Who cares? You can roll around there until you disintegrate. You think I care? You think it matters to me? You're nothing but garbage and I want to thank you for reminding me that the whole world is nothing but garbage. Nothingness tossed you out into world so nothingness could be clean and pure and empty. Lest I forget who I am, there *you* are."

Eventually he arrived at the location he had started out for, his parents' house. From something a little more than a shack in a secluded wooded area on several acres, over the years his parents had transformed it into what Ben Shelley called their 'geekdom'. Now it was a sprawling, eccentric, overgrown oddity with dark blood-red walls of board and batten, yellow window frames flanked by bright red shutters, window boxes overflowing with dangling vines, a green steel roof, a massive greenhouse with an enclosed walkway leading from the main house, and a kind of pandemonium of gardens littered with pergolas, trellises, arbors, and obelisks. The sight of it repelled him. Perhaps because it too closely resembled the meaningless, patternless, disjointed junk-pile of thoughts and ideas he was continually fighting in his own mind.

"Look at this mess," he thought. "What a display! Their own little heaven on earth. How pathetic. The dream come true. Eden in a crazy nutshell. Take a good long look. You'll never see this abomination again. I'll burn it down to the ground inside me as if it never existed!" It was in a way astonishing that this thought should have such an immediate and even refreshing effect on his mood. It had, at least for the moment, stilled his mind. He wondered at this and felt the surge of a dominating optimism as he approached the front door.

He walked in without knocking and found his parents at the far end of the room before the fieldstone fireplace. It was clear that they had been expecting him. "Ben. The bastard!" he swore to himself. He had dearly wanted to surprise them, to give them no advantage, but his uncle had spoiled that, too.

The interior of the house very much reflected the exterior, from the board and batten walls to the wide plank floors stained a deep blood-red. On every vertical surface hung the quilts his mother concocted and on every horizontal surface, even the floor, a collection of flowers, herbs, and vines in eccentric pottery and tall pot stands of intricate metal. In the far corner sat a bronze Buddha, his father's special icon profoundly unimpressed, its eyes closed, its arms folded.

The effect was somewhat overwhelming as a visitor would be assaulted on every side with such a confusion of ornamentation it would be difficult to focus anywhere.

His mother, standing beside her husband who sat on the fireplace hearth, wore an oversized faded denim shirt, gaudy yoga leggings and Birkenstocks. His father, on the other hand, wore a long loose collarless white shirt-dress in deference to the Buddha in the corner. His legs were bare, his sock-less feet strapped into leather sandals.

Nicholas's sense of dominance increased and a derisive smile appeared on his lips. He found this feeling highly enjoyable, the emotional fulfillment of his inner commitment to the attitude of disdain.

His father lifted his head and raised his paired hands in prayerful salute, an action that had become habitual since his sojourn in the Ashram decades ago. A smile appeared on his father's lips which was evidently intended to convey a warm and welcoming peaceful attitude, but to Nicholas the smile seemed merely a silly and cartoonish gesture. Nicholas dropped into the large pink bean bag he'd always sat in when he lived here.

But suddenly his station in regard to them--lower, smaller, subservient--seemed to crush his fragile confidence. Immediately he struggled his way back out of it and hurriedly took a seat on one of the two 'art chairs' set in the middle of the room facing the fireplace. This small and insignificant action, however, touched the tender spot where his new self festered in birthing. He faced his parents, anger and embarrassment rising into a toxic uncertainty, his confidence wounded. "From such a little thing," he thought to himself. "Is that all it takes to wound me? If I wilt under the smallest things ..."

This train of thought came to an abrupt end as his father began speaking.

"My dear Nicholas--" he began in his affected way but he was immediately interrupted by his wife.

"No, no!" she demanded. "No 'my dear Nicholas'! No! Why are you here?" she accosted her son, nearly breathless with anger. "How dare you!"

Nicholas could not help but notice that her skin was creased with fine wrinkles and that her cheeks had begun to deflate. Her marigold-colored hair hung loose in long dry strands and looked if it hadn't been washed in days.

Had it really been that long since--since that day, the day when everything changed for him? He found himself wondering whether he was the cause of this degeneration and hoped it was true. But most noticeable were the ugly red splotches that had suddenly bloomed on her face with his arrival.

"Now Mari," his father broke in. He had a high-pitched voice in normal conversation but when he was under the stress of maintaining a serene presence it escalated to a girlish pitch. "Let's not start there. Let's be calm. He is still our dear Nicholas, even if we have...uh, if we have...taken some steps. Some regrettable steps. Still, though, Mari--"

"Look at him looking at you!" his mother commanded furiously throwing her arm out toward her son. "Do you see?"

And in fact his father did not and had not seen the look on his son's face since his nervous gaze had been drawn to his wife with an earnest almost pleading regard. He did not look at Nicholas even now but instead closed his eyes, sinking into what Nicholas assumed to be a silent mantra.

"How am I looking at him?" Nicholas challenged his mother. He was in a fine mood suddenly.

"Don't play that game with me, Nicholas," his mother threatened and stepped toward him. "I want you to leave. Now!"

His father's girlish voice gushed earnestness. "Mari, such acrimony is really out of place here, under the circumstances."

His wife spun round at him, her eyes wet with hot angry tears. "Are you insane? The *circumstances*? The circumstances are, Ben was supposed to protect us from him and here he sits like nothing ever happened and the ink isn't even dry!"

Quickly correcting himself and visibly unnerved by his wife's vehemence, Kit Shelley stammered, "Sorry--sorry. I mean the, the circumstances of that very, that very agreement. Sorry, Mari. Sorry."

Some Buddhist, Nicholas chuckled to himself as he watched his father's eyes dart toward him, as if to escape another assault from his wife. "His peace is in pieces," he mused, delighted.

"Can we not be calm? You see the value of that, I'm sure, Nicholas," his father sped on, his words running away with him. "We acted with much charity, I venture to say. Yes, yes, and out of concern for...well for peace, you know. Yours and ours. We brought you into the world and provided for you and tried very hard to instill in you a sense of the oneness of things, the wholeness, the...the beauty, if you will, of the intricate web of being that all of us are...are a part of. But from very early on you resisted, Nicholas. You...you were not...like us. It is my sincere hope that you have come in peace with a right mind. We appreciate the shock you must have suffered but I dare believe you see the wisdom of it. And, and, please, please, understand that...that, we, uh, we stand by it, you know, the agreement."

Nicholas listened to his father with a rising sense of irritation tinged with a malicious giddiness. He was so ridiculous to watch! His prayerful hands clasped under his chin, the thumbs tickling the beads he wore around his neck. His bald head gleaming in the afternoon sun splashing through the large windows and washing all contrast from his face. He really did look like the Buddha! Even the earrings he wore reflected the fat dumb structure in the corner for he had gained much weight over the years. And then there were his skinny naked lower legs, like the legs of a flamingo Nicholas smiled to himself.

"He's laughing at you, Kit. Can't you see that?" Marigold wailed, her eyes burning into him.

He turned to her, a slight blush appearing on his cheeks and neck. A pitiful pleading grin deformed his mouth. "Marigold. Marigold," he cajoled, "peace, sister."

"Of course, peace! Peace! Now that he's here to confront us, let's have peace! You f-f-fucking coward!" she cried and stamped her foot.

Shamefaced, Kit Shelley glanced at Nicholas who was watching him with amused interest. He smiled meekly, apologetically, as if to convey to his son that it wasn't as bad as all that and he would easily be able to soothe his wife.

"Now, Mari. Don't do that," he pleaded, his voice tender but at the same time with a wheedling note. Just the way to make her even more crazy, Nicholas observed silently and chuckled delightedly. "Don't be angry. Haven't I often said our minds, they're like a kaleidoscope...we see everything all shattered and crumbled into a thousand pieces. We pick which pieces to see each other through but none of us are that single piece, that shard. We're all of the pieces. You see a coward today but tomorrow you'll see something else, a wise man maybe, but that won't be me either. Only the Buddha has ever been able to focus all the pieces into pure sight. Don't judge, Marigold. It hurts you too much."

"Then what do you see there," Marigold spun toward him pointing at Nicholas. "I see the son that tried to strangle me! Have you forgotten? Your dear Nicholas. His own mother! He would have killed me if he hadn't stopped before I passed out. And here he sits! Like nothing ever happened."

"Ah, yes. There is that. You raise a good point, Mari. But, you know...have...have we ever asked him why he...why?" Kit urged.

Marigold's mind was aflame with the memory of that day. Speaking about it so openly had caused a crack in her anger. The fear for her life she had experienced then--at the hands of her son!--erupted again into full consciousness as if it had occurred only minutes before.

"Why are you here? How dare you come back into this house!" she said through her clamped jaws, all her terrible concentration focused on her son's face.

Nicholas had been waiting for something like this. The moment had finally come. A shiver of excitement thrilled over his whole body.

"You bring up a good point, Kit. Why did that happen?" He crossed his legs and folded his hands over his chest. "It's why I'm here, frankly."

"Don't you dare apologize," his mother hissed, her neck and jaws now locked tight under the strain. "Don't you dare."

"Apologize?" Nicholas laughed. "What have I to apologize for? Not killing you? If you ever knew me, which you never have, you would be the one to apologize, to me!"

"Oh Nicholas, now-now, what is all this?" his father interceded before the interchange became even more abusive. "You're not making any sense. Please be careful...for your health, my dear Nicholas. Think of your health!" As he spoke his prayerful hands trembled and sweat appeared on his upper lip but both his wife and his son ignored him.

"In fact," Nicholas went on, "I never intended to actually kill you, though at the time, bending over you, my hands around your neck, I was surprised to find that the idea of it was nearly overpowering. I nearly threw it all up for the sheer luscious pleasure of finishing you. Surprised? You see how blind parents can be to those they birth. You, Marigold, were my guinea pig, my lab rat. It was an experiment, you silly woman, to test my will and my resolve. In that moment I broke through to the revelation I'd been searching for. I didn't kill you then because I realized what a useless gesture it was. I suppose I should thank you. It came to me in a kind of psychic orgasm. Certainly you deserved to die for the great crime you had committed against me, the greatest of all crimes, but killing you would accomplish nothing. What could it achieve? Only a long prison term. Even though I was justified in punishing you, even so, even though you are guilty, it would have been nothing more than a pathetic, run-of-the-mill murder and all the meaning would have died with you and I would have said my little word and be forgotten forever. And that's why you are still alive and your crime goes unpunished."

"This is very disturbing, Nicholas," his father said frowning, the fear rising in his eyes. "I'm afraid we don't quite follow. What crime are you referring to?"

"As you say, here I am! What am I doing here? The answer is, it's her fault."

"What's her fault, Nicholas?"

"She gave birth to me. Because of her, and because you two rutted like pigs, I'm here. And you cannot ever be forgiven for that. I'm here and what am I going to do about it? That is the starting point of all philosophy. But where all philosophies stop, I begin."

Look at them, Nicholas thought to himself, they're dumbfounded, stupefied, or are they just embarrassed? This is very amusing.

"I know you were worried I might show up to berate you and argue and scream and cry over your little scheme to disown me," he continued in an easy conversational tone. "But in the first place, I couldn't care less. And in the second place, you have disowned me and I'm here to formally disown you. I didn't birth myself, after all. That was your doing. Your decision. And what could I do about it? Nothing! And now you have to live with the consequences of her crime. Oh, I see it on your faces. The real danger. Oh God, please don't let him tarnish the company brand, don't let him disrupt our idyllic life in the country. But don't worry, this isn't about the business or the money or your brand or your comforts. There is only one fact that matters. It was not my choice to be born the first time. That day, with my hands around your neck, that day I call my birth day. I birthed myself anew, under my own authority."

Suddenly, Marigold jumped. Her eyes popped and flamed at something behind Nicholas.

"You were supposed to protect us from him! That was the deal!" her voice a fevered hysterical rant.

Ben Shelley had suddenly appeared in the entryway flanked by Art Gross and Shiney.

Shiney was rocking from foot to foot, his head down, his hands stuffed in his pockets, his bald head shining under the hall light. Art Gross looked even meaner and angrier than when Nicholas had seen him earlier.

"I figured we wouldn't be welcome so why bother knocking," Ben Shelley pronounced as Kit, Marigold and Nicholas all gaped at him and his entourage. "So we were right," he said looking at Nicholas. "Well, c'mon fellas. Let's join in. Don't be shy," he said waving Shiney and Art into the room. "Witness our fond family reunion, all gathered together in the ancestral villa, in love and amity forever, hey Marigold?"

"You're a fool and a clown," Marigold spat at him. "The ink's not even dry and look who's sitting here. The matricide you were to protect us from."

"Please, please, Marigold. Let civility and amity reign. Am I right, Mahatma?" he said turning to his brother. Upon seeing Ben and the two rough looking men with him, Kit's already much challenged Eastern serenity was washed away to be replaced by sheer terror. His face went white and his body seemed to shrink under its long robe.

"Nothing to say? Why am I not surprised? See, Art? See, Shiney? I told you we had nothing to worry about. Oh, I'm sorry. You haven't met my esteemed associates. This is Shiney, aka William Shine, and this is Art Gross, a couple of close mates from my time inside. The witnesses, you know, to our recent legal undertaking on your behalf. And, well, here's the thing. See, the moral side to this means a lot more to them than the legal side. Because like all their kind, having paid their dues, they find themselves...how should I put this...let's say, highly suspicious of the legal side of things. Can you blame them? So what we have here is a couple of signatories--"

"Stop!" Marigold burst out. "I can't listen to any more of this! Good God how I hate you!"

"Well, you know, Marigold, that's not helpful. Really, you're making this more difficult than it needs to be," Ben countered, shaking his head sadly. "As I was about to say, what you have here is a couple of signatories who are, you might say, rich in their newfound moral sensitivities but, on the other, quite unfortunately financially poor. And this inevitably gives rise to inner conflict, doesn't it fellas? So it was only natural that the moral side of things should win out over their, you know, somewhat dented trust in the legal side of things, you see, and that in turn led them to question *your* moral inclinations regarding our agreement. Now, I'm sure you can imagine how they might feel, that it's all too good to be true, you know?"

From the outset of his monologue, Nicholas was struck by the change in Ben since their earlier meeting. Still loquacious and given to rambling around a point with digressions and distractions, he had as well become a kind of lampoon of himself, speaking faster than before with a cringing nervous energy.

"So we had a conference call after our meeting this morning and we agreed that if Nick was heading here, it would be prudent to be represented ourselves, in case our agreement was altered in some way to disadvantage us. It's happened, believe me, it's happened. I've seen it happen. We merely wish to avert such an outcome. We're here to support you in any moral uncertainties that may come up, don't you see? After all, there is such a thing as a mother's heart and who can predict how it will reason? Nicholas has accepted the terms. We simply want to be sure you continue to do so."

Marigold hotly reminded him, "Me accept the terms! What about the terms you agreed to? You agreed not to come here and you were not to allow *him* to come here! Yet here he is and you, too. You bring these...thugs..into our house to protect your side of the agreement? It's not embarrassing enough that they know about...him and what he did to me. No. You bring them here, invited guests, to judge my morality?"

"Yes. I see that now. So I apologize most abjectly though I point out to you that we have not been engaged as his jailers," Ben said. Then turning his attention to Nicholas, he continued, "I should have stopped you when you said you were coming here. You know what you risk and yet you risk it right out of the box! Do you really want to blow up our understanding, your parents' and ours?"

"Haha, Uncle," Nicholas countered, "this is rich! Look at you all. My god. Well, let me set your minds at rest. Not only am I not here to blow up your precious deal, I'm here to ratify it! So worry not."

Suddenly, Art Gross emerged from behind Ben Shelley pushing past him to address Kit directly whom he had been intent on studying since entering the room.

"I'm sick of all this," he said with angry force. Kit cringed, backing away, as if expecting some kind of offense from this gloomy, threatening man.

"I only got into this at first because I owe Ben a lot," he explained in a somewhat lighter tone, seeing how severely his unexpected interruption had affected the man standing in front of him. The others could plainly see the effort he was making to restrain himself. "Yes, the money angle was attractive. He said you had plenty so...but what he did...a son doing that to his mother...anyway, I just want to say, I understand why you...why you did what you did. I don't want the money. I don't like being a part of it at all. At all. And I don't like *him*," he announced, turning to face Nicholas. For a moment, he stood directly in front of the younger man, nearly nose to nose, and with unblinking eyes stared into the black pupils. In his way, it was a kind of charity, a last hopeless attempt to search out some glimmer, some hint, of the normal boy Nicholas must have been at sometime in his life. In resignation, he took a deep breath and then, quite suddenly, shuddered. He had found nothing to hope for in those eyes, but then he hadn't expected to. With a bowed head, Art Gross shuffled to the entryway without a further word to anyone and left the house.

"Hahaha, that Art, huh?" Shiney now popped in, clearly unsettled himself by the turn of events. "Long-time depressive, you know. Clinical!"

Marigold's eyes raked Shiney then turned on Ben.

"He has signed? That one? Tell me has signed!" she implored her brother-in-law.

"Yes, yes, of course he's signed. Of course. It's all tied up nice and tight on our end. It's your end--"

"I tell you, Benjamin, goddam it, 'our end' is not in question. You fool! How could you even imagine--"

It was at this point that, after having wrestled with himself all the while, not knowing how to respond yet feeling acutely disrespected, his relevance diminishing by the second, Kit Shelley suddenly and impulsively broke in.

"We don't feel free, Benjamin. I want to feel free. We deserve it. Keep your end of the bargain. Don't come here to question whether we will keep ours. He should not be sitting here."

"Benjamin?" Ben Shelley snarled at his brother. "My, my, you call me Benjamin? As if you had some authority in this little drama, as if it isn't you who should be held responsible for this...this Frankenstein's monster. It's you who should have spent seven years in jail not me. For child abuse!"

Shocked, Kit fell backward. "I never--"

"I know. You never touched him. But from the time you came out of that ashram, you psychologically abused this kid. His inclinations, God knows, were already clear enough. He was mean. He was sharp. He was conniving. But he was salvageable. He was not fully made. He didn't have to be what he's become. But, oh no! You and your criminal Buddhist foolishness made all that worse. All his worst inclinations--your wife saw them! She was never a fool. Only married to one!--you gave him the license to be his true self. He knew you better than you knew yourself and he played you, you, his father! She had to go and get him at school because the other kids were terrorizing little Nicholas. Remember? Remember? The boy who couldn't stand up for himself? But oh, he was the first one to plot and scheme to get his so-called friends in trouble. How many times did he lie about some kid so that he could see him punished or even expelled? And then run to Mommy when his mean little tricks were discovered. And all the time, you never saw it or cared. Peace! Your peace did that and here he sits. *Your* son!"

Nicholas had remained silent throughout, the better to keep the drama unfolding. It had been years since he had seen the three of them---his mother, father, and Ben---together in the same room. He had been younger then and a mere observer. Their interaction now was intensely interesting and even enlightening, especially his uncle's condemnation of his father. That was a new insight, to be stored away for some future opportunity. It had no emotional impact on him, however, a mere data point. But he had to admit that it had been his father who, from the moment he arrived, had intrigued him most. Nicholas could almost smell the man's anxiety. A slight nausea rose in Nicholas's throat. It was true, he knew himself to be prone to just such cowardly impulses. He had been fighting it down for months. And he felt deeply in his heart that the tension between his goal and the path to the goal was the result of just such a fundamental cowardice.

Another member of the party had also been watching with a fascination perhaps even more intense than Nicholas's. William Shine stood holding his left elbow with his right hand, his left hand cradling his chin and his extended index finger absently tapping his lips. His eyes shifted avidly to each of the others as they spoke and an unconscious knowing smile appeared now and then. To an observer, it was the pose of the professional listener with a touch more arrogance and condescension than would have been appropriate to a psychiatric session.

"May I just jump in for a moment," he now offered.

Marigold was ready to deny his request. She detested the skinny, sloppy, bald-headed intellectual. But at her side, Kit raised his hands with palms open and nodded at Shiney. "Please," he smiled limply, "restore our perspective."

"Well, thank you, Kit," Shiney pronounced in his most soothing professional tone. "I hope I can call you Kit--I must just say that perhaps there is another side to this...situation, so to say...that perhaps we could explore together."

Marigold could not restrain her animosity to the man. His unctuous attitude, his arrogant presumption at this moment were intolerable to her.

"Oh, you awful little man. Get out of my house! This charade has gone on long enough! I cannot bear it a moment longer. If the result wasn't more detestable than this disgusting arrogance, I'd tear our agreement into a million little pieces in front of your damn eyes. But then where would I be?" She glanced at her husband who stood slightly behind her. "Have you nothing to say now? Will you let this go on?"

Kit, caught off-guard, mumbled, "I...uh...I--"

"Oh, spare me!" She resumed her attack on Shiney. "How dare you come here and lecture me! Get him out of here," she pointed at Nicholas. Then turning back to Ben, "and take your appalling little cell mate with you. At least, the other one had the decency to be embarrassed. You stand here, in my house, with a son who tried to kill his mother, who you were bound to keep away from this house. And you dare to speak a single word to me with him sitting right there? You dare to show me empathy? Get out! Get out now! All of you!"

Kit placed his hand on his wife's trembling shoulder and leaned into her. "Marigold," he commanded.

Shocked by the change in his tone, she swung round and with all her strength slapped his hand away. But Kit grabbed her arms and held them tight against her sides. Her eyes flamed. Her breath came in sharp short stutters forcing a line of drool to appear from the side of her mouth and spittle to shoot from between her bared teeth.

"Marigold," Kit repeated, this time gently. "I want to hear what this gentleman has to say."

These words were the last words his wife had ever expected to hear from her husband's lips. Never before had he dared give her a command. Choked with rage, her mind reeling with the enormity of her husband's transgression, she was left speechless which further maddened her. She turned away from him and collapsed in a heap onto the hearth.

"You have something to say," Kit addressed Shiney. "I think I have something I need to listen to." His voice shook and his lips trembled as the realization of what he had just done came home to him. "My son, also. Really, all of us. You, too, Ben. I find myself all of a sudden yearning for a catharsis. All these years..." he said, speaking softly to himself. "Can he be understood? Were we wrong?" His plea was met with a groan of pain from his wife who sat behind him with her arms hugging her stomach.

They took seats, Ben in the art chair next to Nicholas and Shiney on a large padded ottoman. Kit lowered himself into the couch, facing them. There was an uncomfortable silence for several moments, but Kit seemed content to let it continue. Finally, Ben said, "Shiney?"

As Shiney lightly cleared his throat, Nicholas decided it was time to put an end to this charade. After all, he reasoned, he had played his part. He had severed the last remaining human bond between himself and his past. Like a bulimic, he thought to himself. One last purge and I'm empty of it all. To be filled to the brim with a new entity. He had thought he would stand up and mouth some tart insult as a final parting gift to them all, but at Shiney's first words he hesitated.

"Well, you see, I think you've misjudged what's going on here. I mean, this man--your son--is not what he seems. He is not even what he thinks he is. Not yet, at least. But he could be, he very well could be."

"Be what?" Kit whispered.

"How can I express this?" Shiney shifted on the ottoman, settling himself, needing a moment to control his rising excitement. "You see," he began with his hands tightly clasped. His eyes, behind their thick lenses, glistened and sparked. Leaning in toward Kit, he continued, "don't tell anybody but we psychiatrists know there are certain kinds of people even though we proclaim that every client is a unique individual. Well, basically, that's crap. Look, we see so many people in so many similar circumstances, we all yearn for a true individual. Somebody who isn't so goddam boring with their mundane little crises and pathetic traumas and what not. Let me tell you, spend an hour with ordinary clients, all day, every day, and you'd beg to be put in jail with no visitors! I'm only half-kidding, but the point is, most inmates are not so different. Except for the fact that prison may be the only place to find the exception. It's a small sample size but it's rich in disorders, most, as I say, surprisingly ordinary, but once or twice I actually did run into an exception, thanks to my buddy here. Ben let it be known that I would help anybody for free just as he was doing with his jailhouse law practice. Now these couple of guys were different. They were tormented by--well, if you've read your philosophy there have been people--Nietzche, of course, but many others--who have built whole systems around the concept of nihilism. Now, it was the idea of nihilism--though neither of them had ever heard the word--that had captured some part of their minds. How they got there...well, the point is, they did. It held a special fascination for them. They were not what you'd call educated, let alone trained philosophers, nonetheless they got it. They could not conceive how what they had done could be punishable! They knew--*knew*--they were guilty, there was no question in their minds. They never questioned their guilt. They questioned the perspective that judged them guilty! They railed against it. 'Where do they get off judging me!' they'd say. 'Who are they to judge me!' And I really had no answers for them. But I knew their anger was caused by their inability to take it further, 'own it' as they say today. I knew because...well, because I felt it, too. Somehow, someway, it had to be possible. The idea was pregnant, like it was waiting to give birth, begging someone to see!" Shiney paused and wiped his forehead. "And then..." he smiled shaking his head in disbelief,"...there it was. Right in front of me. Nicholas's manifesto. The *reason* my friends could not find a way beyond nihilism! I didn't see it before. Nobody could have seen it before. The ordered mind--such as it is--can only push reality *to* nihilism but no further. That's what's stumped us all. I had pretty much despaired of finding a stance beyond nihilism which can only itself lead to the destruction of the order it hates--*which is the order of its own mind.* Nicholas's manifesto was the result of *a disordered mind*, unhinged, egomaniacal, illogical. Only a disordered mind could conceive of a pure disordered disdain for everything except himself. So--to answer your question, Kit--no, he cannot be understood. To the ordered mind, that piece of paper is ridiculous, childish gibberish, stupid even. You could have had no other reaction to it, and you were right to get out of his way and shift responsibility to Ben before something happened. But you waited too long and something did happen. Yet something even more momentous happened as well: whether he intended this or not, to solve the problem of moving past nihilism, he *negated* it! Your son has negated nihilism *and all philosophy* with two words: Who cares?"

"Oh stop! Stop-Stop-Stop!" Marigold suddenly exploded as her hands tore at her hair, pulling and ripping. In the next instant, she was up, her arms flailing as she launched herself at Shiney, punching and kicking him in a wild orgy of ferocious anger.

So surprising was her outburst that at first the others were stunned into immobility. But then they heard a sound. Whereas Marigold's action had shocked them deeply and could not have been expected, still it made a kind of sense in the context. Shocking, yes, but understandable. This new sound, however, nearly froze their blood. Across from them Kit had recoiled into an upright fetal position, his knees having sprung into his chest. His feet, propped on the cushion edge, were splayed apart exposing his naked genitals. His eyes seemed to have sunk back into their sockets and his eyelids blinked spasmodically. From his mouth, drool trickling down his chin, came the sound that had frozen them. "He-he-he-he. He-he-he. He-he-he." A crawlingly pitiful sound, a barely human giggle that Kit himself seemed unable to control and even unaware that the sound was emanating from his own throat.

Ben Shelley was the first to react. "Jesus, Kit," he cried bounding out of his chair and plowing into the fray between Marigold and Shiney. "Jesus, Jesus! Cover yourself up!" he screamed as he roughly pushed his sister-in-law off Shiney, but tripping over Shiney's foot, he fell against her and they both crashed to the floor. By now Nicholas too was on his feet, his entire attention consumed by the site of the devastated ruin that was his father. Instantly, he recognized that he himself was unable to move as his father was unable to move. And that a fixed gargoyle grin was also straining the muscles of his own jaws. And that this revolting vision was a kind of foreshadowing of what awaited him.

Ben had righted himself and was heaving Marigold to her feet. Shiney was up now and working to straighten his glasses. Breathing hard, Ben yelled, "Nicholas go! Go! Get out of here!" But Nicholas did not hear him. Suddenly Shiney came toward him, his glasses sitting crookedly on his face, grabbed his arm and pulled him away toward the front door. Outside, he helped Nicholas find his keys, opened the driver side door and ushered him into the driver's seat. Before closing the door, he whispered, "You going to be alright?" There was no answer. He continued, "You will be all right. Save yourself. We need you. OK? I'm telling you, you are important. Remember that. You are important."

Nicholas nodded slowly and slowly reached to close the door. With great effort he was able to raise his arm and press the red starter button. The car came to life but it was several seconds before he could focus on putting it in gear and moving off. In the rear view he saw Shiney watching him drive away through his crooked glasses.

The car rolled slowly down the long drive under its own power and into the street. Nicholas realized, almost too late, that he was headed for the ditch on the opposite side of the street and hit the brake. He was stopped crosswise in the street. He yanked the steering wheel hard and touched the gas to get the car pointed in the right direction. A street sign appeared up ahead and he raced toward it, turned onto the street which wound through a sparse neighborhood and then dead-ended at a dirt track leading into a barren field. He stopped the car and turned off the engine. He struggled to open the driver's door but then did not get out, instead slumping in his seat feeling nauseous and exhausted. He began to whisper to himself.

"Every day, I must remember who I am. Every day, I must remember who I am. The old Nicholas has been dissolved and flushed away by my choice. Choice is the universal solvent. By my choice, the new Nicholas will be a black hole dissolving everything into himself so as to annihilate everything that isn't Nicholas. Nicholas is the end of evolution, the end of the struggle, the survival of the one, this is perfection!"

    He slumped back into the seat and in minutes fell into the deepest sleep.

CHAPTER 7 | **The first disciples**

Later that afternoon, Richard was once again peeking into Bella's room and found her asleep.

"Hey," he called softly.

She woke with a start and was surprised to find that she had slept. Perhaps, she thought, eventually your body did what it had to do. She found some comfort in this. At least her body knew what it needed. It could make a decision. It believed in something.

"That's funny," she thought, not finding it funny at all. "Nicholas puts me to sleep."

In fact, it was quite true. It seemed that for hours after reading it, her mind had overstrained itself, wrestling with what she had read and re-read, searching it--and herself--to understand its effect on her.

"But what kind of a person do you have to be to think like that? To think at all when it comes down to it? Most people never think and certainly not like this. We've developed some kind of herd immunity to thinking. I thought I was thinking, but was I? Really? All I've done is stumble around in my head, bumping into the old beat up furniture. The same old questions over and over! I'm so sick of it! Oh, God, to think something new!..but is it even possible to think your way out of this mush of feelings? I'm a pile of mush, that's what I am. An original thought, if I ever had one, would sink in the mush. There's no help for me. I am who am I, what I am. But, God help me, at least I can recognize a new thought when I see it! I mean, I can't be that far gone, right? I mean, that's something, isn't it? Anybody else would write him off as a freak or a weirdo. OK, he is a freak and a weirdo, but maybe that's what you need to be to write something like that. To think something like that. And be able to articulate it. What then? Is he an artist? Is that it? Or a poet maybe? Yes, yes, that makes more sense. He's weird, he's rude, he's moody, he's sick. He's an artist!..." Such were the thoughts that had pummeled one another over and over until finally she had slept.

Unlike before when he had appeared excited and at the same time apologetic, now Richard stood facing her with a serious expression. To her, he suddenly looked older and even intimidating.

"Where does this guy live?" he asked in a quiet but authoritative voice, as if he did not expect her to refuse him. Bella noticed this particularly, this new attitude, and was surprised at the effect it had on her. Her first instinct was to respond to him as was her habit whenever her brother asked for anything: "Get lost." Or "Drop dead." Or just "No". But now he seemed to have found a way--not that she believed he had meant to do this--to preempt this long tradition of brother-sister carping. Further, she felt for the first time the meanness of such a reply and that it was a kind of minor enjoyment she had always secretly relished but was denied to her this time.

"What? No," but her refusal was not heartfelt and made her feel a tinge of shame. "Why? What are you going to do?"

"I told you, I want to meet him."

"What makes you think he wants to meet you? I hardly know him myself. I only met him this morning. I'm not going to sic my little brother on the poor guy."

Richard's attitude did not change. He stood before his sister, waiting for her to come around. It was as if he understood the weakness he had induced in her, as if he could see her struggling against herself.

"Well, you're not going without me," Bella said sounding weak and indecisive.

"I have to do some stuff first then we'll go." And he turned and left the room.

In the car, Richard was having a very hard time restraining himself. He had been working feverishly to launch a new campaign on his dark web site ever since reading the manifesto. This one was no mere prank like the earlier one. He felt himself to be at a turning point in his life and all because of a random meeting between his sister and this Nicholas guy. They pulled into the yard and rolled up beside a car already parked there.

"So he's home," Richard blurted and threw open the door.

"Wait for me," Bella demanded and led the way up onto the porch. She had been steeling herself for this moment and had determined not to think at all but just to raise her arm and knock. Nevertheless, now she hesitated and in that moment Richard slid in front of her and knocked loudly. Almost instantly the door flew open.

"What took you so long--Oh."

The man who stood before them was forty-ish, not tall but thin and angular. From behind his thick round glasses he scrutinized the two visitors.

"Oh. You're kidding, right? In this neighborhood?" he challenged in an irritated and condescending voice.

Bella at first had stepped back as the door sprung open. Expecting to see Nicholas, her resolve immediately crumbled. "No, no, we're not--"

"Don't care," the man replied, dropping his eyes and turning away.

Bella would have preferred to accept defeat and go back to the car but Richard, behind her, was poking her in the back. "We came to see Nicholas," she blurted to make him stop.

The man froze. Then he turned slowly.
"You know Nicholas?"

Even more now Bella wished she could simply disappear. "I was here with him this morning. He brought me--well, I sort of brought him, I guess, after, um..." Her voice trailed off as the last of her courage seeped away. Helplessly she looked back at Richard and moved a step to the side inviting him to come to her rescue. Her face was suffused with the burning sensation of her own cowardice.

Richard saw this, recognized it instantly and stepped forward.

Somewhat nervous himself, he fastened his eyes on the man's belt."Uh, look, sorry about this but my sister did meet Nicholas this morning. She even took a video to prove it."

The man tensed imperceptibly in the doorway, his interest finally engaged. For several moments he stood with his head tilted to one side. He seemed not so much to be looking at them as considering something in his own mind. At last, he stepped back and motioned them inside.

The sight that met them surprised and shocked Bella. Nicholas lay collapsed and deathly white on the couch. His eyes were closed and he was breathing with difficulty. Richard had moved quickly past the man for a closer look at this Nicholas who had so excited his curiosity. Gazing down at him with a kind of idiotic awe he turned to Bella smiling triumphantly.

"Has he had another attack?" she demanded, moved by a feeling of sharp concern.

The man's eyes flashed at her. "You know about that?"

"I...uh--"

"She videoed it," Richard announced proudly. "Standing in the pouring rain, like a statue. Show him, Bella."

Despite the fraying of her composure, Bella felt a surge of anger and this helped her to turn and face the man squarely.

"Who are you and what are you doing here?" she asked in a defiant voice. "I want to know, right now, what's wrong with him?" She actually stamped her foot at the 'right now', something she had never done and had only read about women doing in novels. It always embarrassed her to read of it. That she herself should act like a prissy heroine was mortifying.

"No need for that," the man observed in a calm, sardonic voice, giving her a belittling glance.

"Well?" Bella insisted more harshly than she intended when the man did not immediately respond.

"Then you'll show me the video?" he ventured.

There was a slyness about his whole attitude that finally dispelled Bella's hesitancy and insecurity.

"No, I won't show you the video," she threw back at him. "Not without Nicholas's OK. And if you don't tell me who you are and what you're doing here, I'm going to call the police."

Suddenly, Richard was at her side. "Jesus, Bella. Don't be crazy." Why he should be taking the side of this stranger was incomprehensible. No, it was disloyal. She turned on him, her eyes flashing. But before she could say a word, the man started to explain.

"You say you met Nicholas this morning? That's a coincidence because so did I. We met at his uncle's office. His uncle's a lawyer. My medical friend and I were there to sign some papers. By the way, it's my medical friend I was expecting when you showed up. My name is William Shine. I'm a psychiatrist. It would be helpful if I could see that video."

"No. I'm sorry. Where's your medical friend? Nicholas looks terrible. What did you do to him?"

"Now, you're going too far. I didn't do anything to him," he explained with some heat. "I rescued him. And who are you to come in here demanding things? So I ask you. Why are you here?"

Richard, who had been shuffling his feet nervously as he listened, suddenly lost all patience. "She's here because I made her bring me, Ok?" he confessed. "So now you know. Is he going to wake up or what? Is this the cata--thing?"

"So you also only met him this morning, I take it," Shiney addressed him with an insinuating tone.

"No," Richard admitted.

"Yet you show up here barking at me as if you were his family, which I know you are not."

There was something about this brother and sister team that puzzled and disturbed Shiney. It was strange, wasn't it? Why this interest, this protectiveness, in a person they had only met hours ago? But more to the point, whatever could have propelled Nicholas to befriend the girl in the first place? Why did he allow her to take of a video of him? But did he allow it? And why in heaven's name did the boy, who had apparently not even met Nicholas, seem so anxious to do so, had even forced his sister to bring him here uninvited? Yes, very strange.

Bella and Richard looked at each other, both seeming to realize for the first time that their uninvited appearance and inexplicable forwardness required either their exit or an explanation. They were saved from deciding by a voice from the couch.

"What the hell," Nicholas mumbled, taking in the group of intruders. Then focusing closer on Shiney, he growled, "What are you doing here?"

Before Shiney could answer, however, there was a single knock on the door. It opened and Art Gross stepped in. For a moment, as the others turned toward him, he stood on the threshold, studying with evident distaste, the general disorder and confusion around him. Shaking his head in disgust, he addressed Shiney, "This is how he lives. My God. Let's go."

Nicholas acknowledged him with an angry outburst and a look of deep scorn. "Here he is! Humanity in a nutshell! Look at him. And see yourselves."

Calmly, as if there was nothing here of any interest to him, Art put his hand on the doorknob and said, "I've had enough of this guy for one day. Let's go, Shine."

Shiney, annoyed by this interruption for fear it would disrupt the developing situation, ignored him.

Nicholas, now fully awake, turned his ire on Bella. "And you. You! You're in league with them?"

"No!" Bella said, shocked at such an implication. "I don't even know who they are."

"Don't you remember leaving your parents'?" Shiney said quickly to change the subject. "You drove away in a kind of fog and we were worried about you. Luckily, Ben had arranged to put a tracker on your phone. Don't look at me like that. It was part of the agreement you signed, which, of course, you didn't read. So by the time we left that disturbing scene, he saw your car stopped in a field. 'What's he doing in a field?' we wondered. Naturally, we thought the worst. I drove out and found you behind the wheel in a kind of trance. I shoved you over and drove you here."

"What's the gollum doing here, then?"

"Came to take me back to my car."

"Who's he?" Nicholas barked at Bella.

"My brother," she answered with a note of defiance in her voice.

"Quite a coincidence, wouldn't you say?" Shiney continued. "Things are happening. Momentous things."

"Oh, get out, all of you," Nicholas said in disgust.

"Come on, Richard," Bella urgently whispered, tugging on his sleeve.

"No way!" Richard countered, pulling out of her grasp.

"Richard!" Bella insisted.

"No. You go. I'll find a ride later."

"Don't worry," Shiney offered. "I'll be happy to drive him home. By the way, what is your name?"

"Bella," Richard answered for his sister. "She doesn't get it."

Shiney shot him a glance of surprised recognition. Is it really possible--the thought raced through his brain--that this kid 'gets it'? Momentous things!

"Yes. Of course," Shiney said now filled with a kind of prophetic conviction. "We should leave you to recuperate. But when you feel better, please try to consider what's happened

118

today: that by pure coincidence, this young lady, Bella, met you this morning just as we did, and once again by pure coincidence they are standing right here, right now. See? It's coming to pass as I predicted. You are important. Your first disciples. You don't realize your power of attraction."

From the doorway, Art Gross grumbled, "Or repulsion."

"He's right, dude," Richard excitedly took up the thread. "Seriously. You wouldn't believe the followers I've drummed up for him in, like, hours! Here," he said taking out his phone and scrolling to a site. "Look", he said proudly handing it to Shiney.

This unexpected and stunning piece of information struck each of them differently. Shiney fell back a step, his eyes large and elated, then lunged for the phone. Bella was aghast and blurted out, "What have you done?" Art Gross merely shook his head. Nicholas frowned, cocked his head to look at Richard, then suddenly launched himself off the couch and grabbed Richard's shirt with both fists, shaking him. Bella sprang to Richard's defense but Nicholas just as suddenly dropped his hands, releasing him. Richard, who had been enjoying the effect his bombshell produced, seemed at first terrified by Nicholas's attack but almost instantly he had gained control of himself. He offered no resistance. Only a sardonic, mocking smile played on his lips. Nicholas slumped back onto the couch and cradled his head in his hands. Richard anxiously and excitedly continued to explain his triumph as if nothing had happened.

"I posted his manifesto on the dark web," he began, speaking to Shiney as if to a co-conspirator. "Do you have any idea how many anti-life freaks are out there? Hundreds! They think he's the new Jesus! I mean, it's crazy! They all loved that line about 'you can have the H, I'll keep the rest for myself'. I mean, that was genius."

"The marvels are multiplying!" Shiney intoned.

He had completely forgotten about the video that had so sparked his earlier interest. Had he thought of it now, he would have shrugged it off as insignificant and a mere distraction.

"Oh my yes," he murmured as he read and scrolled. "Oh my...Such comments!...Something is happening here...Quite amazing." Finally, handing the phone back to Richard, he said, "You've really moved the ball down the field, haven't you?"

Behind them, having not moved from his station brooding darkly at the front door, Art Gross fumed, "Oh for Chrissakes! Cut it out! Let's go."

"Yes, yes, we should probably leave Nicholas to recuperate," Shiney agreed. For once, he was grateful for Art's presence. "It's been a long day for him and he is not well." He paused, still facing Richard. "I just wonder, though," he said, lifting his head to peer at the boy from under his hooded eyes, like a predator.

"Yeah?" Richard prompted, his smile dimming slightly. "What?"

"Oh, just curious. I wonder...are you by any chance...a man with a plan?"

It was almost as if Richard had been waiting for this very question. He lowered his voice but his eyes gleamed. "It's just words unless he has a target," he said as if imparting a secret wisdom.

"And you propose one?"

Richard leaned in closely and whispered.

"The fucking Catholic Church!"

For a moment, Shiney was speechless. He didn't know whether to laugh out loud or embrace Richard. It was undeniably a most outlandish and even ridiculous assertion. He was, however, quick to realize that his reaction needed to be neither hot nor cold. On the one hand, he might alienate this precocious young schemer and lose influence with Nicholas. On the other, by endorsing his 'target' too enthusiastically he would appear in the boy's eyes as intellectually inferior and, even worse, sycophantic.

"Let's go, Shine," Art called out, his patience depleted, "Get this day over with. I mean it. Let's go."

Though she had been standing this whole time quietly watching her brother with growing alarm, Art's voice jolted Bella into action, too. She had not been able to hear what Richard had whispered to Shiney but the exchange only reinforced her belief that nothing good would come of their association. She was still angry with herself for allowing Richard to bully her into coming here in the first place.

"Yes, Richard. It's time. Come on." Then she stepped nearer to Nicholas intending simply to say goodbye but at the last moment found herself tongue-tied. Looking down at his figure, a pathetic sight in her eyes, moved by pity, she said the first words that came into her mind.

"You should really clean this place up when you feel better."

Thankfully, Nicholas did not look up at her. Bella, red in the face, stunned and in disbelief that she could be so stupid, turned away.

"Yeah, OK," Richard said. "This has been fun." He took her arm and lead her out of the room.

"So it's happened", Nicholas thought to himself after they all had left. "What you feared above all else. What you wanted above all else. The test has arrived. But you are not prepared!"

He noticed he was shivering violently and threw his arms tightly around himself for warmth. "Why did I send it to her? She's to blame. Goddam her! 'Who Cares?' is a phony. I'm a phony. But now, now, because of her and her goddam brother, I've been thrown into the ring with the whole world waiting in the other corner! I can't stand it! The sneak. The conniver. Didn't expect it of her, did you? So sweet, she fooled you right out of the box. You idiot, you failed the first test because you were too stupid and full of yourself to see danger. 'Who Cares?'--YOU DID. What's worse, YOU DO! Even now."

Shame consumed him, convulsed him, made him nauseous. Suddenly, he jumped to his feet while covering his mouth and raced to the bathroom where he vomited over and over until there was nothing left to vomit. There followed nearly an hour of dry heaving that wracked his stomach and scorched his throat. When it was over, he collapsed to the floor and lay sprawled there, his forehead pressed against the cool base of the toilet.

CHAPTER 8 | Dodging a bullet

    As the opening procession moved up the center aisle at the eleven-fifteen Mass at St. Augustine's Catholic Church the next day, there was scattered applause among the congregants as they recognized Fr. Jim Flynn. He was second-to-last in the line walking just ahead of the Pastor, Fr. Anthony Pattalone. As Fr. Flynn often assisted at the eleven-fifteen mass, everyone knew him but few parishioners expected to see him this particular morning. In fact, there were many open months and wide eyes among those who thought it inappropriate for him to be saying Mass in his current state, even though many of them believed him to be not guilty. Fr. Flynn smiled brightly several times as he passed up the aisle and hands reached out from the pews to touch him. At the altar, he took up his position beside Fr. Pattalone and the Mass began.
    By the time he rose after the Gospel to deliver the homily, the initial shock and surprise among the parishioners had dissipated and, suddenly as one, the whole congregation broke out into enthusiastic applause.
    Fr. Flynn stood at the lectern smiling and nodding, quite clearly moved by their support. He had not expected to assist this morning since the Rector had ordered him to remain inside the residence. Yet there had been news last night about his situation--good news--that he was anxious to reveal today. But even that news had not been enough to lift the sanction

his Rector had placed on him. He was therefore allowed to assist today only because, had the Rector refused to allow it, Fr. Pattalone would have been short-handed. The Jesuit community had contracted to provide a priest of Fr. Pattalone's choice as regular assistant. His choice had been Fr. Flynn. So the Rector had relented. For now.

"Thank you. God bless you," Fr. Flynn said as the applause died down. He bowed his head, folded his hands on the lectern and lead the congregation in the Hail Mary.

"In the name of the Father and of the Son and of the Holy Spirit. Amen." He paused a moment, looking out across the assembly, and then began, "First of all, I must thank my *beautiful* friend, Fr. Tony Pattalone, who didn't blink an eye when I told him the Rector would not stop me from assisting him this morning if he still wanted me. 'Get your Jesuit butt over here and stop messing around.' I think I've quoted you correctly. Thank you, Tony. And thank you all for believing in me based simply on your love for me. I am *so so* grateful. And as it turns out, your faith in me has not been in vain."

There was a rustling of anticipation in the pews as people unconsciously shifted and adjusted positions, some leaning forward, several falling to their knees, hands clasped tightly.

"Because as it happens," Fr. Flynn continued, an impish grin playing on his lips, "our Provincial General--the boss of all the Jesuits in this province--had been making a few calls to the powers that be on my behalf, and let me tell you, you do not want this guy calling you with a score to settle. He finally spoke last night with some high-ranking law enforcement people who he had badgered and threatened into giving him what he wanted. Which was the low-down on my situation.

"Turns out--and I have the Rector's permission to tell you this--there is a national database of priest sex-abuse cases which is maintained by a law firm somewhere. The law enforcement people admitted to our Provincial General that their investigation had determined that this database had been hacked--"

An ecstatic cheer erupted in the congregation and would have lasted some minutes but Fr. Flynn raised his hands signaling for silence. Everyone waited breathlessly for what he would say next.

"It also turns out that this hacker had inserted my name into the database along with the name of my accuser, a student from St. Augustine's College School where of course I teach."

There was a collective intake of breath as the congregation reacted to this unconscionable betrayal. The words 'Oh my God!' and 'Oh no!' Could be heard from all parts of the Church.

"*However*," Fr. Flynn continued, his puckish grin broadening into an open smile, "the trouble was, for the law enforcement guys anyway, this student had died in a car crash two years ago, God rest his soul."

Now everyone in the congregation rose to their feet, hands raised above their heads, applauding and calling out "Thank God" and "God bless you".

"Thank you. Ok, now, *stop* that! We're in Church not at a baseball game." Everyone chuckled and subsided into their seats.

"And believe me, this does not mean that I hit a homer, so to speak," Fr. Flynn continued, now in a serious tone. "Because, you know, a grave sin has been committed. That is in God's hands. But this was a slap across the face, wasn't it?" "*This* face". Here he raised his hand and made a circular motion around his face. "If I am innocent, why was it necessary for God to slap me up side the head. So unfair. So humiliating.

"Yet, it can't be punishment because I didn't do it." He paused again and rested his elbows on the lectern, looking out as if to engage each parishioner face to face.

"We believe God is love. To many people, that phrase is nothing but a t-shirt. But to us Catholics, it is *everything*! Which *must* mean that what happened to me was a--wait for it--a *grace*. Yes, it must be grace, a loving God's loving slap to remind me that in my pride and arrogance I was drifting away from him, concerned more about my reputation, my standing, my self-regard. And in this way he helped me see that our faith is a kind of either-or proposition: either God is love no matter what and that there is eternal meaning in everything, and especially in our suffering, or that God is not love and therefore there is no meaning at all. Pain is just pain and suffering is just suffering. And therefore, if it's true that God is Love, as I believe it is, it can *only* mean that I was *blessed* with this suffering. Otherwise, it came from nowhere, meant nothing, a purely indiscriminate affliction that happened not because God loved me but because some juvenile delinquent wanted to slander me.

"My friends, what we suffer is never meaningless, *even if we can never understand the meaning it has!*

In fact, it is *precisely* this feeling of meaningless, God-less suffering, this soul-killing fear that is itself *holy*!

"Yes. Holy. Because why? Because Christ himself experienced it on the cross. He has been where I have been. Where you have been. And felt what I felt and you have felt. 'My God, my God, why have you forsaken me?'"

Here he paused again, took out a handkerchief from under his chasuble and wiped his eyes. The church was utterly still. Two hundred and forty pairs of eyes were fixed on him.

"Even in His agony, as great an agony as any of us could ever imagine, and like me and like you, crushed beyond human endurance by the meaninglessness and pain and degradation of it all, without hope in his human soul, *still* what were his first words? 'My God. My God'.

"As he did, so must we do in our suffering. Rant, cry, scream at God for forsaking me, for forsaking you. For this too is a *prayer*.

"My God," he said softly. Then again. "My God."

Slowly, Fr. Flynn left the lectern and returned to his seat. Fr. Pattalone rose to begin the consecration. The Church was silent. At the end of Mass in not a few hearts sentimental joyfulness over the priest's vindication had leaked away replaced by an eerie confusion that was almost palpable.

Except in the heart of one parishioner, who, perhaps, had thought more often and more deeply about these things. Angela Benfont's face was wet with tears and her eyes shone. She rose and weaved her way back against the retreating crowd toward the sacristy.

There was the usual crush at the front doors but today the mood was quite different. A very unusual silence had fallen over them. Many faces betrayed looks of sour confusion, many heads wagged back and forth.

One elderly woman with a tight grey bun on top of her head and wearing a long baggy sleeveless shift that exposed her wrinkled, flabby arms, glanced at the gentleman pressing against her shoulder.

"What was *that*?" she whispered conspiratorially.

The gentleman nodded his head sadly. Another man standing behind her, fifty-ish and balding and wearing a red golf polo, said, "I wonder if I will come back here."

"That's what I think," a young woman in her twenties with green hair said. "I agree. I mean, I don't even know...I mean, what was all that stuff about suffering and pain and agony? Was he on something, you think?"

Now a very tall elderly man who stood a head taller than the others spoke, seemingly, for benefit of all. He wore a dress shirt and a bow tie and had longish grey hair, perhaps a retired lawyer or doctor. With an air of professional competence, he explained in a calm, caring voice, "You can tell, I believe, that this controversy was too much for the man. He's taken it too personally. In some way it surely seems to have damaged him...He was always such a joyful person, very engaging, a real catch for the Church in these days." Heads nodded vigorously, until a young father holding his baby in his arms, spoke up. He had been listening intently and was evidently disturbed by the opinions around him.

"Excuse me but can you really think that? Did any of you actually hear what he said?"

"Oh yes!" chimed in a large short woman. "That's the problem," she said glancing rapidly around for any sign of agreement, and there were several nods for her point.

The young father ignored her and continued, as he shifted the baby with difficulty to his other arm because of the crush around him. "I think you're really saying that we never hear sermons like that."

Some titters from his listeners.

"But I think that's exactly the point. We need to hear more sermons like that." He spoke with a nervous tremor in his voice, but he clearly felt that no one was coming to the defense of Fr. Flynn and had stoked up his courage to make a case for the defense. "Not the normal kinds of sermons we always hear. He's the only priest with the courage to talk about, well, you know, the real stuff."

The crowd was moving now as the older folks who had been holding things up hobbled down the front steps. It seemed people were not anxious to drift off to the parking lot just yet.

One woman accompanied by her little boy of seven and a girl perhaps three or four, felt the need to announce her views with the simple declaration. "The children! The children!"

Finally, all seemed to accept the idea, voiced offhandedly by the tall and imposing elderly gentleman as he descended the steps to the sidewalk, that someone ought to have a quiet word with Fr. Pattalone.

It appeared to have been confirmed in most minds (except that of the young father who, as soon as he cleared the exit, quickly left the crowd) that Fr. Flynn had acted inappropriately and that Church was no place for such subject matter. Good Catholics, they all felt, did not come to Mass to have their whole Sunday ruined by a psychologically damaged priest.

Back in the sacristy, the two priests disrobed in silence while the altar boys folded and stored the vestments in the massive mahogany wardrobe. The boys departed also in silence.

"So, what did you think?" Fr. Flynn asked. Fr. Pattalone did not answer, only glancing reprovingly at his friend and then continuing to replace the cruet and chalice in the space made for them in the wardrobe.

"Tony?" Fr. Flynn said.

Fr. Pattalone was a thin, small man with intense brown eyes, heavy eyebrows, a high forehead and large protruding ears. His mouth was fixed in a tight sharp line as if his jaws were locked. He had only to look at someone with his severe even threatening features to unbalance them, which worked particularly well with rowdy altar boys. It was rumored about the parish that he could smile but it was only a rumor.

"Is this how you repay friendship?" Fr. Pattalone said turning slowly to face his friend and crossing his arms as he leaned back against the wash counter. Fr. Flynn was accustomed to this taciturn little man's personality and loved him dearly. He had the highest respect for him as well. There was no cleric more trustworthy, more scrupulously honest, more loyal than Fr. Pattalone. So it nearly broke Fr. Flynn's heart to be addressed by him with such sternness and disappointment in his voice.

"Tony! God help me, I didn't mean to offend anyone!"

"Jim, you damn Jesuit," Fr. Pattalone said with a discouraged sigh. "Those people out there are not your high school students. They're children in the faith, not theologians."

"I didn't mean--"

"You didn't mean to scare the hell out of them? Well, you did."

"But, but, what did I say that was wrong or untrue?" Fr. Flynn pleaded, his hands outstretched.

"Nothing. That's the problem."

"So, we shouldn't tell truths in Church? We shouldn't acknowledge our sermons are mostly pablum? That the people listen to us because they can't get up and walk out?"

"Go home, Jim. I'm going to hear about this. I have to live with it." Fr. Pattalone turned away then said over his shoulder, "You dodged a bullet. I'm glad for you. But some kids at Auggie's aren't fanboys. Watch yourself."

Fr. Flynn left the sacristy in a downcast mood. After Fr. Pattalone's rebuke, his first thought was that he had better use the side door rather than go through the Church to the front doors.

"What, will there be parishioners with pitchforks? Are they hanging me in effigy out there? Will they egg my car?" he thought in angry denial. "'Children of the faith'? Well, who's fault is that? What have we been doing for the last two thousand years that you can't dare to tell the people what their faith is about? Oh no! As long as they believe they're good people, they'll keep coming to Mass and throwing their loose change in the basket. Can't risk *that*!"

But he knew this kind of thinking was poisonous. As he reached for the door to the side entrance, he paused and said his favorite prayer.

"My peace I leave with you, my peace I give to you. Let not your hearts be troubled and do not be afraid."

And as he pushed the door open, there stood Angela Benfont, her face flushed, beads of sweat along her hairline. Her hands were clasped against her heart and her radiant smile hit him like a bear hug.

"Angela!" he exclaimed. "Of all the faces I need to see right now, yours is Number One."

He descended the three steps to where she stood and put his hands on her shoulders.

"A sight for sad eyes," he smiled down at her.

"Oh, Father. Sad? After that tremendous sermon? Why should you be sad?" Angela said earnestly.

That she should be the first person he met struck him forcibly as a great grace, even-- perhaps especially and because--he could still taste the poison he felt. This delighted him. He was firmly convinced that this was a sign of the Spirit working for his salvation, as always.

Fr. Flynn sighed and in that instant knew just as certainly that the Poisoner was there at his side as well, as always. She was being offered up to him as an accomplice. The Poisoner had injected him and was willing him to inject her.

"Oh, you know," he said, ushering her gently along with him toward the side door. As they walked in friendly silence (Angela, who loved silence, reveled in it now) Fr. Flynn again repeated to himself his favorite prayer.

As they left the dimness of the Church and stepped onto the pavement, the bright sunlight caused them both to raise a hand to shield their eyes. Angela could not resist making an appeal she had often made before. It was one of her secret fondest hopes. "You know, you're always welcome at our Tuesday discussion group. My friends would love to meet you."

Fr. Flynn frowned. "I'm afraid the Superior isn't quite ready to stamp my get-out-of-jail card."

"Oh, Father! Why? You've been proven innocent. He let you come here today."

"Yes, well, that was strictly business. The Order has a commitment to Fr. Pattalone. But I am still a risky proposition, you know." He leaned into her and spoke softly, a mischievous grin playing on his lips. "You never can be quite sure if Jim Flynn will behave himself. You never know when he'll do something to embarrass the big boys."

"You never would!" Angela declared.

"Oh, Angela, *never* say never."

CHAPTER 9 | So very French

  Bella sat on her bed in what had lately become her habitual position, legs crossed underneath her, elbows propped on her knees, her head cradled in her hands as it moved unconsciously side to side. Her eyes were closed tightly and her hair hung down over her face, greasy and mussed. She hadn't washed it in days. Her breathing was shallow, short and rapid. She gave every impression of being in pain but, in fact, her posture and movements were the outward signs of a terrible struggle, a kind of spiritual wrestling match with herself. This struggle, albeit at a lower level of intensity, seemed always to be going on inside her. But in the last few days it had become increasingly acute. And she knew for a certainty what was causing it.
  "I feel like I'm in a whirlpool and getting sucked under. What is wrong with me? Goddam that guy! I wish I never--well I did, so quit complaining," she thought to herself with deep disgust. "You are pathetic!. . . What are you afraid of? What? What? That you'll go to hell? Hahaha. Hell. What's so bad about hell?--did I just say that? What's happening to me?. . . It's that stupid manifesto, isn't it? He sure as hell isn't afraid of going to hell! Maybe he's *in* hell, maybe that's what hell is. Total freedom to do anything, say anything, believe anything. Holy shit! Hell is freedom? Oh my God, hell is FREEDOM!--Stop! Stop!. . You're a theologian now?...That can't be right but it

kind of makes sense. Because then wouldn't that mean that religion is anti-freedom? And isn't that the whirlpool? Freedom and anti-freedom swirling around, sucking everybody in...Oh just stop. Please just stop. You're a fucking moron. . . but, but, it's the, I don't know, the goddam *perversity* of it all, this whole Christian thing, it's just plain *perverse*. I mean, you couldn't make it up even if you hated life with all your heart!"

Just then her phone rang. She groped for it listlessly and answered it in a flat, tired voice she almost didn't recognize as her own.

"Hello."

"Bella? This is William Shine, from the other night, you may remember?"

"Uh..." Her mind was in a fog and she was confused by the presumptive friendliness of this strange voice.

"I'm sorry for bothering you on a Sunday morning but I am actually trying to reach your brother. May I speak to him if he's available?"

Without answering, Bella climbed off the bed and in a kind of trance walked across the hall to Richard's room. She opened the door and Richard turned in his chair from the computer screen.

"What?" he said crossly.

Bella tossed her phone at him and left the room. Not expecting this, Richard juggled the phone as it landed in his lap, dropped it on the floor, then picked it up and looked at the screen. There was no name, just a number he did not recognize.

"Hello?" he said tentatively.

"Ah. Good. Richard. This is William Shine, from the other night, you may remember. Thank you for taking my call. You're probably wondering how I got Bella's number. Purely by chance, no subterfuge involved I assure you. When I found Nicholas the other night, I went through his pockets to see were there any pills or anything like that and I found this crumpled piece of paper with Bella's name on it and a phone number. And of course I had no idea who this Bella was, so I thought I'd better hang on to it for him and then, well, there she was at his apartment, with you, and, well, I don't know, was it fate maybe or destiny or one of those jokes life seems to revel in playing on you when coincidences converge, you know? Great jokester, life, don't you think? Well, anyway, to move on, I've been anxious to, hopefully, perhaps meet together, you and me. And of course Bella if you--"

"Jesus, you talk a lot," Richard said.

"Haha. Well there you have it. The essence of my charm."

"Not very charming. Annoying as hell."

"Oh, I'm sure you're right", Shiney agreed.

"What do you want?"

"Since you ask. I am convinced that, perhaps, this time life is not so much punking us as, well, guiding us? And I have this idea that in some way the intersection of our separate orbits, if you will, means something. Think about it. How odd is it that events have transpired such that you and your sister should have swerved into my orbit. And, of course, vice versa. I mean, not in a million years unless—well, leaving philosophical speculation aside, perhaps you can understand why I'm calling."

Clearly losing patience with this conversation, Richard said, "So what you're saying is, you want to grab a latte at Starbucks."

"Haha. Yes, minus the latte and the Starbucks. I wonder whether it wouldn't be to both our advantages to get to know one another better. See where separate interests might coalesce into a...well, a program, as you say. I mean, life has presented us both with an opportunity to, perhaps, do something remarkable, don't you feel that, too?"

"I guess," Richard said. Having gotten over the oddness of the man and unexpectedness of the call, he was beginning to feel a certain cautious interest.

"Oh now don't be coy, Richard. After all, it was you who offered a program so shocking I haven't been able to stop thinking about it. You have me, hook, line and sinker. I'm quite literally vibrating to hear more. The fucking Catholic Church? This is advanced stuff. Between you and Nicholas my mind has been good and properly blown. I feel like I'm chasing the caboose here and I need you to reach out and haul me on board. Will you agree to meet? I'll set it up."

"Sure," Richard answered, careful not to appear too eager.

"And your sister?"

"What do you want her there for? You think I need a babysitter?" Richard challenged him in a nasty tone of voice.

"Oh, come now, Richard," Shiney said, "you didn't strike me as a particularly insecure young man. Just remember, if it wasn't for your sister--"

"Yeah, yeah, fine."

"Will you honor me with your phone number?"

Having gotten the number, Shiney felt a thrill as if their two minds were now directly conjoined.

"Fantastic. I'll get back to you with the details?"

"Whatever."

As much as he desired it, William Shine feared it was a reckless and perhaps disastrous idea. The 'meeting of the cadres' as he had come to refer to it excited him, not least because he loved the sound of that word, the idea of it. <u>Cadres</u>. It had a romance about it. It always rekindled in him memories of his first encounter with The Gospels of the Four Apostles: the writings of Marcuse, Derrida, Foucault, and of course Sartre. Oh, Sartre! Oh, the French! How he loved the French! It was, therefore, a real nostalgia for the French-ness of their ideas, synonymous with seriousness, and their complete success as cultural solvents that had led him to view Nicholas's manifesto as a potentially new word in the canon. It sounded so French. But was the manifesto serious? Serious enough? Or was he being taken in by its audacious tone? He knew he was in danger of falling in love with it for no better reason than its unassailable and arrogant illogic but more for the attitude. So very French! He was especially intrigued by the line he could draw directly from the Gospels' vilification of the bourgeoisie to Nicholas's disdain for the imaginary reader.

He understood that the bourgeoisie—the great enemy of the Gospel writers—was long dead, from suicide, so it appeared to him, since all their structures of dominance had long since been transmogrified as if by some kind of cultural alchemy into a disgusting rush to become backyard socialists and shopping mall activists. In other words, to become like him, but soulessly, unimaginatively, a ghastly flock of unthinking zealots desperate for that badge of higher virtue that came gratis with the veneer of social justice. How wonderful it was now to have such a rich crop of fools to hate once again! *Vive la bourgeoisie*! And Nicholas had indeed captured the proper attitude toward them. "Who Cares?" indeed!

It was simply too wonderful a chance not to place a bet upon it. But how large a bet? After all, there was no body of work to underpin Nicholas's manifesto as the Gospel writers had amassed. There was no prior distinction attached to his name. Had he even a college degree? Thus the possibility for ridicule was real. He needed to be careful.

He decided Nicholas's apartment was entirely wrong for what he had in mind. In truth it was the memory of seeing Bella cringe as she entered the apartment the other night that changed his plan. "No, Ben's office would do just fine," he thought to himself. "Much better, really. We have to convince Art to show up, of course, and he would never come to Nicholas's. This should look like a meeting of the board of directors, with concerned guests. We must not scare her away." He felt much better now about the prospects for the gathering, since, rather surprisingly, the prime invitee--Richard--had already agreed to attend. And Bella, too...ah, Bella!

"Of course," he said aloud. Bella had not been far from his thoughts. "A little leaven of calm and objectivity, a natural doubter, that one. Good instincts. Trustworthy. Ha! Listen to me! She's made quite an impression on you, Mr. Shine. Yes, yes, I admit it. But not in the way you imply. Nothing of that sort. She's...she's...well, for one thing, she may be the only one among us who isn't completely unhinged! Haha!"

This positive attitude evaporated, however, as he began to dial Ben Shelley. They had not spoken since the episode at Ben's brother's house. Which meant of course that Ben knew nothing of Bella and Richard and their independent involvement with Nicholas which was certain to make their conversation awkward. Shiney believed--he had to believe--that he could persuade Ben to accept the situation as it had evolved in his absence, and that, in the end, the Benfonts could be useful in a way that could augment Ben's efforts to exert control over Nicholas without seeming to. In the event he was to be cruelly disappointed.

"That little shit could ruin everything for us," Ben Shelley said, his voice tight with anger, when Shiney explained that a meeting might be a good idea. "If he ever pulls that stunt again I'll do to him what he tried to do to his mother. And I won't let up until his eyes pop out of his head!"

Having been caught completely off guard, Shiney's mind reeled with the ramifications Ben's attitude presented. He was left speechless. A moment later, he could hear Ben take a deep breath.

"Yeah, you're right, though," he said in a calmer tone. "We need a meeting with that nephew of mine. He needs to realize I'll chain him to the goddam bed post if he doesn't do his part. And what is that? Just to stay the hell away from his parents and not cause any trouble. Is that so hard? Oh no, the little bastard had to blow up the whole deal within an hour. Almost. Well, I'm telling you, that's never going not happen again. And he needs to know that."

Shiney readily agreed having only half listened while his mind scurried in search of a way to broach the bigger issue.

"There has, though, Ben, been something of a development." And he went on to relate the arrival of the Benfonts at Nicholas's apartment, painting it as a surprising and perhaps positive occurrence, while leaving out his more personal interests.

"See, Nicholas sort of kind of widened the circle, so to speak," he explained in an off-hand, matter-of-fact tone of voice.

"Wait! Wait! What do you mean, widened the circle?" Ben interrupted. Shiney could feel Ben's anger rising again.

"Damn it!" thought Shiney. "Careful! Careful!"

"Well, it turns out," Shiney began nervously, "he, uh, sent the thing he wrote to this girl, Bella Benfont, who he somehow ran into I guess randomly before he came to the office."

"OK, so what?" Ben asked. "He's got a girlfriend. That's good. We can use that."

"But here's the bit of an issue that's cropped up."

"Yeah? C'mon, spit it out." Ben had never spoken to Shiney this way, with such impatience and ill-disguised disrespect.

"She apparently showed it to her brother."

"OK. So?"

"Looks like this kid is kind of a hacker or something and he, uh, well, he actually posted it on what he calls the dark web, which is a thing, I guess."

"That all?" Ben demanded impatiently, clearly missing the import of this news.

Now Shiney realized fully that he was losing his advantage--if he'd ever had it. Fear rose in his stomach and his voice became constricted with it. "Ben, the kid told us, me and Art and I don't think even his sister knew til that minute, but apparently it was a big hit with the subterranean mob on this dark web. I mean, the kid had drummed up a following for it within hours, so it seems." He took a deep breath, the conviction now settled in his mind that he had handled this as badly as he could have imagined. Desperately, fearing what might be coming, the uncertainty as painful as a migraine, he took another deep breath.

"So, what you're saying is," Ben asked after a pause, "that ridiculous piece of intellectual masturbation is out there, in the world."

The final blow.

Weakly, hardly able to breathe, Shiney heard himself whisper, unable to force the air from his lungs, "I wouldn't call it--"

"Yes or no?" Ben demanded crossly.

"Well, yes, I guess so."

"And that means what, you think?"

He knew now he was totally exposed and said in a deflated, defeated voice, "There's...something to it, I suppose."

"You suppose! You suppose?" Ben exploded. "You're a convert, Shine! You were all in the first time you read that dreck. I saw it in the office and at my brother's. Defending the little bastard to Marigold's face! You got balls, I'll say that. But, God almighty, I'll never understand it. How does an educated mind like yours always fall for the most disgusting philosophical malignancies? And that piece he wrote is nothing if not malignant! So who's side are you on, Shine?"

"Ben, please! You can't think I'd do anything to undermine our agreement. Honestly, I don't see how my interest in...that...will affect it at all."

"So, what you're setting up is a pandering session, is that it? You, these Benfonts, Art? No, no, not Art. Ha. At least he hasn't lost his mind."

"Alright, Ben. That's enough now."

There was a long pause in which each heard the other breathing.

Finally, when Ben came back, his tone had softened. "This freaking kid is becoming a bigger problem than I thought. Anyway, as he says, 'Who cares?' Let's have the meeting. I'm good Tuesday."

"Yes. Yes, sure. Your office?. You'll let him know?"

"I won't give him a choice...what's the matter? Is there something else?" Ben asked. His tone was impatient but not dismissive.

"Listen, I think it's in our best interest to get to know these Benfonts better, you know?"

"Oh, the hell with the Benfonts," Ben said wearily.

"No. Listen. Trouble is--now don't get crazy--I've sort of invited them to the meeting."

"Shiney, I swear--"

"No, listen, Ben, listen. We can't just let them hang out there, you know, unsupervised, can we? I mean, they're connected to us now whether we like it or not. We can't have separate camps. Who knows what trouble that kid Richard could stir up."

"Shiney, goddamit. Now you listen." But then he stopped. Shiney could hear his fingers drumming on the table top. "If this thing falls apart..."

"It won't, Ben. I am on the right side."

"You better be." He hung up.

After this, it was a relief to talk to Art Gross. He was reluctant and petulant but Shiney reminded him that he had signed the papers and was therefore committed. Finally he sent a text to Richard's number giving details for the meeting.

Exhausted, he fell back in his chair and closed his eyes. "..Oh, what are you whining about? You got what you wanted. True, true. Ha!"

CHAPTER 10 | Bats

"Bella, I'm home. You missed a wonderful sermon by Father Flynn. He's been cleared of that awfulness," Angela Benfont called from the bottom of the stairs. Her voice was bright and happy.

Even muffled by her closed bedroom door, her mothers's voice was like a lightening strike in dry tinder. A fierce and fiery annoyance swept over Bella, so strong it actually scared her. Her eyes and mouth snapped tight shut to still her reaction before she screamed as if under torture. Yet like lightening, it was a flash and then it was gone, or nearly so. It left a kind of acrid smoke behind made of anger at her mother and contempt for herself. A minute later, Richard threw open her door. He had just received the text from Shiney with the arrangements for the meeting. He tossed her phone onto the bed.

Bella could not help but notice the difference between his entrance now and a few days ago. He had barely emerged from his room since the other night at Nicholas's apartment and who knew what he was getting up to on that computer of his. He hadn't sat down to a meal since but Bella had heard him up and about, late at night coming and going from his room, she imagined, from the kitchen. He was a different person. The excitement and crazy delight in the stunt he had engineered against Fr. Flynn was replaced now with a tense and unpleasant seriousness, his wild-eyed enthusiasm by eyes like slits beneath a furrowed brow. All child-likeness, which had so endeared her to him then, was gone.

"That catatonic thing, you believe it was real?" he asked in a monotone.

"I suppose," Bella said, watching him closely. "After I walked him home and it wore off, he looked sick as hell."

Richard slowly folded his arms like a man who has made up his mind. "You need to come to a meeting with me. It's time."

"Oh, you've joined a shit-head support group? You're right, long past time." She forced herself to throw off the words in the needling tone they often took with each other but she could feel the hair rising on her arms. There was no reaction from Richard.

"They want you there."

Slowly Bella rose from her usual slumped posture on the bed to sit upright, her arms rigidly supporting her on either side.

"Richard, you're scaring me," she said, unconsciously sliding to the far side of the bed.

"You need to be there. They think you're important."

"OK, that's enough! Stop it right now! Stop standing there like that! Stop looking at me like that! What is going on, Richard? Never mind. I don't want to know. Oh my God, that fucking Nicholas! What is going on, Richard?"

Richard took a deep breath and exhaled it noisily. "That's what the meeting is about."

"I. Don't. Care! Do you hear me? What is happening? To you? What have you been doing all day, every day, in that room?"

Again Richard took in a deep breath and let it out, clearly losing patience with her. "Look, you started this. It was you that sort of broke open the portal and let him out. So."

Bella put her hands to her forehead, digging in her nails. "What are you saying? Let him out? Who?"

"Oh, come on, Bella. Don't be thick. You know who."

"But what did *I* do? I didn't do anything! All I did was video some weirdo standing in the rain! I mean, I thought it was performance art! It was nothing. It was a goddam coincidence, that's all."

Richard smiled at her. It was almost kindly but his eyes were hard. "Well, the cat's out of the bag now. It's trending. It's out of control." He seemed proud of the fact.

"That stupid essay or whatever he calls it? Richard, please! You can't be serious. It was just--stupid. Nobody can take it seriously--"

"No? You did," he said in a mean and condescending tone.

"But--but--"

"Exactly. But-but. I agree with you. As a program, it is stupid because it leads nowhere. 'But-but!'" Richard unfolded his arms and spread his hands out. His voice rose as he spoke. "It's effect, Bella! It's effect. That's what's important. It opened a portal and like bats from a cave out flew freedoms for everyone, whatever freedom they desired could be theirs. And it's trending, Bella. It will grow and more and more followers will be there for the leading!" He dropped his arms to his sides and stepped closer to the bed. "That's why you have to be there."

Bella rolled off the bed and stood facing Richard across it.

"No! No, I don't! I don't believe in any of this! I don't want any part of it!"

"You have a very important part, Bella."

"Don't be ridiculous. I'm just--I'm just--"

"Yes. Just the person who can convince him to do what he has to do."

"Do? Do what?" With her hands clenched at her neck and her left shoulder turned toward him as if to ward off a blow, there were tears in her eyes.

"Lead." Richard turned to the door. "Be there or be square." He closed the door behind him.

Bella's clenched hands pressed harder into her neck as her chin squeezed down on them. Her arms ached as the muscles tightened around her rib cage. Her jaws, her eyes, her mouth, were all clamped tightly shut.

"Wait a minute! Wait a minute!" she thought as a shiver ran down her spine. "Oh God, no. No, no, no, no, no! Bats from a cave? Oh, what have I done? My fault. All my fault. And here I sit hour after hour moaning about myself, whining like a coward. . .He's right, goddammit! It's time to decide, you goddamn coward. You silly, stupid, useless--what? I can't even describe you! What are you? What good are you? What can you possibly be good for? Why are you even here? What a joke you are! What a disappointment!...So the bats are out of the cave. Will I be a bat?"

"My turn," she heard her mother's voice chirp from the other side of the door. The door opened and her mother peaked in around the corner.

"He lives?" she asked with a wide smile.

Bella pivoted away from her in an effort to release the tension in her body. "I guess."

Her mother slid all the way in and sat on the edge of the bed, looking up at her with dreamy eyes. "Oh, Bella, I wish you had heard his sermon."

"Mom, please. Not now."

Angela frowned. She knew she would not get the response she hoped for.

Bella fell on the bed but made sure to lie on the further edge from her mother.

"You know honey, you shouldn't sit in your room all the time."

"But it's OK for Richard," Bella mimicked her mother's tone.

"Sweetheart, Richard is too clever for his own good but he is, I don't know, let's say outward-looking. Your heart draws you inward, Bella. You're, I don't know, kind of a contemplative. Mother's feel these things, you know, when their children are hurting inside. I know you don't like this and I've said it before, but I believe it's true: you're more like me, honey. You're not cynical like Richard can be, and oh brother, can he! You're not sarcastic like Richard can be...but most of all, I love your courage--"

"Ha!" the irony of this remark was almost more than she could bare.

"No, listen to me. You think I don't know you question everything in your heart? You think I don't know you resist giving yourself credit for anything? And always blame yourself before other people? Bella, you are no coward. Yes, I know that too. I fought that same demon for many years. Believe me, honey, you are stronger than it. Don't despair. Whatever it is making you sad, don't despair. It's how God's grace works."

Bella covered her face with her hands and muttered, "That makes no sense."

Angela caressed her daughter's ankle then rose and moved to the door. "Supper in about an hour."

When her mother called her down an hour later, she rose, left her room, and opened the door of Richard's room.

"Alright," she said to his back. She closed the door and descended the stairs.

CHAPTER 11 | Living dead men

When he had awoken that morning to find himself wrapped around the base of the toilet bowl, the first thing he felt, even before his eyes were open and his mind was still clouded from sleep, was not the hardness and chill of the bathroom floor or the pain in his shoulder and numbness in his arm. It was rather the sensation of a kind of lightness in his chest. A lightness that should not have been there, where he had always awakened to the cold, heavy weight of his crushing insecurity.

So unexpected was it that for many moments he hardly even dared to breathe for fear of disturbing it, sure it must dissolve as the fog in his head cleared. But then he realized this was the residue of a dream in which he had found himself in the food court of a large indoor mall, standing on a table. Around him were hundreds of tables at which sat hundreds of people, all eating and drinking in the most ravenous and disgusting manner, like animals. Nobody noticed him and at first he was terrified that they must notice him at any second and swarm over him like hungry zombies. Then an odd idea came to him. If he called attention to himself, all the hungry people would get up and run away. So he began to clap his hands, slowly at first and not too loudly. As he did, a head here and there rose up and turned toward the sound. He clapped louder and more heads looked up but no one in the food court seemed inclined to run away. Instead, they began to peer at him with interest. Suddenly the whole food court broke into rapturous applause. And then he had woken up.

At first he feared to move lest the sensation fade away. But it did not fade away and slowly, slowly, he lifted himself into a sitting position leaning against the tub and remained still, waiting and hoping against hope--and wondering how it had happened at all, even if at any moment it certainly must die away. Yet, it remained and his wonder and delight grew.

"Did I purge my mind along with my guts?" he thought to himself. "All of a sudden you believe in dreams? In signs and portents? But why should I have had such a dream? That particular dream? You can't deny it came from your own unconscious. Which just goes to prove that the unconscious must know you better than your rational mind. It must be a sign, not just the random firing of random neurons. Could it be that my ideas were nothing more than simple egotism? Well, not my ideas themselves but my stance concerning them? Yes, I see it now! I was treating them as nothing more than playthings, a stance and a dance without consequences. Which was precisely what I believed I desired all along! It was just too lovely to sit back and in delicious arrogance imagine their effect on the wider world. But now! Now! Yes! Signs and wonders! There can be no doubt that now I have been given a sign, a wonderful sign that can only mean one thing. It's too obvious to deny. Go ahead, say it out loud. You are the prophet, the apex of evolution, and millions will acknowledge you!

No more fear! No more vacillating! Oh, what an idiot I've been! The one thing I feared--that my ideas would be taken seriously and therefore I would be taken seriously--is the very thing that has happened and it's all because of that kid. I thought I'd be happy with my little plaything as long as I kept it within my little closed circle. But I'm the one who broke the circle by sending it to that girl to spite my uncle! And what happens? Her brother lets it loose and I'm the new Jesus and I can no longer stay hidden and safe in my little make-believe world. There! See? Your unconscious again! That kid did what I didn't have the courage to do. He out-ed me. And the wonder of it is, I'm not ridiculous any more! I can be what I was meant to be!"

    He had spent that day and the following days in a kind of trance, consumed in astonishment as he imagined triumph after triumph and the fear and respect he would instill in those he despised--his uncle and his silly and despicable parents, of course--but also that mindless, undifferentiated horde at the mall, the hungry zombies who would run after him devouring every word that fell from his lips.

    It was in this new mood that Nicholas took the call from his uncle to appear at the meeting and agreed to come without hesitation. Ben had called it a 'come to Jesus' meeting and Nicholas had been savoring the thrilling irony of that phrase. Because 'Jesus' would indeed show up and his 'coming' would not be the one his uncle planned.

Shiney had made sure that they would arrive early to give him time to prepare them. He began by thanking them profusely for coming and then segued to a brief description of Ben Shelley, Nicholas's uncle, a description that cast him as a well qualified lawyer, reasonable and even-handed, no one to be intimidated by (regarding his jail time, he seemed to have forgotten to mention it). "And of course, Art Gross, who you met that night, is Art Gross."

Next, with rising apprehension, he tackled the nub of the problem as he saw it. The first part of the meeting--the 'family' issues--would no doubt be contentious, he explained, a discussion he admitted he could not control, but assured them he would do his best to move things along.

But in the meantime, they might hear things that could be somewhat concerning. "Just family stuff. I'm sure you appreciate that all families have family stuff that needs to be aired once in a while. It's just unfortunate that you two--well, I'm sure you understand." Wisely, he addressed himself almost exclusively to Bella. Richard, he noted with approval, seemed vague and uninterested, hardly listening, but Bella was at the center of his concerns. He had known since that night at Nicholas's apartment that she was the wild card. All his life, he had had an instinct about people like Bella, and always avoided them when he could. She was one of those with a natural immunity to 'bullshit', and though, unlike her brother, she appeared to listen as he rattled off his remarks, he was quite sure she saw straight through him. Which made it more difficult to ensure that she would be a neutral observer.

"It goes without saying, of course, that there is no need for you to feel you must participate in any way. That will come later, when we get to the good stuff! So, just for the first part, I advise simply suffer through it in silence. That's the best course. Let's sit." Sitting next to Bella, his ordeal finally over, Shiney admitted to himself that, "she thinks I'm the biggest asshole she's ever met".

But this was not what Bella was thinking. She was far beyond caring about Shiney's self image. The last days had been a torture for her. She knew in her heart that her brother had crossed some sort of boundary. The change in him haunted her. That was the only reason she had agreed to be part of this meeting: to protect her brother. Now that she was here, her apprehension had reached a fever pitch. That Shine-person's pep talk had not helped. In his rambling unctuous voice, she sensed only fear. In his anxiety to induce in them a nonjudgmental attitude, only a veil of hypocrisy thrown over some other plan. Her whole being told her that there was danger here--spiritual danger--and that this meeting might be her only chance to discover what that danger was--and, somehow, some way, save her brother from it. As a last precaution, she had decided to secretly record the meeting on her phone.

Ben and Art Gross arrived and took seats and a few minutes later Nicholas buzzed himself in. All five heads swiveled as he entered, though Bella, whose back was to him, had snapped a glance over her shoulder and then quickly returned to peer down at her lap where her hands clenched her phone. Richard, sitting beside her, merely stared, unblinking, as Nicholas moved toward them. Shiney actually rose to greet him, a wide smile showing his bad teeth. Art Gross crossed his legs and groaned. Ben Shelley, straight-faced but with a belligerent look in his eyes, sat forward in his chair with his elbows propped on his knees. His left foot was vibrating rapidly up and down. Nicholas noticed this from a distance and realized his uncle was a mass of electric anger.

"Hello, everybody," Nicholas said in a light tone. Then addressing his uncle, he said with a sardonic smile, "I know why I'm here and I am prepared to say, unreservedly, that I accept the original terms of the agreement. So. By the way, I didn't know there would be observers."

"Never mind about that, goddamit!" Ben said. His anger had been building for hours and now it threatened to disrupt the whole purpose of the meeting. There was still a smile on Shiney's face but it had dimmed considerably. Art Gross, in contrast, nodded his approval. Richard glanced at Bella, eyes wide and excited. Bella bent her head down further toward her lap. Nicholas sat and crossed his legs.

"Let me put this in simple terms so you can understand it," Ben began, "because clearly you don't. You agreed--and we have it in writing--to stay away from your parents and to cause them and their business no injury either physical or psychological. And what's the first thing you do within minutes of signing? So, let me spell it out once again and for the last time. If you so much as call their number and hang up, or be seen driving past their house let alone show up again at their door, or speak to anyone about their business or their personal lives, we will stop your allowance in a heartbeat, never to be reinstated. Furthermore, I will personally charge you with fraud on your parents and me and breach of contract and use every legal maneuver I can devise to make sure you end up in my Alma Mater where we still have many friends and clients who owe me favors. Which I will not hesitate to call in. And you can use your imagination what those favors might be for. Do you understand this time?"

Nicholas watched his uncle with a glitter in his eye. "He doesn't see me!" he marveled to himself. "The new me is in the disguise of the old me! It's like I'm Zooming this from Mars!"

"I said , do you understand this time?"

Nicholas merely gazed at him in wonder.

"C'mon, Ben," Shiney pleaded. "You've read him the riot act and he gets it. Can't we move on to the--the new situation?"

"Goddamit, Shine!" Ben exploded. "I brought you into this as a witness. That's it. All you had to do was sit there and shut up. But, oh no! You had to go and encourage him. Even at the house! In front of his mother! Praising that asinine manifesto when anybody could see--Art saw it!--that it was nothing more than a spoiled brat's wet dream! And here we are. Don't talk to me about--"

"Asinine manifesto?" Nicholas asked quietly, surprising them all. "Hmm...yes, yes, utterly asinine, except that it's made me a phenomenon in the dark places of the Earth. A new Jesus, so I hear."

Ben, suddenly perplexed by his nephew's unexpected and confusing reaction, blanched and turned on Shiney. "Goddamit Shine! I told you, if this goes south, I swear--"

But now Shiney, fearing that Richard would see him as a weak collaborator, went on the offensive. "Let's remember who sent the manifesto to his parents? Not me," Shiney countered. "And if everybody could see it was nonsense, why send it to them at all? But if it wasn't for that 'nonsense', don't you realize you'd still be stewing over a family fortune just out of your reach? The way I see it, we both have a lot to thank him for, old friend."

"The fact remains," Ben said, "this is out of control now, don't you get it? We're at the mercy of a matricidal maniac and this dark web delinquent--"

"Matricidal maniac?" Nicholas commented calmly. "Why wouldn't I be? Why isn't everybody? They spit us out into this foul existence and then as if they hadn't perpetrated the most unimaginable injustice, we're supposed to love, honor and obey them. If you want to blame someone, put the blame where it belongs. On her. It's out of control all right. Out of *your* control. Because she birthed me.... So, please, just sit back and let us--"

From a disinterested slouch, Richard had suddenly bolted forward in his chair. He was poised on the seat's front edge, his eyes wide and greedy.

"Why did he call you matricidal?" He spoke as if enraptured.

"There was an incident, that's all," Shiney jumped in quickly. He was unable to disguise his anger as he turned to Richard. This was precisely what he had hoped to avoid. "An argument, really. A misunderstanding. Between them and tempers flared. That's all."

"That's all, huh?" Ben Shelley glared. "What about the part where he tried to strangle her, his own mother? Just a minor detail?"

The others were silenced momentarily by Richard's next question. "But you didn't? Kill her?"

Nicholas, regarding him with increasing interest and approval, answered. "No. She lives. Unfortunately."

But clearly Richard's question had not been juvenile curiosity. There was something more, something that had stirred his imagination. "And...and did you, you know...have an attack after it?"

"What an odd question," Nicholas said. "What an odd kid. Huh. Did I? I don't remem-- yes, actually. That night. I'd forgotten about that."

Richard fell back in his chair. "Oh, my god!" There was a look of wild vindication on his face.

"What?" Nicholas asked, sitting forward himself, anxiously. "You're thrilling me!"

"Oh, for Chrissakes," Art groaned turning to Ben with fire in his eyes. "Are you listening to this?"

For once, Shiney was thankful for Art's presence.

"Look," he offered, sounding calm and reasonable though he wished with all his heart to be left alone with the Benfonts, "the business part of this meeting is pretty much all wrapped up. Ben, you got what you wanted, didn't you? And so I'm just wondering. Nicholas and I and Richard, and of course Bella, we're all anxious--"

"Yeah, yeah," Ben interrupted. "You want us to bounce so you can get on with your plots and subterfuges. Fuck, Shiney--excuse my language--don't you ever get tired of this shit? Constantly bubbling over about revolution and transgressing something or other like water on a hot plate. Jesus, you make me tired. Art, you want to leave, it's ok. But I think I'll hang around a little bit. Just to be sure."

"You stay, I stay," Art said.

Now that his anger had subsided, Ben was determined to assess these Benfonts more closely. Richard, he judged, was young, excitable, unstable and in thrall to Nicholas. Also, he did not look well. Ben noticed he had begun to sweat. But so what? He could not conceive how this kid posed a risk, though the information about online followers was troubling. But there was nothing he could do about that now. Bella, then, the quiet one, sitting there clearly ill at ease. "She's embarrassed, isn't she?" he thought. "To be here and feeling out of place? Yes...but there's something else...her brother. Otherwise, why is she here? She has nothing to say, hasn't uttered a peep. No way she buys into whatever he's selling...What is it?...She's afraid for him? Yeah, that's it...But, wait, then why be afraid? What does she know? Is she afraid for him or of him?...Both?" He leaned forward.

"Hey. You alright young lady?" he asked. "I'm sorry if we've upset you. It gets kind of ugly around here at times."

"I'm fine. Really. I'm just sort of tagging along," she smiled dimly, alarmed to have been noticed. Ben sat back and folded his arms.

For Richard, this had been an excruciating interruption. The look of vindication still dominated his features and made him appear younger, almost childlike. Excited almost beyond endurance, his eyes glued to Nicholas's face, he had several times opened his mouth to speak but Nicholas, distracted by the speakers, kept breaking eye contact, though he too was intensely awaiting Richard's explanation.

But now there would be another delay as Shiney reluctantly turned to Richard. "For the sake of Ben and Art, Richard, just fill us in on your, uh, on the engagements, if that's the word, that you've generated with Nicholas's manifesto."

"I don't know. Lots," he grumbled sitting back in disappointment.

"Hundreds?"

"Probably more. Couple of thousand or so as of yesterday."

"Two thousand? That's fantastic. That's the nucleus of a movement!"

"I guess."

"But Richard, you don't realize--"

Richard, at his wit's end and furious over these delays, exploded."No! *You* don't realize! Who are you, anyway? You are all so stupid! The only question is, what is the end? That's the only question. You gave us real actual freedom for the first time. It's brilliant, really it is. But it's not the end. It only makes the end more...obvious, I guess. You cleared everything away for me, all the underbrush sort of. And...and I saw that the real answer," here he took a deep breath, his eyes popping out of their sockets "...was in the video."

It was clear that no one had expected this. Shiney's head wrenched backward as if he had been punched. He had had the chance to see this video but thought it irrelevant. Nicholas, his head to one side, stared at Richard with an ironic but admiring smile then swiveled to Bella.

"So, you didn't delete it after all. Just saying: I'd like to see it someday."

Bella was watching her brother, hardly breathing, but now blushed in embarrassment. Art Gross let his chin fall to his chest and resumed his disgusted slouch while shaking his head. Ben Shelley, however, quickly sat up, his eyes fierce on Richard.

"The video?" Shiney delicately probed. "You mean the one Bella captured, him in the rain? I don't...I don't see. . . I'm sorry, Richard, I don't see how that ties in with the, you know, the *program*. You know, 'The fucking Catholic Church', remember?"

Bella gasped. Fear gripped her mind and heart. Fear of a brother she no longer recognized, fear of these strangers, of Nicholas, but most of all fear of what she herself had set in motion.

Ben saw his opening and pounced. "What the hell is going on here? You have a video of Nicholas?"

"Yes, they do," Shiney answered, not looking at him, hoping to race through an explanation that would allow Richard to continue. "I haven't seen it but it purportedly shows him in the state of one of his fits. But what has that--"

"So, let me see if I understand this," Ben said, taking control. "You say you have a video of Nicholas. Of course, you obtained his prior permission to record him. You had him sign a consent form, did you? No? Hm. Well, in jailhouse parlance, you're fucked."

Richard, who moments ago would have wilted under Ben's power to intimidate, spoke now with obvious disdain and confidence. "Am I? Have you got a copy of this video yourself? No? Without one, how do you propose to prove anything? And if I did have one, you could never find it."

"Oh, we'll find it."

"You familiar with the dark web?"

"Are you saying it's out there? You posted it?"

Nicholas giggled with delight at this kid's audaciousness. "Wow."

This was what Ben had been waiting for, and fearing. "It's public? You had no right!"

"Well, I wouldn't say it's public. The only people who can see it are the thousands I've attracted with it in a chat room you can't find, let alone get into."

"We have resources," Ben threatened.
"Ha. Good luck."
"Of course, there's always your phone. Or should I say your sister's phone. That's the phone that took the video, I understand. Miss Benfont, may I see your phone?"

Bella shrunk away from him.

"Don't worry, Bella, it's gone," Richard said.

"So you admit it was there," Ben pressed on.

"Sure. And now it's not."

"Ok, look here you little bastard. You think you're so goddam clever but you can now expect a law suit that will cost you and your family your goddam house, your cars, your savings. You'll all be living in a refrigerator box on the street. You get it?"

"Goddamit, Ben! Stay out of this!" Shiney lashed out, utterly frustrated at his inability to control Ben's outbursts and terrified that Richard would shut down altogether or worse get up and storm out of the building.

"I do get it. Yes, sir, Mr. Shelley, I get it. But supposing your resources could get you into the chat room, know what they'd find? It's run by none other than Nicholas Shelley."

"Ha! Whose brilliant now! Kudos, Richard. Set our hair on fire, Richard, you dragon-hearted delinquent! The video, huh? And what is this news about 'the fucking Catholic Church'?... Wait a minute! You're Catholic yourself! Bella told me that priest, the one in the papers, the sex abuser, he teaches at your school, ergo, you're Catholic."

"So they tell me."

"A heretic! My god, you are deep! Go on, go on."

"Jesus Christ," Art Gross mumbled.

"Exactly!" Richard burst out, startling the others and raising his arms in triumph. "Exactly. Thank you. Jesus Christ. Exactly! Sorry, Nicholas, you came close, so close, but that's what you missed. *Jesus Christ!*" Bella especially but also Ben and Art were now riveted to the sight of Richard ecstatically trying to push out his words while at the same time tensing every muscle in a futile and wholly unconscious effort to quell the shivering that was now quite noticeable. "He gave humanity hope for the first time in life after death. But here's the thing you missed: When Jesus Christ rose from the dead, he killed the only thing we owned for ourselves, that we all gained by being born. He killed our original freedom! He had co-opted it for himself and from then on all of humanity would be conscripted into Christian hope, forced to renounced its original nature and its original will and to play by the Church's rules or risk everlasting damnation. And so the whole human race--which supposedly he came to save--was lost to itself. Do you see now?"

"Oooh, this is getting juicy," Nicholas chuckled. "So-so-so? What's the answer?"

"To kill that hope of immortality with a new Jesus."

Shiney was caught completely of guard. "But wait! What is this? That's not in the manifesto!"

"He's ahead of you Shine. And me, for that matter, because it certainly is in the manifesto. Haha. This is crazy! But the kid's interpretation is what I actually intended and didn't realize it. The new Jesus! I didn't use those words but I could have. It doesn't matter now. I mean, this is...I mean, how did you know?" he turned excitedly to Richard. "You read my mind! Maybe you were *in* my mind! I literally had a dream about it. In this dream I was the new Jesus! Shiney, all that negating nihilism bullshit of yours never rang true. I had no idea what you were talking about. But this! You read my fucking mind, Richard!"

Shiney was yet not ready to give in. "Is this what you meant, Richard? I don't...I don't see how you get from there to here."

"Oh, God, Shiney," Nicholas beamed, "how ridiculous you are. Who Cares! Who cares how he got anywhere. He got there, that's all that matters. C'mon, Richard, where's this going? Get to the end!"

"Nicholas, I told you. It's the video."

"Yes-yes! You told me. But *how*? A guy standing in the rain? Unable to move? Hardly able to breathe? That's how you kill hope? You've lost me."

"Look. Life and death are the poles. The ancients saw this and turned to nature and the skies for explanation. They found none, and so had to learn to live and die as part of nature--now do you see how close you came? But then along comes this guy, this Christ, and what does he do? He gives nature and all of life meaning! It's pointed somewhere now, in the future, called Heaven. And *that* changed everything. Overnight, a life that grew up from Nature and decayed back into it and made a kind of natural sense was corrupted forever. Our freedom is still ours but now it is an outlaw, hated and hunted by the Church he founded. All because we *must* believe in the immortality of Christ or face not just a natural death but everlasting damnation *after* death!"

"So what?" Shiney said angrily. "You've forsaken the pristine beauty of the manifesto, the disdain for everything that isn't me! The end of all philosophies, the end of logic. The triumph of the disordered mind! Who needs more than that?"

"I have no idea what you're talking about. Haha!" Richard said, smiling brightly at Shiney.

"The new immortality, then. Which is what exactly?" Shiney asked sourly.

"Well, you agree I imagine, that life cannot be justified, right? We did not ask to be here. And death cannot be avoided, right? So we have to suffer it through no fault of our own--"

"Get to the answer, goddamit!" Ben finally broke in, irritated by the pomposity of the high-schooler. "Jesus!"

Richard merely smiled at him too and continued. "So what are our choices, right? Suicide? But then life still wins. It goes on and we don't. Not suicide then? But then death wins because it's unavoidable. We're stuck, you see?"

"And?" Nicholas eagerly prompted.

"We must cheat them both at the same time. Refuse to play the game. Refuse to live or die."

"Will this bullshit never end?" Art Gross announced.

"Wait a minute, Art," Ben said. "I want to hear the answer."

Richard nodded to Nicholas. "The video was a revelation." They were all shocked when he slid from his seat and went down on one knee worshipfully before Nicholas. His eyes were alight. He held his hands up, clenched and imploring as if in prayer and shaking all over. "We must all become like you! That's the answer! We've got to excite ourselves and defile ourselves and smash every sensibility into bits. Exactly like what you did to your mother in strangling her, but more and more awful and degrading. The point is, you proved that the will to do the worst things can shut down the whole system. And when you said you had had a catatonic fit afterwards, I almost lost my mind. *It proves my point!*" The words came tumbling out so fast, spittle sprayed Nicholas's pant legs. "If we commit acts of utter degradation over and over again, eventually the personality itself has to crash in the form of your fits. Do you see now? It's the only end we can freely choose for ourselves--to become permanent catatonics, alive but not alive, dead but not dead. You see? You see? A new immortality! It's the only way we can take back our natural wills from Jesus Christ! The free spirits of Catatonia, free from life and death forever!"

Nicholas, fascinated, leaned forward and grabbed Richard's shoulders. "But what acts?" he asked in a tense whisper, leering at Richard like a lustful suitor. "What acts precisely? Tell me." Their eyes were locked, inches apart.

Art Gross sat with clenched teeth, his face a tight grimace. But because the spectacle before him was so deeply disturbing, he could not watch it. Instead, he had been observing Bella. Richard's insensitivity toward her had troubled him deeply. She seemed an innocent tortured by this hateful nonsense. Now he could no longer bear the injustice of it. He slammed his chair back and stood, trembling with anger.

"Think you've heard enough, Ben?" he snarled. "How much of this crap do we have to listen to? It's disgusting and degrading."

Ben Shelley pushed his own chair back and stood with hands jammed into his pockets and his thin shoulders hiked up to his ears.

"Yeah. More than enough. And I don't want to hear what comes next," he said. "You two have really stunk up the place. I never figured you'd slide this far into the pit but leave it to you to find a kindred spirit there who's even nuttier than you. Jesus. Just remember what I said before. And as for this...this...I don't even know what to call it, this sickening degenerate life-hating bullshit you're so thrilled by, I'm warning you. Whatever it leads to--if it leads anywhere but the nut house--the name of Shelley is not to be associated with it. Understand? From here on in, Nicholas Shelley is dead, dead, dead. OK, this meeting is over and I wish we never had it. Goddam you, Nicholas."

"No, we're not done here," Nicholas said, smiling up at him, still holding Richard's shoulder. "Go. Go."

Shaking his head in disbelief, Ben said, "Jesus, what a sight! Fuck it. Let's get out of here before I strangle the golden goose. . . Shiney? You coming or what?"

Shiney, who had been the main instigator in setting up the meeting, had been noticeably silent for some time. He peered up at Ben through his smudged and greasy glasses but if he intended to respond he was preempted by Nicholas's quick interruption. "Shiney wants to stay. He's getting a schooling, right Shiney?"

Shiney did not move but looked away sheepishly.

"Art?" Ben called.

Art Gross's eyes had not left Bella as if willing her to look at him. But she remained rigid, her arms wrapped around her body, her head down.

"Yeah, yeah," he answered softly in a worried and disheartened tone. Then he and Ben walked down the long empty space and through the front door.

When Ben and Art had gone, Nicholas released Richard's shoulders and motioned him back to his chair. In the interim, an idea had begun to tease him and had soon fully captured his imagination.

"My God, Richard! This is breathtaking! Isn't it, Shiney?"

"It's depressing," Shiney answered.

"Oh, c'mon, Shine! Cheer up! Listen now as Ricard makes you sick to your stomach!"

Shiney, nearly sick to his stomach already, at last forced himself to address Richard. But the look in the eyes that met his stopped him. A cruel and joyous hatred peered back at him. He looked away.

"But enough about you. I'm intrigued to hear what our silent partner thinks. Bella?"

"Leave her alone, Nicholas!" Shiney suddenly cried coming up out of his chair. "Look at her! Bella, you should leave. I'll take you now. You shouldn't have to listen to this pornography. And, Richard, you are the fool I feared you might be. You have no honor! No. I was the fool I feared I was. Ben was right. I make myself sick."

Still, Bella would not respond.

"Sit down, Smiley," Nicholas ordered the older man. Shiney sat reluctantly but now fixed his eyes on Bella. He could not bare to look anywhere else. "Tell us, Richard, what acts do you contemplate." His voice was that of young boys telling dirty stories.

Richard's shivering, despite his strenuous effort to control it, had only gotten worse. Now even his hair was vibrating. But there was also a marked change in his face. It was as if the sound of Bella's name had caused a flood of confusion and pitiful searching in his eyes. His mouth had hardened giving the impression of terrible distress and anxiety. Indeed, his head began to swivel quirkily as if in search of something or someone. When his gaze found Bella, he seemed at first mildly surprised and his face relaxed though she had been sitting beside him the whole time. He peered at her with the strangest expression, one Bella had never seen before.

"Richard," she whispered showing him a smile that throbbed with love and hope.

"Bella?" Richard said his voice shaking.

"Oh no, Richard, none of that now, my friend," Nicholas quickly forestalled him. He snapped his fingers. "Over here, Richard. That's right. Let's get you back on track, OK?"

Reluctantly, Richard returned his attention to Nicholas. Hearing his voice had broken the spell between himself and his sister. This pained him for some reason and also brought back the shivering attack which had lessened for just an instant. At first, he felt a terrible resentment against Nicholas but then remembered the 'acts' he had yet to reveal. His body jerked and the interlude was forgotten.

"Yes. Yes," he said, intentionally shaking his already trembling head as if to throw off a bad thought. "Well, I p-posted a list of the kind of acts that would have the m-most dramatic effects and asked the chat room to p-pick the five top ones."

"That's smart. Get 'em engaged. Excited. So what were the five winners?"

Richard paused a moment and blinked several times. Nicholas felt that his confidence had been dented and was quick to reassure him. "It's OK, buddy. It's OK. You're the genius here. You can tell me. C'mon now. What were they, the five winners?"

Richard put a hand to his mouth and leaned forward conspiratorially. "Not in front of my s-sister," he whispered.

"Ricard," Nicholas whispered back, "who cares? Remember?"

"Oh," Ricard said quietly. "Yes. I remember." He fell back in the chair. A moment later, the odd twitching at the corners of his mouth returned and he was shaken by a particularly violent shudder as his eyes, bright and beaming, came to life. "Who cares?" he bawled as if the phrase was a kind of war cry. He clapped his hands loudly once and sprang forward again. "Ready? Number five," he began speaking in bursts, "Number five was run over a baby carriage with your car. With a baby in it. Number four was rape your mother. Number three was slice off a girl's breasts. Number two was knife the next person you see."

As he began to enumerate the 'acts', Bella's eyes filled once again with the horror of what was coming out of her brother's mouth. An old memory that had often in the past assailed her randomly and which she had always angrily shaken off before, had come back to her moments earlier. But this time she accepted it, ran to it, grasped it with her whole mind and her whole heart as if her very sanity were at stake.

She had been very young and always at her mother's side at Sunday Mass and Holy Days. It had been during one particular Good Friday service as the Gospel recounted Christ's gruesome path up to Golgotha, that, bored by the long recitation, she had turned absently to her mother. She had been alarmed to see that her face was crushed in pain and tears were steaming down her cheeks. Her mother saw the alarm in her child's eyes and tried to smile in reassurance. Through her tears she whispered, "His poor mother. His poor mother." And now she imagined her mother's face were she here to see what had become of her son and Bella's heart groaned in agony for her mother. For she knew now with terrible certainty that she was responsible for all that had happened, that because of her Richard was lost, and because of her, her mother who loved him blindly would surely lose her mind, her faith and perhaps even her life. Suddenly she threw herself onto her knees before Richard and grasped him madly as she prayed the 'Hail Mary' as fast as her lips would move.

Angry, frustrated and overwhelmed by impatience, Nicholas cried, "Ignore her, Richard! Who cares about her, Richard? Remember? What's Number One?"

But suddenly Shiney was on his knees at Bella's side. "Bella. Please, Bela," he whispered holding her across her back. Half-heartedly, he attempted to dislodge her but she shrugged him off and continued praying the Hail Mary only louder now as she felt her brother slipping away.

"Oh, Christ, Shiney! Get the hell away from her," Nicholas barked. "Never mind them, goddamit! Tell me, Richard!" Nicholas yelled, beside himself.

"EAT SHIT!" Richard called out, his head stretched up as far as possible away from his praying sister, "NUMBER ONE WAS EAT SHIT!!"

Nicholas's reaction was immediate. He sprang out of his chair with an explosion of laughter and began rapidly pacing back and forth, laughing and repeating over and over, "'Eat shit!' Holy shit! 'Eat shit!' Holy shit!" Finally he came to stop in front of Richard and roughly tried to push Shiney aside to get at Bella and dislodge her from Richard's legs.

Shiney resisted. He was sweating profusely and white with alarm but with infinite gentleness he finally dislodged Bella's grip on Richard, raised her to her feet and settled her back in her chair. He stood beside her, protectively. In the course of the last few minutes he had begun to develop a deep dread of Nicholas and a disgust with Richard driven by disappointment, both of which had only grown more extreme. He had now only one compelling urge; to get Bella away from this ugliness.

"I'm taking her home," he said, but his flat tone betrayed him.

Nicholas sneered at him. "Like hell you are." He shook his head. "Look at you. No balls, Shiney. What a joke!"

Then he turned his gaze on Richard. "Now, Richard, calm yourself. Take a deep breath." Richard took a deep breath. "There you go. Now, as inspiring, and I have to say, amusing, as your theory has been, I am curious to know, since you admit posting the list, has there been any. . .response? Has anybody actually--"

"Yes!" Richard cried, the burden of Bella removed. "Yes-yes-yes-yes! You won't believe it! Listen! Listen!" He leaned in again toward Nicholas, enraptured with his news. "There have already been thirty-seven instances across the country. One guy has already raped his mother and sister and run over a woman pushing her kid in a stroller killing the baby. There's another guy who was caught by his wife standing over the baby's crib with a pillow over the kid's face. And get this! He'd written on the pillow with magic marker: Who Cares! Get it? Who Cares! Of course, they're only getting started.

They won't turn into living stones over night. But just yesterday I heard from a doctor in the chat room, a big believer. Somebody had got the members all riled up about the fact that the effect would wear off. But this doctor said he had foreseen this problem and had come up with a pill that would make a shutdown of the nervous system almost permanent! He's got to do some tests. But can you believe it? And look!" He pulled a baggy from his pocket. "He sent me some! You--*you*--proved it was possible! You must keep going, Nicholas. You're the only one with a head start. With these pills you can be the first Living Dead Man!"

Suddenly, Nicholas moved toward Richard and threw his arms around the boy. Then he stepped back and fixed his black eyes on him.

"Oh, Richard," he said, shaking his head sympathetically while a strange smile appeared on his lips. "Honestly, I haven't had this much fun in years, if ever. Because you're right about your theory. It has been proven." Here, he clapped his hands on Richard's shoulders and pulled him close so that Richard could smell his breath. "Only it's the wrong theory. See, the thing is, those thousands you've recruited aren't really your followers, are they? They're mine, aren't they? Let's be honest, Richard. Your ridiculous new immortality is never going to capture their simple brains like its captured yours. So, a few have tried but can you seriously imagine, Richard, that there are thousands out there who want your kind of immortality? Who will follow you down into the debasement basement and live like rocks? You see, in the end, they've already found salvation--in me! I am already Jesus. Those followers of yours are really following me. 'Who Cares' is plenty for them, and so much easier. Your mistake was to think you needed a program and you devised a beaut! But 'Who Cares?' was always just an *attitude.* An *attitude* that anyone could adopt. Richard, you poor dumb fuck, I'm the easy Jesus. You wanted to make me another hard Jesus. But c'mon, who can resist easy Jesus? Have fun! I'm the life-of-the-party Jesus! Find out how free you can be with easy Jesus!" He stopped, nearly breathless with excitement, and gave Richard an endearing hug. "But even so--even so, Richard," he continued, "for all your efforts to build up my following, I believe I owe you. I admit I am damn curious. I had an idea earlier. You're right, I am the perfect test subject. So let's see whether I can become the first Living Dead Man and prove your theory, just for the hell of it. What do you say?"

It had happened so quickly, Richard merely stared into Nicholas's face blinking rapidly, as if his shivering and shuddering had finally reached his eyes. His mouth had gone slack in disbelief. Nicholas's breath on his face felt like radiation. His hands began to shake.

Suddenly, Bella lunged at Nicholas and pushed him away. He fell back several steps while a sly smile played on his lips.

"Stop tormenting him! Can't you see what you're doing to him? Stop it! He's not your puppet." She turned to her brother. "Richard!" she begged, "Richard, sweetheart, listen to me. Can you hear me? We have to leave here. Right now." But Richard did not budge and it was difficult to know whether he had understood her at all. Shiney had in the meantime moved closer to Richard, for what purpose he was not sure, but he wanted to be of use if she would let him. Moreover, he was by now a different man. Such disgust did he feel for himself and for what he had led this poor teenager into, that he was consumed by the most urgent desire to offer some sacrifice in expiation, even if it were only to help Bella get Richard out to their car. He did not realize much less appreciate until much later that this was the first time in his life that he had ever been sorry for anything.

Nicholas, however, found the whole episode entertaining. "How little she understands her brother," he thought, bemused and delighted to see Shiney and the girl fuss over this foolish kid who quite clearly appeared to be on the brink of some kind of collapse. "Well, I guess I better move in before he actually crumbles like a cracker."

He raised his voice to be sure Richard could hear him but also to break in on his comforters. "Richard! Don't you want to hear my idea? Of course you do. I think we should add another act to the list." He grabbed Bella's arm, holding it tightly as he pulled her out of the way. He watched Richard's face closely. It was little more than dumb mask. "I think Number Six should be..." As he expected, Richard's eyes were rekindled. "No, no, I haven't lost him yet," he thought, though he half-feared he himself would be the one who might push Richard over the edge. "Yeah, well," he thought, "who cares anyway." And then he said, "Number Six should be ...'Rape Bella'!"

But surprisingly, Richard did not react except for a just noticeable twitching at the corners of his mouth. This horrified Bella. She wrenched her arm from Nicholas's grasp.

"You bastard!" she screamed and pushed him again. "Richard! Richard! Look what he's doing to you! Didn't you hear what he just said? Richard!" She slapped his face, that ugly, imbecile face, but immediately regretted it and bent close to his ear unable to look him in the eyes. "Come on, honey, it's okay. We're getting out of here right now." She took him gently by the arm hoping he would follow her while a now badly shaken Shiney took his other arm. He, too, was trembling. He moved in a kind of fog.

Richard peered up at his sister but there was no recognition in his eyes. He was feeling the oddest sensation, that he was going blind and that he desired to go blind. These people were impeding him. He shook them off. All that he saw was inside himself now, where in the blackness Nicholas's filthy deceit boiled. But there also boiled even more vigorously Nicholas's offer to be the first Living Dead Man. The two ideas hissed and spit for his endorsement.

"What do you say, Richard? Shall we have some fun?"

Richard thought, "It could work! He's right. If it was ever going to work, Nicholas could make it work. And if he succeeded! Oh, if he succeeded and Nicholas became the first Living Dead Man, all would be validated." And then in a flash of insight he knew what he would do next and was immediately whipsawed by a rush of exhilaration. "And then I'LL KILL HIM!" And out of his mouth came the words that would seal his fate: "Who cares!" The twitching corners of his mouth spread out into a smile of triumphant will.

    He knew what he had done, and what would happen now, and that after this he would be free--if it worked. He would have a delicious triumph over the traitor Nicholas. But more than that, he would never become Bella, the image of defeat and despair, but rather the true savior of the unfree. The hope of the new immortality would be real with its promise of freedom, the wonderful freedom, the freedom from hope and Jesus Christ. And Nicholas would die.

    "Richard!" Shiney cried. "You can't mean that!"

    Simultaneously, Bella begged him, "Richard! What are you saying? Do you understand what he means? Richard, sweetheart!"

    But neither Nicholas nor Richard were moved by their entreaties. Each understood the other and that their intentions were aligned.

    Nicholas reached out and took hold of Bella's arms and in one motion tipped her onto the floor in front of Richard. His strength terrified her. He straddled her body while supporting himself with his hands against the cement floor. Instinctively she raised her hands to scratch at his face, but he caught her arms and was pleasantly surprised when she went limp--intentionally, he was sure of it, and it gave him a moment of pause. He sat back on her holding her arms and looked down at her face with a pleased expression. He wanted to kiss her for giving in so easily.

In a way, he was correct. She had decided not to fight him. The only thought in her mind now was that Richard should not see her in pain, and she turned her head toward him. Smiling weakly she mouthed the words, "It's OK", over and over. Her terror had not lessened but she believed wholeheartedly that all this was her fault. That the pain and degradation she would feel at Nicholas's attack was to be her punishment, that she would endure it for him, Richard, that she would not and must not claim for herself any anger or hatred or fear but instead accept it all for him. Here, in this unbelievable and most terrible moment, what should come to her but her mother's oft repeated phrase--"Offer it up, honey." She would have laughed had she not been torn with fear, for the meaning of the phrase had always baffled and annoyed her. But now she heard it and grasped at it with an inner certainty and for the first time in her life, she groaned and ached for her mother. She breathed and her mind cleared and she prayed, "For my brother, dear God, and my mother. Forgive me." She rolled her eyes back toward Richard, repeating the words, "It's OK". But Richard did not notice. His full concentration was on the traitor Nicholas, encouraging him on in a voice that sounded like an old man wheezing. His sister's mantra went unheard because he was now repeating his own: "It could work. It could work."

The next thing they heard was Shiney's high screech. He was standing above Nicholas who did not turn to him but kept watching Bella's face.

"Jesus God Almighty, Nicholas! Get off of her!" Shiney yelled, disgusted and quaking. Half-heartedly, he bent over Nicholas and grabbed his sides and pulled. Nicholas swatted his arms away.

"Where's the committed anarchist now, Shiney?" he called out while smiling and winking at Bella. "Didn't I hear you say something about how 'Who Cares?' was a new thing, an exciting new thing? Didn't I hear that? You were right. This is exciting! It might even cause me to go all catatonic. We can only hope, hey Richard?"

Shaking with fear and nearly undone by his cowardliness, Shiney desperately looked around, for what, he didn't know. But there was an empty chair where Ben Shelley had sat. It was within arm's reach, so he grabbed it and lifted it over Nicholas's arched back.

"Get off her, Nicholas," he ordered in a quaking voice. His arms were trembling even though the chair was not heavy. "I mean it, get off her. Yes, yes, you're right. I said all those things. My whole life, everything I ever believed in--I see it now--was leading up to *you*. 'Who Cares?' is a lie. And there is only one answer to it. I care!"

He swung the chair down with all his pitiable strength onto Nicholas's back. He heard a grunt of pain as Nicholas collapsed onto his elbows. His face hung over Bella, his eyes burning with pain and anger. She willed herself to raise her head until her lips were close to his ear. "I forgive you," she said, fell back and closed her eyes.

After the first blow, Shiney froze. He could not believe what he had just done. For the briefest moment, he nearly turned and ran toward the front door. The old Shiney would certainly have done so. Yet the words from the girl's small voice so astonished him that it was as if he himself had received a crushing blow. He cried out in a burst of righteous rage that dissolved his self-disgust and a second time brought the chair down on Nicholas's back. Nicholas collapsed fully on top of Bella who pushed his dead weight off and crawled to Richard, caressing him and speaking to him softly.

Sweating profusely and near collapse himself, Shiney staggered around the prone figure lifting and smashing the chair onto him over and over, uncaring whether it landed on the body, the head, or banged onto the cement floor. Out of breath and strength at last, he fell to his knees.

Out of nowhere, two policemen suddenly rushed in with guns drawn and shouting. They rolled Shiney roughly onto his stomach and cuffed his hands behind his back. One of the officers knelt beside Bella and helped her up but she clung to her brother who stared unseeing while continually repeating the odd phrase, "It could work". The other officer was busy attending to Nicholas who was unresponsive. Eventually an ambulance arrived and Nicholas was put on a gurney and wheeled into it. Shiney was settled in a waiting police car, Bella and Richard in another.

There had been an anonymous 911 call to report that there was a girl in distress at Ben's office address. The caller had even provided the key code. The officers had arrived to see Shiney through the glass doors bring the chair down on Nicholas for the last time.

CHAPTER 12 | That God does not exist

Angela Benfont could hardly contain her delight. At last, after many invitations, Fr. Flynn had come to join the Tuesday discussion group. He had arrived as the seven women were taking their regular places in a semicircle with Angela facing them on a hardback chair in front of the fireplace. Eleanor sat facing her in the one large wing chair next to the sofa which the others referred to as her 'throne'.

Pat D'Angelo was perched on a footstool beside Eleanor. She and Eleanor were the two most argumentative of the group. Pat was in her fifties but looked much older. She had a rough smoker's voice that was almost manly.

On the other side of Eleanor, three women sat together on the couch. DeeDee Timperio was a starkly attractive woman with piercing brown eyes and high cheek bones but unusually thin lips and a very narrow chin. She rarely spoke but spent nearly the entire time posed very properly in her accustomed seat on the couch beside Norrie Dunn.

Norrie was a small thin woman with short blonde hair and energetic blue eyes. She was a serious and thoughtful person but at the same time easily excited by fresh insights and new ideas, especially any that promised deeper understanding of spiritual things.

Next to her at the end of the couch and nearly lost in the thick plush cushions sat the oldest member of the group, Jo Bartolotta, Angela's oldest and dearest friend. She was a small mousy woman, sickly, frail, with sparse dry hair and watery eyes behind thick glasses. Though she was the oldest, she had the gentlest sense of humor, like a child's, and she loved to tell jokes. Her jokes were always sweet and childish. Even when she wasn't telling a joke, her voice was full of humor.

Inches from Jo, Shirley Birdsong sat tensely in a straight-backed chair. She was younger than the others and looked even younger. Her skin was fresh and rosy, her full lips and wide mouth gave her a kind adolescent sensuality. Her permanented hairstyle, however, puffed and sprayed into a bouncy blonde helmet, was unkindly regarded by some of the women as a sign of mental and cultural retardation.

Eleanor especially had not been pleased when Angela disclosed a few months ago that she had invited Shirley to join them.

"Where'd you get her? The Lawrence Welk Show?"

Angela, with a tense jaw and blushing displeasure, had not responded. But Eleanor had gone on to say, "It's like Barbie grew up and became a Stepford wife."

Her sister's surprisingly angry response to this remark had only been diffused when Eleanor promised never to say it again, though she still thought it summed up the woman quite accurately. Angela had a special affection for Shirley, even a certain sense of personal responsibility. They had been close neighbors in the old house and it had been to Angela that Shirley had turned in a time of spiritual trial. One day, Shirley had asked, "Will you take me to a Catholic Mass, if...if that's allowed?" Angela had squeezed her hand. "Of course it's allowed."

As Angela looked around the room, beaming, with Fr. Flynn sitting next to her on another straight back chair, her eyes came to rest on Shirley. Knowing her as well as she did, Angela saw that she was uneasy and she knew it was because of the presence of the priest. Shirley had talked often after attending several Masses with Angela about converting but had yet to finally make up her mind. This long delay, Angela also knew, was directly related to the scandals in the Church. And here, not six feet away, sat a priest who had been accused of that very crime! And he was smiling!

Angela also saw that Shirley was not alone in her unease. Pat and DeeDee and of course Eleanor all displayed tight-lipped displeasure. But she was confident that Fr. Flynn would win them over and did not let their sour looks and Shirley's nervous fidgeting diminish her delight.

She went around the room introducing him to the group, coming last to her sister.

"And this is my sister, Eleanor. She's a trouble maker!"

"Ah!" said the priest with his easy flamboyant smile. "A kindred spirit!" He surveyed the women and clapped his hands. "So. What's today's topic?"

"Oh, gosh, Father," Norrie burst out laughing, as delighted by the sight of him as Angela. "I feel we should talk about something big, you know, with you here. But, gosh, I'm afraid we're more like a Christian coffee klatch, to tell you the truth."

"'Wherever two or more are gathered' you know. I'm quite certain that includes coffee klatches."

Suddenly and surprisingly, DeeDee Timperio leaned quickly forward before anyone else could speak, back straight, hands clasped in her lap, her fiercely concentrated gaze burning into the priest. "Well, since you're here and you're asking, I want to know if you think people are evil. They are, you know," she said with finality.

"DeDe," the priest responded, somewhat taken aback by this unexpected thrust. "That might be a subject for another time. Actually, I'm AWOL at the moment. I have to get back soon and my mouth tends to runneth over so perhaps when we have more time...Come and see me."

No one quite knew what DeDe thought about anything. In normal social settings she could be jovial and even giddy and charmingly absent-minded. But she could also be, as now, extraordinarily harsh and impulsive. As usual, she had been listening with serious attention while the other women for the most part had forgotten she was even in the room.

Beside her, Norrie Dunn's head had snapped round in surprise but also alarm. DeDe's tone had been so precise and sharp it might have been a gun shot. "DeDe, you can't think that." Then turning to the priest, she said simply, "Father?"

But DeeDee had the floor and she was not about to give it up. "Think about it. Christ on the cross proves it! It's so obvious I can't get over how people don't see it! 'I have come to save sinners.' That's what he said. He didn't say, 'I have come to save nice people like us who think we're good.' People are so far beyond saving, God himself had to come down to Earth and die on the cross to make it even possible. People are evil! I don't know how you can deny it."

All eyes were on the priest, DeeDee's most ardently of all. He himself had been listening closely and now he smiled at DeeDee.

"Well, you know, DeeDee, I'm very impressed. You're thinking about the big things, not the trivialities and that's good. You are a serious person. But we have to be careful about the logic. What I mean is, if what you say is true, it must mean that Christ came to save not sinners but evil people. And therefore, because he became one of those he intended to save, he himself must have become evil. Do you see?"

"Bravo, Father!" Norrie cried and laughed.

"I--," Shirley began in a tremulous uncertain voice. She had been nervously waiting her turn but also desperate to ask her question. All eyes had turned to her.

"Shirley. Please!" Angela whispered in alarm.

Shirley colored with embarrassment. "Never mind," she mumbled but an undertone of suppressed anger had leaked into her voice.

"Go ahead, Shirley," Pat D'Angelo encouraged. "This priest can take it, I think."

Fr. Flynn smiled kindly at her. "Shirley, I'm willing to talk about whatever you want to ask."

Shirley glanced at Angela who lowered her eyes in worried acquiescence.

"Never mind, Father," she said.

"She wants to talk about you, Flynn. You priests who've--" Eleanor began.

"Eleanor!" Angela exclaimed.

"The kid's been on the verge of converting for years," Eleanor plowed on. "The only reason she isn't a Catholic yet is all these scandals."

"Eleanor!"

"That's all she ever wants to talk about. Frankly, I wish she'd just stay home. But since she brought it up--again--well, let's see if you want to face the music," Eleanor concluded, critical appraisal flashing in her eyes.

Fr. Flynn had taken an immediate liking to this big woman who watched him like a hawk. He knew better than to underestimate her and suspected her brain was as big as the rest of her. It was quite clear to him that she held the group in thrall and was possessed of an unshakeable confidence in herself. Yet, he did not get the impression that she was doctrinaire in her thinking. It was the confidence that showed in her eyes. They looked like thinker's eyes.

"When it comes to facing the music, Eleanor, I'm the first in line!"

"So, give her the pitch."

"Eleanor! No more!" Angela demanded, nearly frantic with anger and dismay.

"No, no, Angela," the priest calmed her. "We deserve it, us priests, to be grilled over the hottest of hot flames."

"Oh, Father. I'm so sorry," Angela said, moved nearly to tears, shamed at having invited him into this trap.

Fr. Flynn lowered his eyes and clasped his hands. He might have been praying. When he looked up again, his face was severe, the brightness of his personality replaced by deep somberness.

"Perhaps, if you will allow me, I would like to address myself to all of you. Thank you, Shirley, for your courage. I hope you won't mind if I take it that you were speaking on everyone's behalf, even if you didn't intend to." He paused and once again lowered his eyes. "I have spent many hours thinking and praying over this issue. Some priests I know personally have...fallen." He spoke slowly now, measuring his words, not looking at any of them directly, focused at a neutral spot of the rug. "I say to myself, how can God allow such degradation? What kind of God is this? These poor, innocent children." He stopped. No one spoke. He continued slowly and softly. "We must all feel that to speak of him as Love is nothing but the most profoundly evil lie ever uttered." He heard several women gasp but went on. "Yet the alternative is, there is no God, and suffering is nothing but an endless, meaningless, organic phenomenon, hopeless, unbearable, and unavoidable."

Angela, who had been one of the women who had gasped at his words, was about to speak but the priest, without looking at her, simply raised his hand.

"We all want an answer to these abuses. In our hearts, even justice is not enough to satisfy us. Any decent, loving God would never allow them to happen in the first place. But," he paused and looked up, "this is sentimentality, not Christianity."

All the women were watching him, scrutinizing him. Jo Bartolotta looked frightened, her eyes big and wide behind her glasses. Norrie Dunn sat rigidly forward, her elbows on her knees, her chin in her hands, her face hardened with concentration. DeeDee Timperio sat primly but with her eyes closed, perhaps also in concentration, though no one ever really knew what the famously silent woman was thinking.

Pat D'Angelo was enjoying herself. The consternation displayed on the faces of the other women made her feel for the first time that she was glad she had shown up.

Eleanor, defiant and on guard with a heightened wariness, tensely alert for the merest hint of hypocrisy, suddenly thrust her head back, raised a censorious eyebrow, and waited.

Angela, too, was uncomfortably alert. Her icon of faith, she feared, was on the verge of falling off his pedestal in full view of her friends to whom she had lauded him so highly.

Having surveyed them and felt their agitation, he brought his eyes to rest on Eleanor. He was very curious how she would respond.

She did not disappoint him. "And yet here you sit," Eleanor said with undisguised contempt. "If that's what you believe, you should have shot yourself long before now."

"Ha!" Pat laughed.

"Eleanor!" Norrie cried.

"Oh, Eleanor! Apologize!" Shirley pleaded.

"Hear, hear!" DeeDee said and made the other women jump. Her hands had sprung away from her lap as if they had minds of their own. Chagrined, she slammed them together and down onto her lap.

"My young nephew had your number, Flynn," Eleanor continued, confident and scornful. "Black is the color of cowardice!"

"I'm not so sure you're wrong," he said, which surprised Eleanor though she controlled herself and showed no reaction. But Angela understood, and smiled. He turned and continued to the group. He spoke from a deep authority but his voice was not angry or harsh. He had compassion for them, knowing how their hearts were troubled, and yet he also knew that they, like virtually all Catholics, were woefully--almost sinfully--ignorant of their own faith. How often had he spoken with troubled Catholics whose anguish was caused by a life-long, incurious, unthinking and unchallenged sentimentality about the idea of God? Sadly, too many times. He believed it was precisely his vocation, therefore, to pierce this veil of sentimentality whenever, with kindness, he could do so.

"Now listen to me. The God we all say we believe in, this God who should never allow suffering in the first place, is a false God. That God does not exist. He never existed. But he is the only God humans can imagine. He is a God of our own creation. We believe he exists because someone must be to blame for all this suffering. This is why our hopes are always disappointed. Hope is in our nature but we have placed our hope in a phantom. But we would never have known this and we would have gone on forever looking for hope and answers from a God that was never there. There was ever only going to be one way that we could come to know the real God. He would have to reveal Himself to us." Now he turned back to Eleanor and smiled at her. "So I don't wear black because I'm a coward, Eleanor. I wear it to proclaim the death of two Gods. The one that does not exist and the one that does. We are free to choose one or the other, hope in Christ the real God or hope in the hopeless phantom God of our sentimentality. Choose one and we will still know that suffering exists but we will know what to do about it. Choose the other and we will still know that suffering exists but eventually we will quit caring about such things altogether because caring is meaningless and ineffectual and hurts."

"What?--Oops!" Norrie asked sliding even further forward, nearly slipping off the couch. She caught herself and laughed. "What? What is it? What we can we do about it?" she asked eagerly, readjusting herself one the couch.

The priest now gazed at them and his face was stern.

"We can bind ourselves body and soul to Christ on the cross so that we can do what He did and pray for the suffering children of abuse, to make their abuse *our* sin as he made our sins His...Yes, what a disappointment, huh? Prayer! That's the only answer I've got? But if we're honest Christians, we will always worry and agonize over these questions. And then, one day, we will get to the point of such intolerable despondency that all our prejudices against it will fall away and we must give ourselves up to prayer. At the end of hopelessness, there is only prayer or the abyss. We all have that choice to make, somewhere, sometime in our lives. We are free to choose one or the other, hope in Christ the real God or hope in the hopeless God of our sentimentality. That is the freedom and the hope Christ bought for us."

He smiled around at them but none of them were smiling back.

Just then, Jo Bartolotta's mousy voice rose into the silence to relieve her own discomfort and the others', too.

"Father?"

"Yes, Jo?"

"Uh, oh," Pat said. "Here comes another Jo joke."

"Perfect timing, Jo," Eleanor said.

"I do love God, Father," Jo began, a twinkle in her eye. "You know why?"

"No, Jo. Tell me."

"Because he's got such great hair."

"Oh, Jo!"

"You're a hoot."

"Good one, Jo."

"Better than the last one anyway."

There was scattered applause. Jo waited a beat, then said, "That's where His Son got His."

More applause, friendly groans and gentle mockery. Jo beaned at them.

When Bella unexpectedly walked through the front door just then, she saw the group bantering among themselves, unconsciously thankful for the relief Jo had provided.

Fr. Flynn had thought the women must have been praying the whole time for him to shut the hell up, and Jo's sweet little joke had been the answer to their prayers. He himself was relieved. He leaned back and his eyes fell on Bella in the foyer.

"Why, HELLO! AGAIN!" he called out. Everyone turned to see whom he had greeted. Bella stood rigidly with her head down and her arms tight at her sides. She had left the front door open.

"Shut the door, Bel--" Angela said and then froze.

Two men now entered the house behind Bella. After settling the scene at Ben Shelley's office after the arrival of a supervising detective, they had determined that Bella was well enough to drive her own car home and they had followed behind. The first through the door was an older man in a loose-fitting crumpled suit and a tie that was too short to cover his large stomach. He had an inquisitive, searching air about him.

The second man was taller, younger, and dressed in the uniform of a City policeman. This younger man softly closed the door and stood, his eyes downcast. His hair was black and buzzed short. He had a well-shaped head, a slim sensitive nose, a strong chin, and wore rimless glasses.

At the sight of them, Eleanor immediately came lumbering out of her chair to face them. "What the hell is this?" she demanded fiercely in a sharp, loud voice. "Bella?"

Fr. Flynn and Angela rose up beside her. Now all the women were on their feet and, in a rather unseemly rush, gathered together surrounding Angela.

The man in the suit had shuffled forward unimpressed by the crowd he could not have expected to encounter. The officer, behind him, had not moved and stood with his head down and his hands clasped in front of him.

Surveying them, the man in the suit said in a business-like way, "Mrs. Benfont?"

"Who the hell are you?" Eleanor boomed.

The man, taking his time, with no sense of urgency but rather in a relaxed automatic movement he had evidently made thousands of times, reached into his coat pocket and withdrew a wallet-like article and held it up.

"I'm Detective Sergeant Robert Houselander. This is Officer Stan Buckley." With the same automatic movement he replaced the wallet. He addressed Eleanor. "Mrs. Benfont?"

"I'm Mrs. Benfont," Angela said. Eleanor rotated herself toward her sister and saw the whiteness of her face. She herself was flushed and sweating. Helplessness assailed her and above all things she disdained helplessness in herself. Yet her sister's eyes were hard and focused and her mouth was set in determination. Eleanor recognized this look. It came from a depth of strength her sister rarely exposed.

"Can we have a word, please?" Houselander said, gesturing with his hand for her to join them.

Eleanor watched as Angela, bravely composed, took the priest's arm and moved to the foyer. It almost brought tears to her eyes. All the others followed with their eyes. It was at once something terrible and utterly gripping.

Angela and Fr. Flynn joined the two men as Houselander motioned them into the dining room.

"I suggest you send your friends home," he said in his off-handed manner, expecting to be obeyed. But Angela ignored him. It was Bella she had come for, not the detective's summons.

"Bella. What's happened?" she asked as her voice shook.

"Oh, Mom," Bella moaned. There were tears in her eyes.

Detective Houselander glanced at Fr. Flynn with special interest, even pausing momentarily as if surprised by the priest's presence.

To Angela, he said, "Please, Mrs. Benfont, if we can have a word. We'll explain everything."

Angela left Bella and walked into the dining room with Fr. Flynn followed by the two men.

"I think it would really be better if you asked your lady friends to leave," Houselander recommended again. Angela ignored him and went round to stand behind her chair at the table. Houselander was about to pull out a chair across from her but took a step back to peer once again at the priest.

"Friend of the family?" he asked suspiciously.

"Yes," Fr. Flynn said smiling, holding his hand out over the table. "Jim Flynn." They shook and he took the chair next to Angela.

"Stan," Houselander said, still looking at the priest, "bring the girl in."

The officer escorted Bella to a chair beside her mother. They both stood, holding hands.

"Please," Houselander said, gesturing toward the chairs. The two women sat. He glanced into the foyer to see that an audience had converged there. The women, Eleanor foremost, were watching them with intent, fear and fascination on their faces.

"No doors on this room, I see," Houselander said, mildly exasperated. "Stan, you ready?" The officer had pulled a chair into the corner, behind Angela, Bella and Fr. Flynn. His pad was on his knee. He held up a pen and nodded.

"Alright. Now, first, Mrs. Benfont, let me say that Bella here is not in any kind of trouble, you understand."

"Oh, thank God!"

"However--listen to me, Mrs. Benfont," he rushed to intercept her reaction. "However, she has been the victim of an attack--

"Bella! Oh God!" Angela groaned.

"Mrs. Benfont, I know this is tough but let me assure you, I assure you she was not hurt. It was an attempted assault that was interrupted by a man at the scene. She was not injured, only knocked down."

"Well, but what did he want? Who was he? Where did this happen? Did you catch him--"

"Please bare with me, Mrs. Benfont. It appears that another man tried to--well, he apparently intended to rape Bella--"

Angela gasped. Murmurs and gasps erupted from the women looking on.

"But he came nowhere near that. As I said, the other man there beat him pretty severely to get him off her. This man who stopped the attack is now in custody where he may face charges. The man who attacked her has been taken to the hospital."

"Oh sweetheart! Oh, Bella!" Angela said as relief flooded through her.

Houselander allowed some moments to pass as the mother and daughter consoled one another. Angela then turned to address her friends. "It's all right. Don't worry." She smiled weakly. The women, slowly with timid waves and a few blown kisses, left the house. Only Eleanor remained on guard, her arms crossed, leaning against the door frame. The despised feeling of helplessness had not left her. There was nothing she could do.

The detective, relieved somewhat, went on. "There is another matter, however. It concerns your son, Richard Benfont."

"Richard!?" Angela cried, sitting up.

She released Bella and fell back staring at her with a strange look that distorted all her features. At the mention of her son's name, the deep strength that Eleanor hoped would keep her sane left her soul as if it had never existed. Her mind scraped itself raw with fear.

"He was with you?" Angela hissed at Bella. "What was he doing with you? Why didn't you protect him?" she cried. Fear for her son made her voice ugly. It shocked the detective who was not easily shocked. It had propelled Fr. Flynn to jump out of his chair. He fell to his knees beside Angela, whispering her name over and over but she did not notice him. Eleanor, from the doorway, saw with horror the crushing effect it had had on Bella and instantly her helplessness evaporated. With power and authority she rushed to her niece and grabbed her by her shoulders, lifting her out of her chair.

"Angela! Control yourself!" she ordered. "What's wrong with you?" She marched Bella away to the living room.

Insensible to anything but her fear for her son, Angela turned on the detective.

"What's happened? What's happened to my Richard?" she demanded in a voice so fierce Houselander half expected her to come at him across the table.

"Nothing!" he exclaimed, raising his hands at her. "He's not hurt."

"What then?" Angela screamed. "Where is he?"

Houselander attempted to calm himself before responding but he was unusually rattled. He knew that this was not the only shock this poor woman would experience this evening. This was why the presence of Fr. Flynn had caught his interest.

"Mrs. Benfont, there is nothing physically wrong with your son," he explained, his voice almost pleading. "He was not involved in the altercation between the two other men though he was present. But he seems to have had...well, we don't really know, some kind of breakdown as it was described to me. He was taken to the hospital for observation. He's at Mercy General. You can see him."

Detective Houselander did not dare explain further, for instance, that he and Buckley had been shocked when arriving at the scene by Richard's utter disregard not only for the fact that his sister had nearly been raped in front of him but also that a man clearly known to him had been beaten to within an inch of his life, and that Richard was babbling something and wouldn't stop, and that he was in the Psych ward not the hospital proper.

"I, uh, well, I guess that's all...Stan?"

Detective Houselander rose slowly from his chair looking pointedly at the priest. Catching his eye, he subtly tilted his head toward the foyer then moved there. Fr. Flynn got up and followed him and they were joined by Officer Buckley. Houselander did not speak immediately but gazed at the priest with a concerned, almost regretful look. Finally, he said in a low voice so as not be heard in the dining room, "Listen...I'm swerving out of my lane here but you should know, the Feds have been granted a search warrant for these premises."

Fr. Flynn was rocked backward by this. "Why, in God's name?" he asked, his eyes wide with disbelief.

Detective Houselander frowned. His lips opened and closed twice before he was able to articulate the answer. Then shaking his head sadly, he said, "The kid, that Richard, he's the one who--he's the hacker."
"No, God! No-no," Fr. Flynn whispered pathetically, a pitiful expression on his face.

"Yeah," the Detective said in a dejected tone, then paused. "Look, Father, this isn't going to get any easier for her. I don't know when they'll show up, maybe in minutes, maybe later. I imagine she'll want to go to the hospital. Up to you whether you take her now but you can be pretty sure they'll be here when you get back...I'm sorry. I just...well, if they show up here now..." he said looking meaningfully at the priest, "...ok...Good luck." His voice trailed off and he and the officer left, closing the door very quietly behind them.

Fr. Flynn gathered himself though the shock of what he had been told lingered in his face. A terrible anger flared up inside him at what Richard had done to him but even more so at what he had done to Angela. Yet, this anger disgusted him and his heart battled mightily to suppress it. He forced himself to move with calmness back into the dining room as he silently repeated his favorite prayer. Angela did not resist his suggestion that they leave now for the hospital.

CHAPTER 13 | Visit from the police

As they rolled up the long driveway to the Shelley house after leaving the Benfont residence, Detective Sergeant Houselander and Officer Buckley looked at one another.

"Some joint," Houselander commented.

"Rich bitches," Buckley sneered.

They exited the car and approached the front door which opened as it seemed automatically. From the other side of the door peaking out at them a head slowly came into view. It didn't move or speak or reveal any other part of its body.

Houselander said, "Uh, Mr. Shelley?"

"Yes," the head said cautiously.

Houselander held up his ID. "I'm Detective Sergeant Houselander, this is officer Buckley. May we come in?"

"Why?" the head said, but then seemed to sense its own ridiculous position, and revealed itself as Kit Shelley. He had evidently recovered from his earlier hysteria. "Never mind. I know why you're here." He stood aside to allow them to enter. They blinked around at the profusion of color and images while he closed the door.

"I've been meditating," he explained. "I felt a crack in my aabha as soon as you pulled in the driveway...You have no idea what I'm talking about...sometimes neither do I. I often have to ask my wife."

"How do you know?" Buckley asked sharply, repulsed by the man.

"Know what?"

"Why we're here."

"Why else would you be here? He's done something. I can tell you, though, my wife is not going to take it well."

"Oh, yes?" Houselander responded, curious what would come out of this strange person's mouth next.

"Oh, yes. If you have a personal mantra, I urge you to--"

"Oh, no! No-no-no-no!" Marigold exclaimed, stopping dead in the hallway. "Get him on the phone! Right now!"

"Excuse me," the man said and drifted away.

Buckley whispered, "Nut house."

Houselander cleared his throat. "Uh, Mrs. Shelley, we need to talk to you about--"

"No!" she yelled turning her back on them and waving her hands in the air as if to disrupt the photons flowing from their direction.

"Mrs. Shelley," Houselander tried again, "it's about your son, Nic--"

"I won't talk to you! You'll have to talk to Ben."

"Who's Ben?"

"My brother-in-law, the bastard!" Then she screamed out, "Did you get that bastard on the phone yet?"

"He's not answering," the man's voice, barely audible, came from another room.

Marigold began writing on a piece of paper. She rushed forward and handed it to Houselander. "Now get out!"

The two policemen gladly left and dutifully proceeded to the address on the piece of paper. It was Ben Shelley's address.

After informing him of the events that had transpired at his office, his nephew's condition and whereabouts and Shiney's arrest and asking questions rather diffidently as if they were bored by the whole thing, they stood to leave.

"Wait. You're kidding right? Shiney? *Shiney*? I mean, Shiney hasn't got a belligerent bone in his body."

"Tell that to Nicholas Shelley," Buckley commented wryly.

"So, what, he's been arrested?"

"Yeah. They took him to County lockup."

"Holy shit. Well, thanks. Good to hear the kid wasn't badly hurt. And of course that the girl's OK. I can't believe it about Shine, though...By the way, how'd you know this was all going on. I mean, how'd you know it was at my place?" Ben asked casually.

"Anonymous 911," Buckley answered.

"Uh-huh." Ben thought a moment. "Fucking Art Gross!" he cursed to himself.

The officers turned to leave.

"How'd the parents take it?" he asked to their retreating backs.

"We got asked to leave before we could tell them anything," Houselander explained, turning to him. "I guess that's up to you now. Good luck," he threw over his shoulder as he followed Buckley out the door.

Ben Shelley had waited until he was sure they were out of earshot before yelling, "Fuck! Fuck! Fuck! Fuck!" at the top of his lungs.

"What if goddam Shiney had killed him? Oh, he's so lucky that kid is still alive. What the fuck was he thinking? The whole deal would have come crashing down on my head!"

He paced rapidly up and down his living room muttering to himself and shaking his head in raging disbelief at how close he had come to the abyss. He eventually brought himself under control. "Ok, ok, we're good, we're good...of course, I'll have to let them know...but that's ok, just a speed bump, nothing's really changed..Shiney, though. Jesus!...if Nicholas presses charges...do I give a shit?...Oh! That means maybe we can cut him out of the deal!...I mean, we can't have a felon *in locus parentis*, right?...got to talk to Nicholas...tomorrow first thing." Then he pulled out his phone and called his brother. "Well, that was easy," he said after hanging up. "What a family!"

CHAPTER 14 | Revelations

Fr. Flynn and Angela had left for the hospital, too distracted to alert Eleanor and Bella and had gone without a word. It was just as well. Eleanor wouldn't have allowed Bella to go with them even if she had wanted to but she had not even noticed their exit. Now, alone together, her niece slumped on the couch, her head in her hands and her aunt in a straight back chair leaning close to her, knee to knee, Eleanor asked as sympathetically as she could manage, "What the hell happened, Bella?" Her big body felt as if it was bubbling over with a fevered pity for the girl. The vehemence of Angela's outburst against her daughter had so shaken Eleanor that she had for the first time experienced fear for herself, for her own inner integrity. In that moment, she knew hysteria.

Bella rocked her head back and forth but didn't look up. "It's all my fault, Aunt El. It's all my fault."

"Stop that, right now. What's the matter with you? I thought you had more brains than that. It's never your fault when some guy tries to--"

"No, no," Bella mumbled. "I don't mean that. I mean...everything. The whole mess. Oh God, Aunt El! What have I done?"

Eleanor sat back, relieving the pressure on her stomach and folded her arms. These last few minutes had been a struggle for her. The fear for herself had frightened her as few things ever had. But the greater fear for what it must have done to her niece saved her.

"Well, your mother...you wait and see. When she gets home I'm going to smack her right around the room. How she can talk to you like that!"

"Please, Aunt El!" Bella said looking up, her eyes red-rimmed. "You don't know! I should have protected him! But by then it had all gone too far. It never should have gone that far. It never should have happened at all! I caused it, Aunt El. Me."

Eleanor fixed her with her commanding gaze. "All right. I'm listening."

"Oh, Aunt El, it's so awful. I was just--no-no-no--I can't justify myself. I *meant* to!" and she dropped her head.

"Meant to what?"

Bella looked up again, glanced at her aunt, took a deep breath, then closed her eyes. "I should never have shown him that...that manifesto."

"Richard?"

"I don't know why I did that--no-no-goddamit! Yes I do! He had just told me about what he'd done and...and...I couldn't believe it. It was awful but I was, I don't know, sort of morbidly excited by it. I felt so guilty! But at the same time, I *wanted* to feel guilty. I was feeling so dead inside, and this guy Nicholas sent me this thing he'd written and it...oh, it was so stupid but it was so...so different! I couldn't understand how anybody could even think like that! And when Richard came in to tell me--god, was he excited--that he was responsible for that priest getting charged with sex abuse--"

"What?!"

"Oh, no-no-no. It was a prank, that's all."

"A prank? A prank? That little sonofabitch! When I get my hands on that little bastard, I'll show him a prank--"

"Stop, Aunt El! Please! That's not the point."

Eleanor, her eyes ablaze, clamped her lips and fell silent. Bella took a breath and continued.

"I showed him the manifesto and he read it and, I swear, it was from that moment something happened to him. You see? It's my fault! I just felt...oh, I can't believe I'm saying this...I just felt I wanted to...join him, sort of. To be bad! Oh God, could I sound any stupider?"

"Ok, wait a minute. So Richard reads this manifesto thing and, what, he loses his mind?"

"Yes. Kind of. I mean, not literally, but he became obsessed with meeting this guy."

"This guy Nicholas."

"Yes."

"Where is it, this manifesto? I want to read it."

"It's not important now."

"Well, first all, stop beating yourself up. Everybody wants to be bad once in a while. More often than you think. Keep talking. Get it out."

Bella suddenly covered her mouth with her hand. "I think I'm going to be sick."

"No, you're not going to be sick. Put your head between your knees." She leaned over and slapped her hand on Bella's head and pressed it downward.

"Ouch!"

"Just a love tap," she laughed as she gently slid her hand down the side of Bella's face to lift her hair away, holding it against the side of her head and patting her. They were quiet for a while.

Eventually Bella looked up and said, "I can't talk about this any more." Suddenly, her lips began to tremble as she fell sideways onto the couch and broke into a torrent of heaving sobs. With surprising agility for a woman her size, Eleanor rolled off her chair and knelt down beside the couch. Her big arms caressed the girl's throbbing shoulders. She laid her cheek against Bella's head.

Many minutes later, as Bella's sobs subsided, Eleanor lifted herself grunting to her feet. "It's all right, honey. It's all right now," she said lowering herself heavily back onto her chair.

Bella sat up wiping her eyes. "It's not all right, Aunt El. It'll never be all right...oh, poor Richard. Oh poor, Mom. My poor, poor, Mom!" Again she shook with sobs, hugging herself and rocking back and forth. "It's all my fault. Oh, God!"

Eleanor, shaken by these revelations and feeling helpless to ease her niece's pain, finally voiced what she had been anxiously waiting to understand. "But Bella, why is it your fault? *What's* your fault? What didn't you protect Richard from?"

Bella, feeling her aunt's anxiety through her own misery, gathered herself, took deep breaths, and then with an effort reached into her pocket and took out her phone. She scrolled and then held it out to Eleanor.

"Here," she said softly, but then quickly said, "No. Wait." She reached into another pocket and removed her earbuds. These she handed to Eleanor. "I don't know why but something told me I should record it. I can't listen to it."

"What do I do with these?" Eleanor asked as if they might explode in her hand.

"Stuff them in your ears and press the play button. You're such a dinosaur," she said with a wry, sad smile. Then she lay back down on the couch and closed her eyes.

For nearly an hour, as Bella slept peacefully, Eleanor endured the most harrowing experience of her life. The voices on the recording assailed her mind with such smug and loathsome perversity it was as if they emanated from some other vile reality. And the vilest voice she heard was that of her own nephew. Several times she had to pause the recording, so constricted had her heart become by the ridiculous and shameful words he uttered and more so by the insufferable glee in which he uttered them--oh, poor Bella! This sleeping child could no more be responsible for Richard's descent into this madness than...her mind could not discover an analogy vile enough since her imagination was incapable of vileness.

Yet she continued listening. "I must hear this to the end if it kills me," she said to herself. "How she made it through such filth!...oh, good God this kid is brave."

Finally reaching the last moments, she listened as Nicholas attacked Bella and taunted Shiney and Richard. Then came the sound of metal creaking and a thud followed by a groan. Then after a pause another thud, and another and another mixed in with the loud bangs of metal hitting cement. And also something softer, something she almost missed. Bella's voice. Eleanor thought she heard the words, "I forgive you" and at first couldn't believe her ears but a second later her body collapsed in on itself. She cried and cried as she had never cried in her life. She cried for Bella, for her sister...and for her nephew who, if she ever got her hands on him. . .

Suddenly she slapped her hands down on the chair arms, rose up with purpose, and pounded out to the garage. She located Richard's baseball bat and grabbed it. Back in the house she climbed the stairs to his room and kicked open the door. It had been a long time since she had been in this room, years perhaps. Who in their right mind would want to enter a teenage boy's bedroom! But now she had her reason. There, all his technology was arrayed. Little lights blinked everywhere. She had no idea what any of it did. All she knew was that it all represented degradation, vileness, and perversity. Thirty minutes later, it all lay in shards of glass, crushed plastic and beaten and dented metal thingamies.

CHAPTER 15 | A warrant is served

At the hospital, Angela and Fr. Flynn were informed that Richard, as the detective had said, was physically fine but nonetheless was being kept under supervision. There was some hint that the doctors thought he might be capable of hurting himself, though the word 'suicide' was not uttered. Purely a precaution in cases like this, they said, protocol.

They found Richard in a room in the Psychiatric Ward. Richard lay in the fetal position facing the wall. The nurse explained that he had not spoken since arriving and had refused to acknowledge the hospital mental health professionals who had visited him. She also told them, reluctantly, saying she was not technically authorized to report it, that he had been heard mumbling quietly to himself. She couldn't be sure but it had sounded to her something like 'it could work' but, again, she couldn't be sure. The nurse had left them alone with him. Fr. Flynn moved a chair close to the bed and helped Angela to it.

Slowly, slowly, Angela lowered herself onto the chair as if she feared to disturb him. Then also slowly she leaned over him and said his name but there was no response. She waited. Then turning to the priest, with an agonized questioning in her eyes that nearly defeated him, he smiled and nodded for her to try again.

Hovering closer, she whispered, "Richard, it's Mom." She waited, then said,

"Richard...Richard. . ." She touched his side. Violently he shook her off. Her hand recoiled. Her head fell onto the bed and she sobbed.

Fr. Flynn felt helpless, the natural reaction in the presence of someone else's misery, and knew it was for that reason insincere. Instead, he prayed in fervent silence for the grace to take her suffering on himself, and to resist this natural urge to be like Job's counsellors, to help with words whose only motivation was to give to their own discomfort at another's suffering more value than the sufferer's. His strong desire was to ingest her pain and make it his own, because after all wasn't that the whole meaning of the Eucharist?

At last, when it was clear to both of them that Richard would not respond even to his own mother, he put out his hand over Richard's head and quietly intoned his favorite prayer.

"My peace I give to you, my peace I leave to you. Not as the world gives do I give. Do not let your heart be troubled. And do not be afraid." Then he blessed the boy tracing the sign of the cross over him. He was able to release Angela from her death grip on the bed sheets and they left the room. In the car on the way home, Angela had not said a word.

As the car turned onto her street, Angela and Fr. Flynn were met by the sight of police cars, strange black sedans with blacked-out windows and big black vans crowding the street in front of the Benfont house with lights flashing red and blue. Angela, seemingly comatose just seconds before, now sat up as her hands flew to her mouth. A wild look was in her eyes as her head snapped left toward Fr. Flynn.

The convoy of Federal agents and local Sheriffs had rolled up half an hour earlier, presented the search warrant to Eleanor and were well into the search by now. Their first objective had been Richard's bedroom, where they found the result of Eleanor's explosion of temper.

After parking the car on the street several houses down, Fr. Flynn opened the passenger side door for Angela but for several minutes she refused to exit the car. But eventually, she stepped out and moved shakily with him beside her. They weaved their way through the crowd and walked in through the door which was braced open. Agents in blue jackets with yellow letters on the back screaming F.B.I. were crawling around everywhere and filing up and down the stairs like ants, some carrying boxes to be taken away.

At first, Eleanor and Bella did not notice their entry, but as Fr. Flynn led a wide-eyed and terrified Angela through the foyer, they both jumped from the couch where they had been sitting clasped around each other, and rushed to her. She seemed unable to direct her own movements and even seemed to need the priest's assistance to stay upright. But nothing shocked Bella and Eleanor more than the look on her face. Her eyes, wide open, unblinking, stared at them unseeing. It was a crushing, frightening portrait presented to them of a woman they barely recognized. The three of them helped Angela to the couch, their pale, pathetic, anxious faces locked onto hers, their hearts aching with consolation, but she took no notice of them.

Eleanor and Bella had not been alerted to the impending arrival of the F.B.I but when they had opened the door to the agents, it had barely surprised them and they had offered no resistance. They had taken their seats on the couch as the agents had directed and had made no comments nor asked any questions. Everyone's fate seemed to them to have been sealed in that moment. In fact, before Angela and Fr. Flynn had entered they both had dozed off in each other's arms from sheer emotional exhaustion, despite the noise and activity all around them.

While still in the car as it was approaching the house earlier, Fr. Flynn had responded to the wild look in Angela's eyes by pulling over slowly and stopping the car. He had shifted toward her and took her hands. He had smiled bleakly and said, "My dear friend Angela, God has rested a great a burden on your soul and...it will get heavier, my dear. Please remember, this is how he treats his best friends--which is why He has so few. . ." The famous line from St. Catherine of Sienna fell flat.

"Can it get worse?" Angela whispered.

"Angela. . ." but he could not find the words and lowered his eyes. He rubbed his face and eyes and exhaled heavily. "Angela, it was Richard who...oh, God, Angela, it was Richard...the accusation against me. Oh, I forgive him with all my heart! And I would never have said a word about it, never, but...you see, it's a federal crime. That's the F.B.I. at the house."

Angela's head began to tilt from side to side and her eyes narrowed as if suddenly everything was out of focus. They searched his face for a long moment then looked away to stare out the front window. She leaned back into the seat. That hard bitter expression Bella had seen in the dining room was fixed now, perhaps even harder, more bitter.

"Take me home," she had said with a harshness to match her expression.

But as Fr. Flynn had opened the car door for her, she had murmured without looking at him, "I never want to see you again." This was why she had refused to get out of the car. She had not wanted his help nor had she wanted to set eyes on him. However, the priest had decided to simply wait her out. He had no intention of leaving her alone and would have stood there all night if it were necessary, holding the door for her.

Realizing this, she had finally stepped out of the car but after her first few steps, her legs nearly gave out and the priest was there to keep her from falling. She allowed him to assist her into the house but not once did she look at him.

Now sitting on the couch between Eleanor and Bella, Fr. Flynn back in the chair facing them, Angela seemed lost within herself, breathing shallowly with now and again great intakes of breath. On her face, the hardness had taken on an almost inhuman rigidity as she stared ahead of her, her head slightly bent forward, her hands locked tightly together, white-knuckled. Appalled at the sight of her, the two women peered at the priest for the answer to the unasked question whether Angela knew what was happening--and why. The priest nodded.

They sat this way, not speaking, huddled around Angela, for nearly fifteen minutes, when suddenly she pushed herself up and off the couch and moved toward the stairs. Fr. Flynn immediately jumped up, took one step, then stopped. He saw that she was walking quite steadily on her own and stood watching as she pulled herself slowly up the stairs. No one tried to stop her. The ascending and descending agents politely moved aside for her.

CHAPTER 16 | In the hour before dawn

That night, Angela fell ill. She spent most of the evening and early morning hours in the bathroom, on her knees, retching violently. Eleanor, who had decided to stay the night, and Bella became increasingly alarmed. After an hour the retching had not stopped and Angela was in terrible pain. Only spittle and bile came out of her yet it seemed her system was incapable of righting itself.

The sight of her sister sprawled on the bathroom floor, exhausted and besmeared with drool and sweat, yet having to lever herself back up onto the bowl for the next wave when there was no strength left in her tortured body, nearly drove Eleanor mad. She finally called 911.

Now, as they stood beside her hospital bed, Angela was a pitiful and heart-rending vision of inner pain and turmoil. Her hands were clenched at her sides, there was a rosary in her right hand, her eyes and mouth had almost disappeared within the grimace that constricted her face. Most disturbing were the sporadic and violent jerkings of her head as if in her tortured mind ever more torturous visions were assailing her. But after an hour of this, Eleanor could stand no more and the thought that her nephew lay only two floors above them, oblivious to the pain he had caused, made her boil with rage.

Finally, she announced, "I'm going to the nut ward."

Bella had been gently caressing her mother's hand holding the rosary. "OK," she whispered but then a dark frown appeared and she stood.

"No. Wait." She leaned over and kissed Angela's forehead. "I'll come."

Eleanor had determined on the long walk to the Psychiatric Ward that there would be no pussy-footing around with 'this one' and marched on with her arms swinging. Arriving there, she accosted the desk nurse and demanded to know the room where they were holding her nephew, Richard Benfont as Bella looked on from behind her. The desk nurse seemed confused and embarrassed.

"C'mon, honey, what's the problem?" Eleanor said, impatient and aggravated by the woman's dithering.

"He..he's not here," the nurse managed in a flustered voice.

"What do you mean, he's not here? Where the hell is he?"

"Well, they...they took him. A whole bunch of F.B.I. people and cops and they put cuffs on him and walked him out a few hours ago."

The two women started back to Angela's room, dejected but not surprised.

"They've probably thrown him in some dungeon somewhere to rot. I hope!"

Bella smiled sadly but didn't respond.

They re-entered Angela's room to find a commotion in progress. Eleanor cornered a nurse and was told that Angela had suddenly awakened and called out crazily, "Richard".

Bella rushed to her mother's side to see that she was sitting up and in distress, looking around wildly, a drip attached to her arm to stop the vomiting.

"Mom! Mom! It's ok. I'm here!" she said, caressing her mother's arm.

Eleanor pushed through the attendants to reach her sister's bed and leaned over her. She took each of Angela's hands in hers.

"Now, listen to me, Angela. Will you listen to me?" she said in her commanding voice.

Angela looked up at her, then, suddenly, her face contorted and her head dropped onto her chest. For a moment, she seemed hardly to be breathing but after a while she looked up at them and they saw the old Angela, but with her face white and strained. Now back in control of herself, she let out deep breath and forced a small smile onto her lips, not because she felt like smiling but because she felt they needed to see it.

"Hello, you pain in the ass," Eleanor said softly with a tender smile in response. "Welcome back."

Bella, in an uprush of emotion, threw herself against her mother's chest and held her tight, rocking her and silently sobbing.

"Let's get you home," Eleanor said.

The two woman helped her up to her room and into bed. Bella slid the drapes closed since when the Sun came in up in the morning it would be in Angela's face. Now, alone, quiet in the darkened silence, she lay on her bed staring at the ceiling holding her rosary against her chest. Her mind and heart were struggling terribly with something that had begun while still in a semi-coma at the hospital. A kind of spiritual accusation had assailed her then and consumed her unconscious mind in a fevered self-interrogation. Her questing, troubled heart had seemed to be fighting for its very life, wanting the answer as desperately as it tried to avoid the answer, until with the cry of 'Richard!' she had awoken with a pain in her heart that had not left her.

Bella and Eleanor had quite naturally assumed she had wanted to see her son who had caused her such pain and had then remembered all too quickly why he was not with them.

But they were quite wrong. 'Richard!' was the accusation. From the very instant when she had turned on Bella in the dining room the night before, in such anger nearly approaching hatred, the seed of guilt had been planted, terrible guilt. But it was only in that moment when she had screamed out his name that she understood and acknowledged in her heart an even deeper failing: she had not known her son at all!

Since that moment, her soul had been locked in upon itself, flaying itself over and over with the question, how could that be? How could I not know my own son? And how could I do that to my own daughter when I knew the pain it would cost and did it even so? How can I call myself 'mother'? How can I?"

This questioning had gone on for a long time but finally, exhausted and bitterly ashamed, she fell into a troubled sleep. Her mind, however, seemed detached from her will as if it had a kind of mind of its own, the mind of a mind. She watched this mind wandering, but not aimlessly, looking for something. It found the memory of the discussion group and stopped to remember Fr. Flynn say, '...hope in Christ the real God or hope in the hopeless phantom God of our sentimentality'. Her eyes had snapped open. "Oh, my Lord! Is this what You're telling me?" she prayed silently. "Yes! Oh, yes! I have been in love with the wrong God! Or I would never have hurt Bella like that... but, Oh!, how I have failed Richard! Oh, God!" Tears gushed from her eyes as she mercilessly interrogated her heart. "What have I done? What have I done? So proud in my faith I never saw it was just as Fr. Flynn said. Sentimentality! Me! Me! All along, I was nothing but a stupid, proud, sentimental--Oh, God, crush me, crush me to pieces like the Israelites for having believed in false gods. I made You in my image, You were my very own golden calf of the Israelites and in my blind sentimentality I actually believed I loved my children. But look how I harmed them! *Love does not harm its children!* My shame...I have shamed myself and You. . .*and I have shamed my children*! Oh, my children!"

Her sobs finally subsided and she discovered that she had rolled off the bed onto her knees, her hands covering her eyes. She raised herself up and drew back the drapes to see dawn just breaking. Without thinking, words as if inspired by the dawn came to her and she said them out loud. "It was the hour before dawn when the women came to the tomb. . ."

She stood up in awe at the words she had spoken and fell to her knees again, praying earnestly, overcome with joy.

"You rose so I can rise! How holy was the sin of your crucifixion that it made possible the resurrection! And so how holy must my sin be that you raised me up from it so that I can look my children in the eye again and know how to love them as You have loved me! Oh dear God. . ." She fell silent for a while, happy just to revel in the glorious mystery of it. When Bella peaked in later to ask if she felt like breakfast, she smiled at her warmly and they went downstairs holding hands.

As they sat around the kitchen table, Eleanor and Bella agreed that Angela seemed well but her face had lost much of the beautiful rose tint and her cheeks had sagged. However, when they pressed her to eat more, she replied sweetly, "It is so wonderful to be home." For a while, they talked easily about nothing in particular as Angela sipped her coffee, clearly relishing the ordinariness of the moment. Eleanor and Bella knew that sooner or later she would need to ask what had happened to Richard and they would have tell her the awful truth, though now they both sensed that she must already suspect the worst. But when the moment came, they were surprised that she didn't ask about Richard but rather reached over to take Bella's hand, peered at her with the most kindly look, and had simply said, "Tell me everything, sweetheart, from the beginning."

And so Bella told her everything, from first setting eyes on the man standing in the rain and meeting Fr. Flynn through to Nicholas's attempted rape and his beating by Shiney. She left--almost--nothing out, not even

Ricard's critique of the freedom stolen from humanity by Jesus Christ, his concept of the Living Dead Man and his dark web following. The 'top five' abasements were too awful to recount. Even without them, it was a harrowing litany for all of them but Eleanor broke the somberness of the moment by relating how she had demolished Richard's technology, which made Angela laugh harder than they had ever seen her laugh. In the end, tears were rolling down each of their cheeks and not in pain but in a kind of loving and joyous togetherness.

But still, they knew the question of what had finally happened to Richard the evening of the F.B.I. raid must come. When it finally did, Angela received the news quietly and without comment, then, thoughtfully, she raised her coffee cup to her lips but put it back down on the table without taking a sip.

"You know, Bella," she said softly, "I think I'd like to read that manifesto."

Bella did not question her and handed her the phone. But she was suddenly seized by the crazy, irrational fear that the phone would somehow magically play the recording she had made instead of displaying the manifesto. Crazy or not, her mother should never, ever, hear that recording!

Angela took a long time to scroll through the document, stopping often, rereading occasionally, and at last set down the phone. Her face betrayed no reaction, but a moment later she offered a comment.

"Seems rather silly, doesn't it?" she said almost as if to herself. "But, you know, I think I understand what Richard could see in it. He's very silly himself when he thinks he's being clever. And this manifesto is clever in a way. I do so love that about him...and what about the video?"

Bella, again without questioning her, found the video and slid it over to her. Angela pressed 'play'.

When it had played through (it was not very long), she said, "The poor man. Perhaps this condition affected his mind. But isn't that lovely how Fr. Flynn stands with him?" she said, now with a frown as she remembered what she had said to the priest. As she handed back the phone, she said, "We must pray for that man."

Eleanor, who had been paying little attention, satisfied to watch her sister being herself, now spoke up, the spell broken.

"Pray for *him*? Angela, the guy's a monster! Good God, you're back in form all right."

Angela smiled at her, in her own way as deeply gratified to receive her sister's barbs in this lovely recovered normality as Eleanor was to launch them. Then she rose and climbed the stairs again into her room.

CHAPTER 17 | The new man

When Detective Houselander and Officer Buckley showed up at his bedside the morning after the events in Ben's office, Nicholas greeted them civilly. He had spent a restless night in and out of a drugged sleep but at least the pain in his head was much lessened now, though his back ached and was covered in large bruises as was his left thigh.

"Freakin' Shiney," he thought to himself with a bitter spiteful smile on his lips. "Couldn't even kill me right."

The Detective asked if he felt well enough to give a statement and Nicholas laughed which made his head ache again.

"Ouch! Shit!...give a statement? Why should I?"

"Well, Mr. Shelly, we need a statement from you if you'll be pressing charges against Mr. Shine so--"

"Ha! No-no, Detective, I will not be pressing charges. I'm considering sending him an ice cream cake!"

He lifted himself into an upright position and turned to Officer Buckley. "Hand me my clothes," he said. With his back turned to Houselander as he dressed, he said, "So I guess the girl's not pressing charges." There was no response.

Dressed and swaggering, he slid past the two men without a word and checked himself out of the hospital. He called an Uber to take him to Ben's office where he retrieved his car and drove himself back to his apartment. On entering, he stood a while just inside the doorway surveying the space with a fond smile. Then he began a slow walk around the room, still smiling fondly as if he were seeing it for the last time. Finally he climbed onto one of the chairs at the table, crossed his arms, sat back and stared contentedly into space. It was now all worked out in his mind.

    An hour later, Shiney appeared in court for his arraignment. Sitting at the defendant's table in his orange jumpsuit, his hands in shackles, he seemed to be dozing. As the judge brought down her gavel, he jumped. He was not afraid of prison. He had been there before. But this time was different. He felt no rancor as before. No self-pity. No desire for revenge on society for the injustice of having been caught. This time, there was an odd kind of pressure on his heart that was not exactly physical pain but rather the sense of an unravelling, as if his personality were sloughing off pieces of itself under the pressure. For a trained psychiatrist, he was discovering the surprising and now upsetting fact that his inner life had been to him nothing much more than a phantom. As a consequence, he saw now that his professional practice had been one lifelong session of arrogance toward and disdain for the suffering of others. This was the pressure he felt weighing on his heart. In the last few hours as he sat in his cell, he had begun to go over in his mind the many faces he had looked down upon from his high position. He wished with all his heart to ask to be forgiven by each and every one of them but there was no hope of that now.

"Mr. William Shine," the judge intoned. There was a look of disgust on her face. "The court has been informed that the victim of your assault has declined to press charges. Therefore, you are free to go."

Ben Shelley had called the hospital as planned first thing in the morning and was told that Nicholas had already discharged himself.

"This fucking kid!" he cursed to himself as he headed to Nicholas's apartment. He did not bother to knock but pushed his way inside to find Nicholas facing him.

"That didn't take long," Nicholas said, smiling broadly.

Ben's anger had grown with every mile closer he came to the apartment. Now he was rigid with outrage, breathing shallowly and hissing. His eyes blazed and his teeth hurt as he exploded through clenched jaws, "I told you, I *told* you what would happen if you messed this up! Are you out of your goddam mind? You think maybe raping that girl was within the bounds of our agreement?"

Nicholas seemed to be enjoying his outburst as if it had nothing to do with him.

"Oh, relax," he said, "you know that agreement was all bullshit. Your threats were a joke! What, you're going stop my allowance now, prosecute me for fraud? God, you're ridiculous. And where will that leave you and your buddies? Huh? You think she'll keep paying you if you cut me loose? What leverage will you have then? But, hey, as much as I enjoy your theatrics, I have good news for you. I'm actually feeling a little bit jumpy with excitement. Because, Benjamin Shelley Esquire, you will soon have your heart's desire, courtesy of your nephew, the New Nicholas."

"Oh, God, another one?"

"Ha! Crazy, right? Nicholas 3.0! I'm planning a coming- out party and you're invited."

"Jesus God, are you ever going to quit screwing around? OK, you're right about the deal. You've got me over a barrel, Ok? Why are you trying to ruin me? This is my one chance--"

"No, Benjamin. You're one chance is coming up. And it's a beaut! Believe me, I've got your back. No, seriously. This is the new me. I'm a new man, thanks to our pal, Shiney. Ha! You might say he knocked some sense into me. It came to me last night. Like a flash! And you are going to be the big winner!"

CHAPTER 18 | A legal strategy

    Before the other two had come down for breakfast, Eleanor had put in a call to Dominic Mancini, a well-regarded defense attorney and, more importantly, a close personal friend of the Antonelli girls with whom he had grown up. The Mancinis had lived two doors down from the Antonelli house and the children had played together and remained close since then. Dom was always the smallest among the kids on the block but he was wirey, sharp-tongued, aggressive and fearless. The girls each had had a crush on him as children even though they were both bigger and taller than him. But he was the perfect picture in their minds of the true Italian male. Slight and compact, beautifully proportioned, with thick black hair and eyebrows, dark, deep-set brown eyes placed with almost divine perfection on either side of a powerful, straight, chiseled nose. And that smile! It could charm anyone's mother (which often came in handy) and deflate the meanest of bullies, especially since he had pummeled the biggest of them one summer on the baseball diamond. Everyone had seen it and everyone remembered it. Best of all, he had always been there to stand up for young Eleanor who was the slowest and largest girl on the block.
    Eleanor explained, in outline, what had happened and asked Dom to find out where the F.B.I. had taken Richard and what he was charged with. Dom was shocked that no one from the Bureau had reached out to the family. What

he didn't say was that this was a bad sign. It meant the Feds were taking this case very seriously and that Richard could be in grave danger. Computer crime was a big one at the Bureau. They loved to bust hackers. The kid was probably soiling himself by now! He was back to her within the hour having talked to the Special Agent in charge.

"I reamed the bastard pretty good, El," he told Eleanor. "They've got him at the County lockup. They want to take him in front of the magistrate tomorrow morning--they don't dawdle on these cases--but I told him don't make any plans for a preliminary hearing until I've seen him and can tell the family that he hasn't been beaten within an inch of his life. So I'm heading over there now. Don't worry--yet."

The lawyer came to the house later that day after having met with Richard, cautioning him to say nothing to anyone unless he, Dom, was sitting by his side. He had also met with the District Attorney and the Special Agent in charge of the case. He also explained that Richard was being charged with hacking with the 'specific intent to commit fraud or cause harm' which, unfortunately, was precisely what he had done, committing fraud against and causing harm to Fr. Flynn.

"But Fr. Flynn will never press charges!" Bella objected.

"Doesn't matter. The Government is pressing the charges."

Though this meeting with the lawyer concerned such serious business, it was impossible for the two women to resist comparing this older version of little Dominic Mancini with their memories of him. He had not lost his sense of style. He had arrived impeccably attired in an expensive-looking suit, highly polished shoes, with a large Rolex hanging on his thin wrist. Yet there was very little left to remind them of the sleek, tightly muscled, beautiful young boy he had been. What they saw now was a somewhat pudgy, somewhat soft middle-aged man who might have been Dom's uncle back in the day. Now he walked with a slight hunch in his shoulders which was accentuated as he sat facing them. His once lovely thick hair, still black and lustrous, had receded upward until his gleaming forehead extended to the middle of the top of his head. His wire-rimmed glasses sat high on his nose and because of the hunch of his shoulders, he was forced to peer up at them so that, from their point of view, his still thick eyebrows were magnified astonishingly. Nonetheless, his eyes were sharp and had a biting quality that demanded attention and his smile had lost none of its brilliance. Nor had time diminished his energy while it had accentuated his aggression and fearlessness. He was quite literally feared in the halls of justice for his tenacity and utter inability to back down. In short, Dominic Mancini would once again come to the aid of the Antonelli sisters in their time of greatest need.

    So it was a stunning shock to their confidence in him when he laid out his plan for Richard's defense. Sitting back, he spread his hands and said, "We're going to plead guilty." His was prepared for their reaction which was immediate and would have been much louder if not for fear of disturbing Angela upstairs.

"Alright, alright! Calm down! Are you two the lawyers or am I? You want to know what happens if we plead not guilty? Huh? There will be a preliminary hearing. It's sort of a trial before the trial with one big catch. The defense, that's me, cannot object to any evidence the prosecutor wants to throw out there, OK? He can introduce any piece of crap 'evidence' he wants, even evidence that would never be allowed at a trial-trial. You following this? OK, so what, right? Well, the judge at this call-it-a-mini-trial, is going to decide whether or not the prosecutor has introduced enough evidence to show probable cause. In other words, that Richard is guilty. Ok. Now think about this. Who do you think will be whispering in the prosecutor's ear the whole time? The Feds! And they want--oh, boy, do they want--a trial! Hacking cases get big headlines, OK?. And the only options this judge has legally are, go to trial or drop the charges and dismiss the case--don't even start! There is no chance in hell this case will dismissed. Why? Because the damn kid is guilty! Listen to me! Richard is a talented hacker, no doubt. But he was cooked as soon as he pressed 'Return'. Look, this is the F.B.I. Cyber Crimes division! They've got hundreds of the smartest hackers on their payroll and all the money they want to chase down people like Richard. And these guys nailed him. Believe me, the evidence is rock solid. So, if we go to trial, he gets convicted and spends the next one to twenty years in jail. Want to chance it?...I didn't think so.

And don't think we can make a plea deal with the prosecutor. The Feds will be all over him to put Richard away. It's the judge we have to concentrate on. He's the only one authorized to impose a sentence. So, we get a little bit of insulation there from the Feds who are rabid dogs on this stuff. But, Richard *has* to plead guilty and then we basically throw ourselves on the mercy of the court, meaning the judge. That's the situation."

Eleanor turned to Bella with a questioning look then slowly turned back to Dominic.

"Listen," she said sitting forward, her hands clasped on the table top, a kind of worried intensity showing on her face. "There is something else."

Both women, without conferring with each other, had been careful to make no reference to the recording of the events in Ben Shelley's office which, if revealed, would put Richard in a much less sympathetic light and might even bias the lawyer against him. So Eleanor's decision to reveal it surprised her.

"El!" Bella whispered.

"No, he should know about it."

"What should I know about? Better tell me. Whatever it is, I guarantee it'll come out," Dom said.

"There is a recording Bella took."

"Yes? Of what?"

"Of the scene at that lawyer's office, where it happened."

Dom eyed the women intently. In his experience, there was always 'something' that never arose in initial conversations with defense clients but that surfaced under the mounting pressure of their situation.

"Ok, good." He wrote on his pad, tore off the page and handed it to Eleanor. "That's my email. Send it to me. I'll review it later. Do it now. Right now."

He knew they would have an argument about it as soon as he left and that Bella would almost certainly refuse to do as he asked. If she didn't send it while he was sitting there in front of them, he would have a much more difficult time persuading her to release it to him. Clearly, whatever the recording revealed, it would not reflect well on Richard and if so he, Dom, needed to be prepared, for whatever *could* come out *would* come out. The first rule of defense.

Reluctantly, Bella took out her phone and attached the audio file to an email. But before hitting send, she suddenly jumped up, cried "Dad!" and rushed to the front door.

CHAPTER 19 | A surprise arrival

Ray Benfont, standing in the foyer, had entered wearing a hostile look but smiled broadly as Bella approached and embraced him.

"You've come," Bella said softly, pleased just to look at his face and also relieved that the email remained unsent. But Eleanor had already picked up Bella's phone and sent the email which quickly dinged on Dom's phone. Now she watched with distaste as Bella greeted her father.

Ray looked straight at Dom Mancini. "So it's your car outside. Since when do lawyers make house calls, huh, Dom? What did I miss? Anything important? Like maybe my son's life?"

"I didn't know, Dad, when I talked to you. We only called Dom this morning."

On his way here, Ray Benfont had actually been smiling until he saw a car in the driveway he did not recognize. Then the smile cracked and an irritated and defensive frown replaced it. They were ignoring him! As if he didn't matter at all! As if they had forgotten he even existed! All except Bella, for sure. Not her. Not Bella. She had called last night and explained about the hacking prank and all that had happened afterwards and told him, point blank, that Richard needed his father at a time like this, and that he should come to the house in the morning. Anticipation at seeing Bella again (he hadn't been to the house in several months) had put the smile on his face. It did not strike him as odd that seeing her had nearly erased from his mind all thought of

Richard and his situation. The truth was that he had always cherished Bella more than her brother whom he had never understood and quite frankly did not much like. Richard had always been a blank slate to his father. A smart kid, a really smart kid, but this was not a positive trait, not something that stirred pride in Ray Benfont's heart. Resentment thus became the basis of his relationship with Richard, but not only with Ricard.

Raymond Benfont had had an easy path in life. He was a big muscular man, over six feet tall, with dark red hair brushed back from a significant widow's peek. His complexion was noticeably red as if from high blood pressure or perhaps sunburn. His arms and neck too were just as red and were covered in red freckles. Because of this he had picked up the nickname 'Red' so that now he was known everywhere as Red Benfont. People called out to him, "Hey, Red!" Or "Red! How ya doing?" or sometimes he overhead as he passed by, one person ask another, "Who's that?" and the other would answer, "That's Red Benfont. Great guy!" This pleased him enormously, so much so that he came to consider himself the 'great guy' all who knew him proclaimed him to be. And who could blame him, really? It wasn't his fault that other men instinctively looked up to him, that he elicited in other men almost instant respect--along with an equally instinctive understanding that certain lines could not be crossed. The normal antics of camaraderie among equals did not apply to Ray Benfont. One did not mock him or kid him or try to put oneself above him. Within these lines, he was a great good friend and everybody desired to be his friend. Yet Ray Benfont was astute enough to have recognized early on, even from his high school days, that this reaction among friends and acquaintances almost always cost them an uncomfortable feeling of their own insecurity, that he somehow diminished them. He understood this viscerally and appreciated that he could continue to enjoy his natural dominance provided he never let them see how much he enjoyed it. This long practice in his role as a dominant personality who charmed precisely by not overtly dominating had made him a subtle and accomplished actor. So it was not surprising that everyone who knew him imagined that his wife must be very proud of him and that his home life must be better, happier than their own with Ray 'Red' Benfont as father and husband.

There was, however, a darker side to him: the ease with which he had reached adulthood meant that he had not faced any big challenge either socially or psychologically. This left him unprepared for life with Angela Antonelli. In his frankly blind lust for her he naturally expected the deference from a wife that he experienced everywhere else. And at first, he was very happy. She did defer to him for she herself was madly attracted to the big man that everyone hailed as 'Red'. But, as with most actors, Ray Benfont lived for adulation. He had no conception of what life would be like without an audience, let alone an audience of one who soon found his performance stark and cruel. They had endured one another for fifteen years 'for the sake of children' until finally Angela had served him with divorce papers. The thought of her and their life together produced the only reaction he was capable of: constant, intense, burning resentment. An irony: Angela's lawyer at the time had been Dominic Mancini.

"Where's your mother?" he asked Bella abruptly, sounding mean and resentful.

"She's upstairs. Recovering."

His attitude changed quickly, though. He could appreciate how awful this must be for Bella. But his tone was neutral, betraying only an acknowledgement of an obvious fact. "Yeah. She's taking it hard, I imagine."

"Well, she seems a little better--"

"Bella!" Eleanor called out in a peremptory tone. "Where do you get off barging in here like you own the place?" she accused Ray.

"I do own the place. That's how," he threw off, evidently not inclined at the moment to battle with Eleanor. Turning to the lawyer, he said, "So, what's your lawyerly advice, counselor?" Now he stepped down into the living room and stood over Dom Mancini, his hands in his pockets.

"How you doing, Ray? Long time," Mancini said effortlessly, immune to the larger man's intentional brow beating. "Well, Eleanor, I'll be leaving." He stood and the contrast between the two men was comical. "Good to see you," the lawyer said, passing Ray as he went for the door.

"Hey, hold up," Ray said to his back. "I want to know what's been decided, Dom," he said sounding bitter and disrespected.

"You're not my client, Ray," Dom answered easily. "Have a nice day". He opened the door and walked out.

"What the hell's going on, Eleanor?" Ray now turned angrily on his sister-in-law. His face was redder than ever and his eyes were hard and mean.

"Dad!" Bella interrupted before Eleanor could respond. "Nothing's decided yet. We'd never decide something without you."

"So what, you just chatted about old times?" he shot at Eleanor.

"Sit down, Raymond, and stop being such an a-hole."

Thirty-five minutes later, Ray Benfont was driving fifteen miles over the speed limit. "No goddam way!" he thought, for about the tenth time. Twenty miles further down the road, his resentment boiling over at that lawyer and that sister-in-law of his, he shouted at the windshield, "They got to be out of their goddam minds! My kid is *not* pleading guilty! You hear me, Eleanor? *No goddam way!*" He seethed impotently for several more miles until his swirling resentment came to rest on the one person who had been the first great challenge to his life's easy path. Angela. "She must have agreed to this," he reasoned. "...maybe...yeah, Lance Paul! You're not the only one's got lawyer friends, lady!"

This idea kept him calm for a while but it did not last. Lance Paul was his lawyer in the divorce proceedings against Angela but Ray knew he would be no match for Dom Mancini. And besides, he was already beginning to wonder whether he was getting his money's worth. In the end, he didn't call Lance Paul. Instead, he decided to rely on his own personality to disarm Mancini and bring him around without interference from goddam Eleanor. It was a measure of his arrogance and a not too penetrating intelligence that he imagined Dominic Mancini would wilt under his charm offensive.

He looked up Mancini's office number and called. His receptionist said, yes, Mr. Mancini will see you and he arrived at Dom's office a half hour later.

Dom Mancini had listened to the recording as soon as he got back to his office after leaving the Benfont's. He had been feeling queasy ever since. He had seen and heard a lot as a defense attorney over the last twenty years but never something like this. And that this kid was the son of Angela Benfont! It was unbelievable. But now, he found himself in a quandary. What was he to do with it? Following the first rule of defense, what could come out would come out, his plan to go for a guilty plea was called into question. Should he proceed on that strategy and the prosecution somehow become aware of the recording, what little pity he might have been able to engender in the judge would be moot and she would throw the book at Richard. The Preliminary Hearing had been scheduled for the next day, Thursday morning at ten.

He had been ruminating on the problem for a while when Ray Benfont had called--and suddenly, the problem was solved. Yes, he would agree with Ray. Richard would plead not guilty thus keeping Ray in his corner but more to the point, providing the strategic pathway for a more compassionate sentence from the judge. It was Dominic's only reasonable option and at least now he had the evidence to support it: not guilty due to diminished capacity. The recording should work for them and not against them as it would surely do if discovered by the prosecution.

Ray Benfont was not a naturally suspicious man. When not in a resentful mood he tended to take people as they presented themselves to him, which, because of his easy sense of dominance, was almost always pleasant with a touch of sycophancy. So when the little lawyer greeted him with just such a display, he produced his signature sheepish actor's grin which never failed to charm the other by suggesting that such a man was capable of an endearing humility.

Dominic, a connoisseur of insincerity, played along masterfully. After listening to Ray with attention and respect, Dom had agreed that Richard would plead not guilty by reason of diminished capacity. Ray was more than satisfied. He himself was charmed by the discussion, his own performance especially. They shook hands warmly and Ray left, pleased with himself and smiling at how the little man had belittled himself before him.

CHAPTER 20 | Behind closed doors

The preliminary hearing for Richard Raymond Benfont got off to a rocky start even before the judge took the bench. It all began in the judge's chambers early Thursday morning. Though it was a closely held secret that the government had pressured the Presiding Judge to choose Judge Mary Elizabeth Deacon for the hearing, secrets did not stay secret within the Halls of Justice. Judge Deacon already knew of it as she entered the corridor to her chambers. Mary Elizabeth Deacon was a fair-minded jurist, a straight-shooter, and she expected all parties coming before her to leave the game-playing in the parking garage. The government, however, was playing every card in its considerable hand to get to a solid conviction in this case. They had lobbied for her precisely because of her reputation as a preemptive move against any chance of an appeal. Now with all the lawyers in her chambers arrayed around her desk in chairs, she bent a merciless eye on the three F.B.I. lawyers, and spoke to them directly ignoring the prosecutor and Dominic Mancini. After revealing her knowledge of their behind-the-scenes lobbying, she said in an icy tone, "...so, gentlemen, as they say, be careful what you wish for. You wanted me and you got me." Then she looked at Dominic. "Mr. Mancini, you requested this meeting."

Dominic Mancini shifted in his chair. He had watched with hidden satisfaction as the F.B.I. lawyers stumbled all over themselves to assure the judge that their only motive was to guard against an appeal by ensuring that a judge with a spotless reputation would be on the bench. "No, that won't cut it, gentlemen," she said holding up her hand to Dominic as she turned back to the offenders. "I resent the implication that a fair trial in this building cannot be expected by the government as if this court house was in some Third World country. I suggest the real danger here is that the government, not this court, is the entity less concerned with fairness. I have been the recipient of much brow-beating this last twenty-four hours as you have applied pressure up and down the hallway for an outcome that you have, it seems, already pre-determined. Your fingers are on the scales, gentlemen, and if you aren't careful they can get burnt!..Now, Mr. Mancini. Please."

After Ray Benfont had left him, the day before, he had arranged for this early morning meeting in the judge's chambers. He was convinced that the audio recording was his only chance to gain an edge over the government's intense pressure for an incontrovertible judgement and an onerous sentence. Further, he knew both Angela and Ray would be in the courtroom, as well as Bella and Eleanor. They were probably arriving even now. His great care, however, was for Angela who he knew had been kept from hearing the recording. To hear it for the first time in open court--he couldn't even imagine how awful that would be and so his gambit was as much to shield Angela from having to sit through that as to produce compelling evidence for his plea. Which he now proceeded to do.

He explained that he had received new exculpatory evidence which he intended to put before the court. However, because of the nature of the evidence, he requested that the judge--and the opposing lawyers--hear the evidence *in camera* and not in open court. The judge agreed and he played the audio from his phone propped up on the judge's desk. The effect on them all was as he expected, and hoped. After much arguing back and forth among the lawyers, with the judge listening in silence, she eventually ruled. While the evidence had no direct bearing on the facts of the case as the government and prosecution contended, it certainly opened a window into the mind of the defendant. She did not see the justice of treating this defendant as among the professional hackers for whom the government's sentencing guidelines had been adopted. Thus, she accepted the defense plea of diminished capacity and pronounced the sentence:

"One year incarceration in the Psychiatric Ward of the County hospital where the defendant will undergo treatment by Court-approved specialists, with a review of progress every three months and a final determination as to further treatment or release to be made by this Court after one year. Thank you, gentlemen."

The lawyers filed out and returned to their tables in the courtroom, the judge followed shortly after. Now in her robes, she read the verdict and, as a concession to the government, announced that bail had been denied. Bailiffs came for Richard.

When Dom Mancini returned to his table he saw that Richard's demeanor had not changed since their meeting the day before. Then he was a terrified kid staring at him with wide frightened eyes who had just spent his first night in a jail cell. This morning, he was a convicted cyber criminal with court bailiffs standing by to remove him to a place that would become his home for the next twelve months. And yet, there he sat, his wide-eyed stare locked onto his face. Dominic knew that look. The shock and terror of the unbelievable when it becomes unavoidable. Rising with the help of the bailiffs, he neither spoke nor looked around at his family but shuffled as if in a trance out the side door.

The lawyer swung round to address the parents. "It looks a lot worse than it is," he told them in an authoritative voice. "It's not like jail. You'll be able to visit him as often as you like."

Angela listened with a sad, almost apologetic little smile, her head tilted to one side, her eyes red and watery. Bella, sitting between her mother and her aunt, was bent forward with her head in her hands. Ray Benfont frowned, angry and flushed with resentment, at the lawyer. Dominic saw this but ignored it. He knew what Ray was thinking. He'd gotten what he wanted, a verdict of not guilty, but it had come at the price of four extra words--due to diminished capacity. Hearing those words in court, in public, attached to the name Benfont, infuriated him. What did he expect after yesterday's hand shake?

While the lawyer was still hard at work reassuring the women, Ray suddenly shot to his feet and marched down the aisle to the exit. If he hadn't left then, he most assuredly would have attacked Dominic Mancini for betraying him. Yet, as he well knew, the lawyer had not betrayed him. He himself had approved the plea. He had even shaken hands with the little man! But this too was Mancini's fault. "Tricky little bastard," he thought, letting his fury carry him away. "He tricked me! I don't know how he did it but..." Yet he did know how the lawyer did it: he had let him. The awareness of his own complicity--that handshake!--was too raw. He shook his head violently to dislodge it, returning to the standard target for his resentment. "...and I'll get back at her, you can be sure of that! You just wait, Angela, you schemer! Think I don't know you're behind this? Ha! It stinks of your perfume, which I always hated by the way. Yeah. I did. You undermined my good name. The whole world knows you're divorcing me! And now this! My son! Where'd this diminished capacity come from, huh? He wasn't living with me all these months, was he? But now the whole world will know my son--Ray Benfont's son--is locked up in a psycho ward!" Flushed and shaking, he pulled out his phone and dialed Lance Paul.

Dominic Mancini packed up his briefcase and prepared to leave the courtroom. He leaned over the railing to shake hands with Angela but Bella was draped over her, hugging her

252

desperately. The lawyer was close enough to hear Bella sobbing into her mother's shoulder.

"I'm sorry, Mom, I'm so sorry. Forgive me."

Angela, with tears running down her cheeks, murmured, "I know, sweetheart, I know. Of course, I forgive you but you have nothing to ask forgiveness for. Someday, you will forgive yourself and on that day, forgive me too."

As Dominic straightened up he glanced toward Eleanor. A very different vision met his eyes. The big woman seemed to be trembling, he thought from rage. Her face was colorless, like rice paper. Veins stuck out throbbing on her forehead. Her eyes, half-open, burned into the distance. He was not wrong. Like her brother-in-law, the proceedings had infuriated Eleanor. She, too, seethed with shame and injured pride that the Benfont name would now carry the scar of Richard's criminality. And, again like Ray, she knew she must move quickly before her fury overpowered her and she lashed out at Angela and Bella.

"He didn't even turn around to say goodbye to his own mother!" she fumed to herself. And yet her fury quickly turned to her niece and sister beside her. "Forgive each other! *For what*? Goddam this Christian mush, goddam it to Hell! Their son and brother gets his ass dragged off to prison--for a year!--and 'forgive me', 'forgive me'! It's...it's...*unnatural*! It's disgusting! Are they crying their eyes out over Richard? No! Oh, no! A year in jail and he's not even eighteen yet. But, oh no, our poor Christian consciences are troubled! Oh, if He were around today, I would...I would...I would *sit on him*!"

Back at home after the preliminary hearing, Angela, Eleanor and Bella once again gathered around the kitchen table. Bella could feel that Eleanor was struggling with some powerful feeling. Her big arms were crossed over her breasts. There were circles of blush on her cheeks and she was breathing noisily through her flared nostrils.

Angela, in her quiet way, smiled at her sister. "Eleanor?"

"Yeah? What?" Eleanor huffed.

"What's the matter, honey?" Angela asked.

"What's the matter? Your son's the matter. That's what's the matter!"

Angela did not respond, only frowned and lowered her eyes.

"Go ahead, tell me you forgive him. Go ahead, I dare you!"

"But...but I do."

"You're lying!" Eleanor accused her. "Did you see him walk out of that courtroom like a criminal without even saying goodbye? He didn't even peek at you the whole time, Angela. And you expect me to believe you feel nothing!"

"You don't feel forgiveness."

"Oh, pardon me, so you can hate how your son treated you but forgive him anyway?"

"No, I don't think it works like that. That's putting all the responsibility on him. You can't forgive anyone unless you take responsibility yourself."

"In other words, it's your fault?"

"Well, I don't know about 'fault' but, yes, it is my responsibility--"

"Oh, what pride!"

"I was going to say, and yours too, and everybody's for everybody. Then it's forgiveness."

"And that's how you see it, huh?"

"I'm trying."

"Aha, so you admit you're only one-tenth a Christian and nine-tenths a hypocrite."

"Aunt El, stop," Bella said. "Mom, we've got something important to tell you...Dad was here."

"Yes. Yes, I saw him. It was good of him to come."

"No, I mean he was here, at the house, yesterday. I called him about Richard."

"Really?"

"You were upstairs. We figured you had enough to think about...

"Oh...well, that was good of you, Bella. Yes no, that was the right thing to do."

"Dominic Mancini was here, too. We were discussing Richard's case."

"Oh, dear, your father must not have liked that too well."

"No. He kind of stormed out."

Angela nodded but said nothing.

"Don't worry. He's still the same old asshole," Eleanor said.

Bella had changed the subject so abruptly because her mother's words had stung her. She did not realize at the time that this was due to the fact that her mother's understanding of responsibility was of a different order than her own. To Bella, forgiveness was very definitely a feeling, the feeling she had experienced when she whispered those words in Nicholas's ear, that they protected her in some way because she had done a good thing under great duress. Immediately she felt herself a spiritual midget beside her mother and she didn't know why.

"I'm sorry," Angela said, "but I have to do something."

"Where are you going?"

"I spoke to Dom about visiting Richard and he told me I had to go online and register. I have to see him tomorrow."

"Oh. Yes. Sure. Do that," Eleanor said encouragingly noting a certain anxiety in her sister's voice. She wondered at it but Angela quite often baffled her and she let it be what it seemed: why wouldn't she want to see her son at the earliest possible opportunity?

CHAPTER 21 | In the middle of nowhere

With Ben out of his hair for now, Nicholas went about preparing his Coming Out party in an extravagant mood. There was not much to do, just buy a couple of items. He had promised himself that this day would mainly be spent pleasurably rehearsing and re-rehearsing what he called his 'opening monologue' while imagining the reactions on the faces of his invited guests. This dreamcast thrilled him immensely. In fact, none of his earlier self-iterations had thrilled him as much.

"I mean, The Evolution of the Individual? Oh, God, that was a great one, that was incipient genius! 'Who Cares?' Man, that was something, really something. All alone on the mountain top, the apex of evolution, beating my chest and screaming into the wind. But then what? You get hoarse from screaming and nobody's listening and then all of a sudden--old Shiney got it--all of a sudden, you do care! Oh, well. Attitudes wear off, that's all. But, oh man, it was a kick! And how they all got so worked up over it! Phew! But 2.0 was a big breakthrough, really. That kid! I mean, that kid had something there. Ooo, it was a thrill- ride. Thousands of followers for me before I even knew his name! Now I would have company. A wrecking crew of misfits, nut bags, and whack jobs. Like a band! But would we ever play to a full stadium? Happy, footloose, party-down-Jesus! Yeah, but it could only last about five minutes before you'd get bored to death. You know, it's always other people, isn't it?" At which point, he could constrain himself no longer and burst into a fit of laughter. He had the answer.

An hour later, he was splayed on his couch breathing hard from the effort to clean up the apartment for the first time since he had moved in. It was an odd kind of cleaning, however, for all his belongings were piled up neatly in the center of the floor. "Like a monument to a dead hero," he thought to himself, delighted, excited, but at the same time entirely content.

It was then that he picked up his phone and composed a text. In his exultant mood, the slight tremors that had begun to run through his body hardly registered on his consciousness.

"El, please," Bella asked. Eleanor had let out a long deep breath when they were alone and placed her elbows on the kitchen table, her wrists crossed. With her left hand she drummed a tattoo as she stared scowling at nothing. At Bella's request, she absently drew her hands together and clasped them in front of her overhanging chest. They had been sitting in silence (except for the tapping of Eleanor's fingers) for several minutes after Angela had walked off.

"What's happening here?" Eleanor asked quietly in a flat voice as if she were talking to herself. "It's too much for me, I can tell you that. I feel like I'm in a leaky lifeboat in the middle of nowhere. . ."

Bella watched her aunt with a tender frown.

"How did it all begin, this mess?" Eleanor continued. "I don't know...I don't know."

Just then, Bella's phone chirped with a text. She opened it to her message app, saw the number, did not immediately recognize it, then, in one violent motion suddenly jumped out of her chair sending the phone sliding wildly across the table, where it bumped to a stop against Eleanor's arm. She looked up startled.

"What? What's the matter with you?" Eleanor, surprised, demanded in a tone that was harsher than she meant. "Don't you start now. We've had enough drama around here. I'm worm out."

Bella stood before her, both her hands knotted into fists and held tight against her throat.

"It's Nic---...Nicholas."

"Give me this goddam phone," Eleanor said, excited to have the enemy so close at hand if even over the phone. She held the phone to her ear. "Hello? Hello?"

Bella shook her head. "It's a text."

"Oh. That his number?"

"Yes."

"Well, just delete or whatever. Don't torture yourself. Don't respond."

Eleanor handed the phone back to Bella who took it by two fingers as if it was covered in filth. She sat back down placing the phone between her hands which lay flat on the table.

"Well? Come on. I'm telling you to delete it. There's no law you have to respond to that...that--"

"El," Bella stopped her with gentle authority. "It's not over yet. The 'mess'. Clearly, it's not over yet."

"Oh, yeah? Give me the damn phone. I'll hammer it to smithereens like I did Richard's stuff. I'll buy you a new one. Hand it over."

A surge of the greatest tenderness swept over Bella.

"Oh, El," she said, "you are the love of my life."

Eleanor raised an eyebrow at her.

"Yeah, well, give me the damn phone, then. I'll flush it down the toilet."

"It won't flush," Bella said laughing.

"The disposal, then. That'll work."

Bella tapped on the messaging app and slowly slid the phone over to her.

"OK," Eleanor said.

"Will you read it? I can't."

"What? No, I won't read it! Read it! Huh!.."

"El, please. I have to know because it's not over yet and he's not going to just go away, apparently...Please."

"Goddam it...How do I.."

Bella reached over and tapped the text for her.

"'Yes. It's me,' Eleanor read. "Hah! The little...'I'm inviting you to my COMING OUT party.' What, he's gay? Did you know about that?"

"He's not gay, El. Just read it."

"'For the new Nicholas 3.0.' What the hell does that mean? 'I'm a new man. Please

260

believe me. You MUST come. Tomorrow at 2. You'll be safe. It's at my parents' house. And they will be there like in high school! HAHA.' What's this?"

"Link to the address."

"He's got a set! Well, you're not going."

CHAPTER 22 | Visitor's day

The F.B.I. wasted no time. As soon as Richard was delivered to the facility, he was ushered into a small bare room with a table and an empty chair for him. Two F.B.I. interrogators were already seated and waiting for him.

The remainder of that first day was taken up with interviews. They came at him from every angle asking him the same questions over and over while altering slightly the words they used--this in a sneaky effort to catch him in inconsistencies. Mostly, they drilled him on his online life. For Richard, this was a mind-numbing, grueling, and exhausting experience. Yet it had the beneficial effect of distracting from his own inner turmoil. He cooperated fully with the agents. He was docile and forthcoming, never questioned them and never refused to answer their questions. All the while, his demeanor remained that of a terrified young man, overawed by his circumstances. Even after sitting for hours in the harsh light and hard metal chair, his eyelids never sagged from fatigue, his wide open eyes fixed and staring at his questioners.

When the session was suspended for the day, he was returned to his room. This, he knew, would be his punishment, to be left alone with himself. Even for those first few minutes he could not bare it and quickly set out to lose himself in any distraction he could find. There was a sign pointing to the Common Room and with great trepidation he followed it, his imagination inflamed to expect a scene from a horror movie though even that would be preferable to being left alone with himself. Instead, stopping inside the door, he witnessed a quiet, open space with people seated around tables or slumped watching the television or simply staring. Cautiously, he stepped inside and paused. His entrance had gone unnoticed. Before long, he was wandering freely between the tables, surveying his new home. So he was relaxed and his back was turned when

sudden shrieks rent the quiet. A small wiry figure had burst into the room followed at a distance by two large attendants, out of breath from what must have been a long chase. The little man raced around the outside of the room and noticing a figure standing among the tables, lurched at Richard who now turned and sprinted back toward the entrance but the little man cut him off before Richard could stop and the two of them collided, sending the little man onto his back. He leered up at Richard out of two small slits from behind a cascade of grey greasy hair that hung over his face. The attendants now arrived breathing heavily and roughly and effortlessly lifted the figure to his feet and easily dragged him away, ignoring Richard entirely. He watched in horror as the little man stared back at him, pointing wildly at him with both index fingers, his gargoyle personality etched on Richard's retina. He knew now that he had just been initiated into the overpowering miasma of destitution and bleak hopelessness. He stumbled himself into corner, desperate to make himself invisible. Tears began to drip from his eyes.

In that moment, the last shrinking vestiges of his personality were dissolving: his belief in his intellectual superiority, his free-form smart-ass disdain, his prankster arrogance. But in a last terrible effort of prideful resistance, he forced himself to look around with his old eyes. A wave of nausea rewarded him. He turned his body into the corner and sobbed, great silent crushing sobs.

The next day, Angela arrived early and stood in line at the guard station with the other relatives and friends. She carried a paper bag of sandwiches, fruits and candy bars. When the guard eventually motioned them forward, she filed into the visitor room, inspecting it closely. It seemed cleaner and better lit than she feared it would be. She took a chair at one of the tables which were all bolted into the floor and placed the bag on the floor beside her.

Richard entered in a long file of patients. Though her smile was kindly and consoling as he approached, the change in him overnight took her unawares. He seemed a husk of himself, a gollum of her beloved son. He meekly took the seat across from her and bowed his head. There were tears in his eyes. Angela reached across the table with her hands open, awaiting his. For a while, he did not react. But soon, his hands appeared and slowly, not reluctantly but from shame, came to rest in hers. Neither spoke. Angela watched her son with the gravest attention as if her eyes could pierce his heart and inject her love into that suffering muscle. She had come with no expectations, no fears, no anxiety. It was a kind of indifference to whatever she might find, not uncaring but rather trustful, even serene, in her profound belief that she should not presume anything either of Richard or herself and that Love would see to all. Angela presented Richard with the paper bag. He took it and slid it over to his side of the table but did not look inside it. Angela waited patiently for him to speak, if he would. If he wouldn't, it didn't matter. After a while, however, she could see that the silence was beginning to annoy him. He was becoming restless. He began sliding the paper bag two inches one way and two inches back.

Tentatively, she asked him, "Would you like me to leave, Richard?"

"No. . .," he mumbled not looking at her. But she was correct. The silence was too much for him. Simply for something to say, he began to tell her about the people he had seen in the common room the night before. His attempt to make this sound like a casual pass-the-time monologue (because, she was sure, he did not want to cause her worry) was only half-hearted. Within minutes, his voice began to fail him.

"I know, sweetheart, I know," she consoled him in her gentle mother's voice. He stopped talking and harshly wiped his face with his hands and then his head, scraping it as if wiping out thought.

"Richard, I want to tell you something."

He was listening now, relieved from the vision of madness.

"There's something I must ask you to do. I had hoped to spare you this until...I want you to promise me. . .," now tears filled Angela's eyes but in her face there was no touch of sadness, "promise me you will look after Bella and Aunt Eleanor...because...I may not be allowed to wait until you get home."

"What...what...are you going somewhere?"

Angela laughed like a child. "My poor Richard. Sweetheart, I'm dying."

She was confirmed in this belief by the little pain in her heart that had not gone away since first coming to her in the hospital. To her, it was less a pain than a gentle reminder and an invitation to be ready. *He* was here, with her. With every beat of her heart she felt the signal language of Love: Be patient. I'm coming. Be patient. I'm coming.

Richard sprang out of his chair and moved away from her, nearly colliding with the table behind them.

Angela frowned. "Please, Richard, sit down."

But he didn't move. He glowered at her, resenting her, disgusted with what she had just told him. He felt sick.

"I know this is a shock, but, Richard, I couldn't just pretend it won't happen to spare you this. It needs to be faced, honey. And I wanted you to hear it from me that I am not sad or frightened and I don't want you to be. I couldn't live with the thought of you finding out while you're in here. I just couldn't. Please understand."

"*Understand*?" he cried. "I'm in jail. In *jail!* For a year! And this is what you come to tell me? On my first day? That you're dying?"

"I know, I know," Angela conceded.

Suddenly, he swung with all his might at the paper bag on the table sending its contents spilling out all over the floor. He turned and walked away.

CHAPTER 23 | The Coming Out Party

All the next day, Ben Shelley was a mess. What was this 'coming out party' anyway? He sensed disaster but at the same time, what did Nicholas mean that he, Ben, would be the big winner? He had always feared something like this, but what was the 'this'? His plans were hanging by a thread, a thread tied to his idiot nephew. He writhed in bitterness at his stupid, stupid decision to guarantee the monthly share payouts to Shine and Gross *from his own resources* to guard against either of them pulling out of the deal. "Who's the idiot now?" he castigated himself. If this deal blew up, he could be stuck with monthly outlays to those two for--oh God, he couldn't think how long! He had never put an end date on the document. "Some lawyer I am!"

His desperation reached such a pitch that he found himself grasping at a long-shot: the possibility the thread might actually hold. All it required was that Nicholas's claim to be a new man was not just another egomaniacal flareup but the actual truth. In which case, the deal would hold because Kit and Marigold would never believe 3.0 would be any better than 1.0 or 2.0. They would continue paying him even if Nicholas joined a monastery.

"Yeah, and I'm Santa Claus," he thought, revolted at himself.

By the time two o'clock rolled around, he had managed to steel himself against the inevitable by centering his mind on a plan of escape, just in case. He had packed two bags and set them by the door. He checked his phone one last time--no texts since Nicholas's invitation text yesterday. He popped the sim card, flushed it, and hammered the phone to shreds. This made him feel much better. He threw the bags in the trunk and drove off.

Nicholas was in a state nearing euphoria. The anticipation was as intensely exciting as the event itself promised to be. The tremors he had been experiencing were becoming more numerous and these added to his euphoria a pleasant physical sensation, a jittery energy that tickled him and would not let him relax. It had kept him up all night making sleep impossible and he was glad of it since he did not want to sleep ever again. And then finally the time had come. He needed to arrive at his parents' early to ensure everything was made ready. Joyfully he picked up the gas can which was one of the two items he had procured and poured gas on the monument of his belongings in the middle of the floor. He lit it with his Zippo lighter and stood back to admire his work. Then he picked up the other item, a length of rope, and carried it and the gas can out to his car.

Up ahead, Ben Shelley saw a car pull into the driveway of Kit and Marigold's house. It was not Nicholas's car. "Who the fuck's that?" he wondered. His face darkened in suspicion and irritation. He sped up and turned in behind the car following it closely up the driveway, trying to see who it was through their rear window but his view of the person's head was hidden behind a high headrest. He parked beside the car and jumped out. To his momentary surprise, Bella Benfont emerged from the driver side door but almost instantly Ben thought to himself, "Yeah. Of course." But she was not alone. The passenger side door flew open and Eleanor Antonelli hauled herself out.

"No. I said you're not going. That's it," Eleanor had announced. They had been avoiding this argument all morning knowing that Angela would soon be leaving for her first visit with Richard. Coincidentally, visiting hours began at two o'clock. When Angela left, Bella had picked up her keys and with determination started for the door. Eleanor moved in front of her, blocking her path.

"El, please. I have to," Bella pleaded, slipping around her. Eleanor, too, was determined and moved surprisingly quickly closer to the door, barring Bella from reaching it.

"Listen to me, dammit! You can't think I'm going to let you go to this lunatic's coming out party after what he did to you."

Bella frowned. "Aunt Eleanor. I am going."

"Oh, yeah?" Eleanor said. "I don't think so, girly." She backed toward the door until her body was up against it and spread out her arms. She knew how ridiculous she must look and smiled in mock victory. "Come on, let's see what you got."

Laughing despite her anxiety, Bella grabbed her aunt around the waist and heaved once to no effect then fell against Eleanor's vast chest.

"Oh, God, I love you, you big fat doll!" she said, burying kisses in the rolls of her aunt's neck. She stepped back and wiped her eyes. "Are you going to move?"

Eleanor stepped away from the door and bent an eye on her niece. "OK, let's go."

"What? No, El!"

"You are not going there alone. That's final. Who knows what that shit might do. Oh, brother, I hope he tries something! Please, God, let him try something."

Bella was silent and concentrated as Eleanor drove. "Everybody is responsible for everybody," she kept repeating in her mind. Her mother's words troubled her because she already felt so strongly her responsibility for everything that had happened. Then what was the reason those words troubled her so? Why did they fill her with such shame and this grinding sense of inadequacy? "What am I missing?" she thought. "I need to know! I *am* responsible for all this, I know it, it's true, I'm not just flagellating my conscience, I'm not!" If she had never shown that damn manifesto to Richard none of this would have happened. That was just a fact. At least this time she had been invited and so could claim some minimal justification for inserting herself back into the flow of 'all this'. It might be stupid but it was not wrong. There was something else as well, a sense of fate perhaps, a connection to some kind of bigger meaning in which she was an important element and not merely a pawn on a chessboard with no squares.

"And who are you?" Eleanor asked in a belligerent tone as she exited the car.

Ben introduced himself as Nicholas's uncle. For a long moment, Eleanor studied him with grim distaste which unnerved Ben. He turned away from the hard eyes to address Bella whom he had not seen since the debacle in his office.

"You got an invitation, too? My God, I can't believe you showed up after...well, all I can say is how terribly sorry I am for what he did to you. I didn't see the attack, of course. If I had been there maybe..."

Bella did not feel sympathetic. "No, you left. Just in time."

Ben took a deep breath and said, "Well, I guess we should, uh..." and took a few steps toward the house.

"Wait a minute there, mister," Eleanor demanded. "What's going on here, anyway? What's this party thing? You must know, being his uncle."

"I don't know. Honestly. I'm in the dark as much as you."

"We'll see," Eleanor said ominously shifting her attention to the house. "Good lord, look at this joint!"

Ben gave her a wide berth letting the two women precede him. Bella reached the door first, paused, look back at Eleanor helplessly then knocked. From inside, they heard a loud "Come in! Come in!"

Gingerly, Bella pushed open the door and stepped inside but did not venture any further until the other two were inside with her. Now Ben stepped past them and whispered, "Wait here a sec." He took a caution step forward to the edge of the entry into the living room. He inched past it and immediately sprang back yelling, "What are you doing!?" Bella and Eleanor now joined him and their jaws dropped.

Nicholas stood smiling madly in front of the fireplace. In front of him in the two art chairs sat his parents, Kit on his left and Marigold on his right. They were tied to their chairs with rope and duct tape covered their mouths. Both parents were struggling terribly and their muffled voices were from a nightmare as they shifted and pulled and strained against their binds, their eyes crazily spinning in apparent pleas for help as their heads rocked and jerked in terror. As the three 'guests' stared at the incredible site the stench of gasoline reached them. Eleanor was the first to react.

"No-n-no. No you don't," she cried flying into the room to rescue the hostages.

Nicholas, evidently expecting some kind of reaction like this, laughed. "Whoa fat lady!" he said and raised his right hand in which he held a Zippo lighter, its top open. With his thumb he turned the wheel to ignite the wick. Eleanor came to a stumbling stop.

"What kind of devil are you?" she spit at him.

"Back up there, fat lady. Who are you anyway? Not that it matters. The more the merrier."

"She's my aunt," Bella now spoke up and stepped down onto the living room rug.

"Well, welcome, Auntie! And welcome Benjamin. And a particularly heart-felt welcome to our Bella," Nicholas said in his most supercilious tone. "Welcome to the Coming Out party for Nicholas 3.0. Oh, I forgot to introduce my parents. Kit," he said tapping his father's shoulder, "and Marigold. Now, I know you all want me to get to the big event. But all big events need an introduction." As he spoke, he snapped the Zippo open, lit the wick, then snapped it closed. He repeated this incessantly throughout what followed.

Ben had recovered from the first shock and was now standing perfectly still. He barely drew breath so intent was he for any hint to direct his next action, whether to stay or flee. He was beginning to perceive that there might be a real positive outcome here if he just kept his head. He had not moved out of the foyer so he stood a step higher than Bella and Eleanor. He never took his eyes off Nicholas, though for each of them the moaning and muffled screams from Kit and Marigold and their erratic, pathetic struggling against the ropes, the terror in their eyes, was too much to bare. Yet each of them knew they must withstand it lest a wrong movement or comment cause Nicholas to drop his lit lighter. Only Bella dared to inch closer, slowly, very very slowly. She thought she saw the slight suggestion of a shiver twitch Nicholas's shoulders.

"You see, my friends," Nicholas continued, "as I explained yesterday to the eminent jurist, Benjamin Shelley, Esquire, I am a new man. I have been resurrected! I thank William Shine, the cowardly weasel, who while trying to bash in my brains during our frolic together, Bella, must be credited for the new man you see before you. It was such a revelation! When I began to wake up, before there was a thought in my head, before I was even consciously aware of my surroundings, I felt deep inside me such a cauldron of hate for Shiney that I was nearly sick to my stomach. The point is, I did not consciously summon it up myself or think first about Shiney and then came the hate. No! *The hate was there!* Do you see the incredible revelation here? *The hate was there before I was there!* I understood then why all my former ideas failed to satisfy me. I had never recognized where they came from! They came from hate! Hate had generated every thought I ever thought in my entire life. Now I see it all so clearly. As consciousness returned and my mind was working again, I solved the whole dilemma: my genius came from hate and was made for hate! Can you believe it? I even came up with my perfect motto, the words that explain it all: I AM, THEREFORE I HATE. Clearly, you must see the genius here--GODDAMIT!"

During it all, Bella had been inching ever closer as Nicholas appeared more and more insensible to her and the others' presence. He was nearly shrieking to be heard over the cacophony produced by his parents. But his unexpected outburst shocked her backwards and she fell over the foot stool behind her, the one Shiney had sat on. She crashed to the floor and from there watched as Nicholas in a rage sprang between the two chairs and fell onto his knees in front of the two hostages.

"ENOUGH!" he boomed and landed a punch beneath Marigold's chin that snapped her head back with such violence it ricocheted forward and fell limply onto her chest. Then he shifted toward his father who was screaming hoarsely through the duck tape and straining and twisting in his bindings. Blood flowed down his arms where the rope had cut into them. Nicholas swung with his other fist connecting with his father's cheekbone and knocking him unconscious. Nicholas stood up, his pants legs soaked with gasoline from the rug.

"Finally! Peace and quiet," Nicholas said.

This distraction had given Bella the opportunity to
lift herself to her knees and crawl forward beside Marigold. One close look at her bruised and blackened neck told her the woman was dead.

Now Eleanor, who had been mesmerized into silence by the horror of what she was seeing, turned furiously to Ben. "Stop this, you goddam fool! Stop it! You're his uncle. This is your brother, for Chrissakes, and it looks like he's just killed your sister-in-law! *Do something*!" Ben did not move or speak. He thought he saw where this was going and the last thing he wanted was to intervene prematurely.

While Eleanor's head was turned away, Bella got to her feet and positioned herself as close as she dared beside Nicholas who had moved back behind his parents' limp bodies. What she had just seen, so terrible, so vicious, so unhinged, convinced her that she must try something, anything, she must find a way to reach him before all was lost for him. Touching his arm she felt the tremors running through him. Urgently, she began to whisper to him as fast as her mouth could form words, words that seemed to come from outside her. "Please stop this. Let me help. Please, Nicholas, you *are* a genius. Of love! Yes, you are. Your love is for the wrong things, that's all. Just give that hate to me and you can spend your life finding the right things to love. And I promise you I'll keep it safe for you. I will dedicate the rest of my life to turn your hate into something lovely. Please, Nicholas, let me try. I can do it because of your great ability to love. We'll help each other. Let's do it together, Nicholas." His reaction saddened her. If he had heard her, he ignored her, but she believed now he was simply unreachable. Her heart sank and she felt faint.

"You ever wonder," he continued, "why haters hate the ones they hate and seek to outlaw their hate? Because hate is too precious to be shared. Consider the other so-called sins. Pride is merely an itch. Greed is an itch. Lust is an itch. Gluttony is an itch. They all need to be scratched. But hate, oh hate, hate is automatic! *It costs nothing!* Hate is not an itch, it is a switch. On-off-on-off! You see? But just imagine the true hater. His sweetest, most satisfying, most truly human experience in life *shared by those he hates*!" Bella found herself squeezing Nicholas's arm tighter and tighter as his voice rose. She feared any second he might drop the lighter while it was lit because of the tremors or because a fit would overtake him. Bella herself was unaware that Eleanor, too, had moved in closer and was hissing at her, "Bella! Bella!" But all her attention was on Nicholas.

"And, oh, he hates them for this reason. And finally to blot out the whole hateful population of them all, he must destroy himself. This is the true trajectory of evolution. We are on this path and it will come about. It must. We are born to hate. We live to hate. The Earth shall be covered in the bodies of haters who killed the whole world rather than face a life of shared hate. Where else can humanity end up? Here I st-stand, the ava-ava-avatar of all human-k-kind. I am, theref-f-fore I *hate*!" He was visibly shivering now. His eyes were glassy and his lips were locked into a vile leer.

Eleanor could stand it no longer. She lunged for Bella and grabbed her arm. She did not care whether this movement would cause Nicholas to drop the open flame onto the gasoline soaked rug. Let them all go up in flames! But Bella resisted her.

"No, El, no. He's my responsibility. Let go!" and she pulled her arm free of her aunt's grip.

Eleanor bore down on her now, mad with fright an anger. She grabbed the girl around the waist and lifting her off her feet carried her toward the entry way huffing for breath and tottering with every step.

"You will *not*--" she said in one heavy breath, "sacrifice yourself--" she said in the next, "for some goddam--" she said now breathing with great difficulty, "*Christian conscience*!" Then she dropped Bella but kept hold of her arm and with all her remaining strength dragged her toward the door. "You are not responsible for any of this, do you hear me?" she said grunting out the words.

Bella, weakened from fear and the crushing conviction of her own failure, surrendered to her despair and Eleanor's greater strength but she did not take her eyes off Nicholas.

It was at this moment that Ben Shelley made his decision. He ran from the entry way and grabbed Bella's other arm helping Eleanor move her to the door.

"Get your hands off her!" Eleanor commanded, furious that this useless excuse for a man thought now to come to her aid.

"You've got to get her out of here," he said as Bella struggled at his grasp. "Please, go-go-go, so I can get to the that lighter before he drops it. I can't be responsible for more deaths. Please! Go!" he begged.

Bella wrenched herself free and turned back to Nicholas but Ben caught her and held her tightly and muscled her back toward the door.

Bella cried out, "Nicholas! I can help you. Let me! Let me!"

"Goddamit, Bella, please!" Ben beseeched her.

"He won't drop it. Look, he's frozen," Bella cried.

But Ben and Eleanor now were of one accord. Together they lifted Bella off her feet and carried her back to the entry way.

"Go now! You were never here, OK? I'll take care of everything. You were never here," Ben demanded opening the front door. "Go! Please. Get out of here!"

He pushed Bella roughly from behind as Eleanor pulled her through the door and out to the car. Meekly, Bella allowed her aunt to shove her into the passenger seat and then squeezed herself under the steering wheel and sped down the driveway.

Ben Shelley shut the door. At last, he was alone and his plan was assured. Kit and Marigold had been silenced, thankfully. Their struggles had sickened him but he had stayed strong and now his reward was within reach. Trembling with anticipation, he approached Nicholas frozen now into a harmless, hateful catatonic statue.

"Well, well," he said standing before his nephew with his arms crossed. "And here we are...look at you, some genius. I knew you'd fuck this up. I just knew it." He reached for Nicholas's hand that held the lighter and its dangerously dancing flame and carefully snapped it closed. "Because of you, the whole thing nearly went down the toilet. If Shiney had killed you--and what if that girl had pressed charges? Be hard to cash those nice big monthly checks with you in jail or dead. But then you hooked me. Oh, yes, good and solid. How, I wondered, would this certified maniac make me the beneficiary of today's comedy? Didn't take me long when I saw you standing there with that lighter and these two all bundled up. But I had to watch and be sure. Knowing you, you'd fuck this up, too. So I watched and sure enough, didn't you go all catatonic. That's when I made my move. I had to get those women out of here first before they saw you weren't going to drop it. The girl saw but she was raving. I could see the sky opening and a fortune raining down on me. I was making good money from your parents but to them it was a pittance. Now, though, here I stand on the threshold of my dream coming true." He paused and bent down to Marigold. He began undoing her rope. "See, you *will* drop that lighter but not before I arrange the scene by loosening these ropes so that when the investigators come they will assume someone tried to save her but was beaten back by the flames and had no chance to untie the other one." He stood and picked the lighter out of Nicholas's hand. "So this is farewell," he said flipping it open and lighting the wick. "I'm only completing what you intended to do. It's not my fault that time stopped just moments before you would have set the whole place on fire and killed your parents and yourself, leaving poor uncle Ben as the sole remaining Shelley and heir to the whole kingdom!"

    He dropped the Zippo and stood back as the flames roared to life around the three figures inside the gasoline soaked circle. Slowly, he walked backward, fascination and exaltation alternately playing on his face. Very soon, though, the flames had engulfed the far end of the room and reached the ceiling. The roar was deafening and the heat was already singeing him. He left the door open as he jogged to his car.

CHAPTER 24 | A death in the parking lot

For a long while, they drove in silence until Eleanor asked, "What were you whispering in his ear?"

Bella turned in her seat to face her more squarely. Something about her was different, Eleanor noticed. That annoying hang-dog, suffering-soul attitude was gone, thank God.

"It was the strangest thing, Aunt El," Bella explained. "I don't know where it came from but I...I wanted to help him with all my heart, that's all I knew and I started trying to distract him but it didn't work. He didn't even hear me, I mean, he was already so far gone. But I just knew I had to try and then I found these words! I mean, they just started coming out of my mouth from somewhere because I'd never had any thoughts like that, you know? And I knew it was hopeless...for him, yes, but for me, it wasn't! Because I felt so certain that they were words Mom would have said! It was like she was there, right next to me...so strange! The thing is, they didn't seem to help Nicholas at all and yet maybe they weren't for Nicholas, maybe they were for me!"

Eleanor shook her head. "Well, anything to get you back to normal."

Bella slipped back into her seat and stared out the window. "I know what he's going to do, El."

"What who's going to do?" Eleanor asked.

"Ben Shelley. He's going to light the fire himself and burn them all up, Nicholas included."

"Oh, for Gods sake!," Eleanor said.

"That way, he gets all their money."

"And how could you possibly--" Suddenly she remembered what she had heard in the recording Bella had made. "Oh, Jesus!"

"Should we go back?" Bella wondered.

"If he was going to do it, it's already done by now...I did think it was funny, what he said about we were never there. Why'd he say that? Who would ever know we were there anyway? He was up to something all right. But not that! How could he? His own family!" She sighed deeply, shaking her head in disbelief. She glanced at her niece and said in a commanding voice, "Don't you dare blame yourself. That whack job was going to do it anyway. He wasn't kidding."

Bella said in soft rejoinder, "But he was frozen, El. I saw him. I was right next to him. I knew it was coming. And as soon as it did, who comes to our rescue? He'd been watching and waiting. He knew, too. That's all he'd been waiting for. How perfect. Nicholas threatens to drop the lighter but goes into a catatonic fit, with the lighter in his hand, and suddenly we have to be rushed out the door because our lives in danger?"

"Oh, the hell with it all! It's over now, anyway. All I want to do is go home and stand in the shower for a week!"

But when they got home, they saw Ray's truck in the driveway.

"Shit!" Eleanor said.

She entered the house ready for battle with a hard, challenging look on her face but that instantly changed when she saw the look on Ray's face. Bella, coming in behind her, stopped dead upon seeing him, then ran to her father. Ray Benfont was a different man. His signature red complexion was ashen. Only his eyes were red. Red and sore and bloodshot. Green-grey bags of skin puffed beneath them. His always perfect hair was roughed up and ragged as if he had been tearing at it. His mouth sagged open like a drunkard's and his hands, hanging between his legs, shook. He sat on the edge of the couch in utter dejection. Eleanor followed Bella and took a stand I front of him. She peered down at him, unnerved by the sight but suspicious. Bella sat next to him, pressed against him with her arm thrown over his back, staring terrified at his terrified face.

"What is it, Ray?" Eleanor said with a calmness in her voice she did not feel. Ray looked up at her, then at Bella, then dropped his head.

"Ray!" Eleanor commanded, losing patience as her apprehension grew.

Ray took a deep breath and turned to Bella.

"Bella, it's...it's your Mom."

"Mom?" Bella said. Tears had already appeared in her eyes.

"She's...she died, Bella. She died--"

"What do you mean, she died?"

"They found her, in her car in the parking lot at the Psych Center. She'd been to visit Richard."

Bella slumped off the couch, uttered one agonized groan and fell forward onto the floor in a faint. Eleanor's hands flew to her face as she wobbled back two steps and fell heavily into her 'throne' chair. Ray dropped his head again and sobbed pathetically.

"What happened," Eleanor asked in a small voice.

"They...they say it was a heart attack."

"How'd you find out?"

"Richard told them to call me."

Eleanor had to catch her breath before continuing.

"A heart attack? There was nothing wrong with her heart."

"They're pretty sure. She hadn't started the car. She was holding her rosary. They think she felt it coming and was praying."

"But she never said anything about her heart!"

"She told Richard...he said she told him she might not be around when he finished his time. She said she was dying...He didn't...He didn't want to believe it and he...he was...not nice to her. He's a mess, El, the poor kid, he's a mess. . ."

Eleanor wiped her eyes and blew her nose. "Help me get her up," she said. She and Ray lifted Bella onto the couch. "Get a wet towel. Cold."

Ray staggered into the kitchen while Eleanor smoothed Bella's hair.

"Where is she?" Eleanor asked as Ray came back with the towel. She laid it over Bella's forehead.

'They...oh, God, they wanted to know which funeral--"

"Call Petrilli's."

"No, I can't. Don't make me."

"Call them, Ray. Right now. They're in her little book."

Ray found the little book of telephone numbers in the drawer of the side table. "Oh," he said remembering what was in his pocket, "they found these in her purse. There's one for each of us and Fr. Flynn, too." He handed Eleanor four envelopes. To this, Eleanor had a strange reaction for she knew why Angela had decided to inform them this way: the shock would be harsh and sudden but, if she had told them face-to-face, who knows how long they would be forced to live in constant anxiety while she lingered at death's door? It was so kind of her...it was how she loved them...it was--it was--.

"Watch after her," she moaned to Ray, her eyes gushing tears, as she rushed to the stairs and climbed them with all the speed she could muster. She stormed into Angela's bedroom, slammed the door behind her and threw herself onto Angela's bed. She buried her head in a pillow. It smelled of her sister. She wailed into it at the top of her voice, her great body heaving uncontrollably, her fists pounding the bed viciously. This lasted several minutes until her strength was spent and she lay sprawled on the bed sniffing and breathing erratically. With a great effort, she at last rolled onto her back. There was a crucifix on the far wall.

"You bastard. You...You...*ugh*! All she ever wanted was You! The only man she ever loved! This is how you reward her? Well, let me tell You something: she damn well better be seated at Your right hand side. You hear me? Don't You dare send her to Purgatory! Don't You dare, or I'll--or I'll--I'll rip that goddam crucifix off the wall and break it into a hundred pieces...Oh, Angela! Angela!...Damn you, you've taken my heart! I would have given it to you if you'd told me you had a weak heart. Why didn't you tell me? You could've had mine! And now you've got it where you don't need it! What good is my heart to you up there?...Goddam you! Don't you understand? *You were my heart!*...Oh God, oh God, I want to die! See? See, Angela, what you've done? You've made *me* weak!" Tears were streaming down her cheeks. She lunged over onto her side so as not to have to look at the crucifix. She lay like this breathing heavily. Fits of sobbing came and went. Her thoughts were wild, confused and anguished and she could find no comfort anywhere. It was a long time before her breathing relaxed and she almost slept. But the darkness that filled her future without her sister weighed on her yet. She was a spent force, a wrecked personality, a body with a self she no longer recognized. On the edge of sleep and only half conscious, she felt the pressure of hopelessness so strongly it numbed her. "Is this Him? Is this what He wants from me? Tell me, Angela? Is this Him? I'm nothing anymore, worthless. He wants my carcass, He can have it, the sonofabitch."